The Golden People

The Golden People

Pat Lacey

ROBERT HALE · LONDON

© Pat Lacey 2006
First published in Great Britain 2006

ISBN-10: 0-7090-8157-X
ISBN-13: 978-0-7090-8157-9

Robert Hale Limited
Clerkenwell House
Clerkenwell Green
London EC1R 0HT

2 4 6 8 10 9 7 5 3 1

Typeset in 11½/14pt Revival Roman
by Derek Doyle & Associates, Shaw Heath
Printed in Great Britain by St Edmundsbury Press
Bury St Edmunds, Suffolk
Bound by Woolnough Bookbinding Limited

I

'They say it'll all be over by Christmas.'

'Hope to God it's not! Even my mother sees I've got to learn to fly now.'

Mathew Holker and his new friend, Derek Pugh, were sitting in the bar of the Eastgate Hotel in Oxford. One week into the Michaelmas term, they were still finding their way around the labyrinth of university life but already pleasantly aware that it was full of the most exciting possibilities, even in wartime.

'Your mother,' Derek observed, 'sounds remarkably like mine. Still wants me tied to her apron strings.'

'Mum and Dad have always been wonderful at letting me make up my own mind about things. From the way they carry on, no one would guess that Dad was an earl and Mum a countess. They hardly ever use their titles although Dad does sit in the House of Lords sometimes.'

'Good God!' Derek, whose father was a country vicar, goggled in astonishment.

'For heaven's sake' – Mat glanced around cautiously – 'keep your voice down! I don't normally mention it. Dad had to sell most of the estate to meet death duties and the ancestral pile is now a housing cooperative. We live in the Dower House with my aged but adorable great aunt and Dad makes a living running the family pottery. He rather hopes I'll go into politics but I don't see it myself.'

'My old man wants me to be a bishop!'

They chuckled at the extraordinary eccentricity of fathers.

5

'Like another?' Courtesy demanded that Derek enquire although a sudden shameful attack of flatulence made it seem most unwise.

'No, thanks. I promised I'd go and see my grandparents in the wilds of north Oxford.' They rose to their feet a trifle unsteadily. 'Now, there's an interesting combination for you – an ex-washerwoman married to an ex-professor of sociology. And happy as Larry. Want to come?'

'Thank you! Sounds fun!'

They emerged into a golden afternoon. 'Let's walk,' Mat suggested. Not only would the parks be an exceedingly pleasant place in which to stroll, the fresh air might clear his slightly fuddled head. Scuffling through drifts of crisp autumn leaves, they sauntered along a river bank where willows trailed and an occasional punt made leisurely progress through the leaf-strewn water.

Leaving the parks, they walked up the Banbury Road and eventually turned into a small, modern housing estate where Derek fully expected Mat to stop outside one of the many bungalows; a desirable residence, surely, for elderly grandparents. But instead he walked on to where asphalt gave way to a rutted country lane.

'Not much further now,' he encouraged and true to his word, there was only one more bend to negotiate before they came to an open five-barred gate that, clearly, was never closed. Dried panacles of hemlock pushed between the bars and ivy wreathed the hinges. 'There!' said Mat, pointing beyond the gate. 'Moneymoon Manor.'

Derek was entranced. Like the ancient vicarage inhabited by his parents, whose upkeep was the bane of his father's life, the house was three storeys high if one counted the dormers set snugly into the eaves. He thought it to be of grey stone but this was only apparent around the doorway and windows where some attempt had been made to control the ebullience of the scarlet creeper that otherwise would have covered the entire façade.

'It's magnificent,' said Derek reverently.

'Wait until you see the back garden,' Mat chuckled. 'It's like a

South American rainforest!'

But viewing the South American rainforest had to be put off to another day. Mat's casual opening of the front door and his bellow of 'Gramma! Gramps!' into a stone-flagged hallway brought a little old lady rushing out of an open doorway. At least, Derek assumed she was old because her hair, worn in a large bun on top of her head, was pure white and her rosy cheeks were netted with wrinkles, but the speed at which she moved could have been that of a young girl.

'Dearest Mat! How lovely to see you!'

'You, too, Gramma! And this is my friend, Derek Pugh.'

'Welcome to Moneymoon Manor, Derek.'

He was led into an enormous kitchen and again he was reminded of his own home; the same clutter of books and news-papers at one end of the big table, the same row of copper pans above a black-leaded range where an armchair was drawn up beside the brightly burning fire. Even the figure in the chair looked uncannily like his father, except that instead of sober clerical garb he wore corduroy trousers and a thick scarlet sweater and, Derek was amused to notice, odd socks: one scarlet, the other bright blue.

'My husband,' Mrs Moneymoon introduced him, 'and,' turning towards the window seat, 'our granddaughters, Polly and Stella.' Two girls of perhaps ten years of age rose simultaneously and solemnly extended their hands. From the sleek caps of dark hair down to the scuffed toes of their strapped black shoes, they were identical. Two pairs of hazel eyes twinkled disconcertingly as two synchronized right hands were extended. 'How do you do?' they chorused.

'How do you do?' With commendable aplomb, Derek shook each hand in turn.

'Provided one keeps one's head,' Mat said, 'they can be iden-tified. Look carefully and you will observe that one has her hair parted on the left. That one I call Port. The other has her hair parted on the right and that one is Star – short for Starboard. Ingenious, don't you think?'

'Don't they – er – don't *you* ever change your partings?'

'Once we did!' came the chorus.

'Once too often,' said Mat darkly, 'and if they ever do it again, I shall personally ensure that they are immersed, head down, in a certain horse trough I know of.'

'Dad wouldn't let you,' Star said.

'We'd see about that,' said Mat. 'Anyway, where is Uncle Dan?'

'Gone to join up,' the twins informed him.

'But he's far too old!' Mat turned back to his grandparents for enlightenment.

'Only thirty-six,' said the professor mildly, 'although no doubt that seems like Methuselah to you.'

'He says he missed the last war by a couple of years and he'll be damned if he'll miss this one,' said Mrs Moneymoon sadly. 'He's gone to have it out with his boss.'

'And what does Aunt Mary say to that?'

'Just hopes – as I do – that they won't take him.'

'Anyone heard from Rosie lately?' Mat enquired. 'She's owed me a letter for months.'

'You know your cousin,' said Mrs Moneymoon. 'She can't be rushed.'

Greenwich Village
New York
November 1939

Dearest Mat,

My usual apologies for not writing sooner but I thought I'd wait until I'd sorted myself out a bit. I still haven't but maybe, if I put it all down on paper, it will help me reach a decision.

It all comes down to this business of being half Yank and half Limey. You know how easy I found it as a child to switch accents when it suited me? Well, it isn't just accents these days. One minute, I'm seething with anger at Hitler daring to threaten little old England and the next I'm looking at Mom and Pop and even pimply old James and thinking this is where I belong.

And then, what about my CAREER? I'm only halfway through drama school and really enjoying it but I guess *you'll* have to break off your studies, so why shouldn't I?

We've always been buddies as well as cousins so I'm relying on you to help me to decide. I've tried talking to Lotte about it because she's also of mixed nationality – English mother, German father – but she doesn't have a problem. She hates Hitler's guts so much she'd die sooner than go back. As I expect you know, she and her family are living over here now. Maybe we'll brave the U-boats and cross the Atlantic together. I know you've never liked her and she's no relation, but she's got her head screwed on the right way.

When you think about it, our parents are a weird lot, aren't they? *Your* mother marrying into the English aristocracy but doing her best to ignore it, mine marrying a Yank, which must have been quite something for a Limey lady back in 1917. Lotte's mother marrying a German POW and *her* mother the result of a union between a parlour maid and another scion of the nobility. Really, the only normal one of that celebrated foursome of nurses we're always hearing about seems to have been Aunt Megan, now living in Wales. I can't remember the last time I met her and I don't think I've ever seen her daughter, Mair. Mom says Aunt Megan's the salt of the earth so that probably means she's dull as ditchwater, Mair, too.

Anyway, please take pity on your coz and tell her what to do.

Yours ever, Rosie

Oxford
December, 1939

Dearest Rosie,
You don't deserve such a quick reply but I can see you have problems so I've decided to forgive you. My advice

for what it's worth is to stay put – for the time being at any rate. There simply isn't anything happening over here and things can't be too unhealthy or they wouldn't have let the King pop over to visit the troops as he did the other day. I'm going ahead with the university air squadron just because it's the perfect opportunity to learn to fly without Mum breathing down my neck and I daren't miss it but I'm beginning to think I'll never actually pilot a fighter or a bomber. However, a Tiger Moth will do me nicely for now!

You're right about me not caring overmuch for Lotte. In spite of her ginger hair and freckles, I remember her as a pretty cold fish. And I know it wasn't her fault she had to wear steel-rimmed spectacles and a brace like a portcullis but they did rather make her look like Attila the Hun. But full marks to her for hating Hitler's guts. That couldn't have been easy in pre-war Germany.

About Mair Corben – I'm one up on you because she and her parents stayed at the Wittenham cottage one summer and we drove down to see them. I remember Mair as small and dark and so fat that when she tripped over on her way down the Clumps, she rolled all the way to the bottom! Non-stop! I was terrified she was dead. But she just picked herself up, shook herself like a little dog, said, 'Well, at least I got here first!' and stumped off. But she stood up for me when we got home and Mum started sounding off about me letting her get so dirty.

I have made a good friend here, one Derek Pugh, who is joining the air squadron with me. I took him over to Moneymoon Manor the other week and found all well there. The twins are as obnoxious as ever, bless 'em! Uncle Dan's a bit miffed because they won't let him join up. Instead, he's being directed into something hush-hush that he's not allowed to talk about. The twins think he's going to make bombs but I can't believe that an English language tutor would be any good in that direction.

Love to Aunt Priss and Uncle Hank and a pat on the head

to young James – or a kick up the butt as you so elegantly put it, if more appropriate!

Your loving coz, Mat

Lotte Schreiber hunched her shoulders against the breeze blowing off the Hudson River across Battery Park and glared at the man who had dared to sit at the other end of her bench. She'd been coming here most afternoons for weeks now to gaze down on the transatlantic liners steaming majestically across the bay towards the narrows, bound for Liverpool, and flirting with the idea of actually becoming a passenger on one.

After all, she didn't *have* to wait for Rosie; neither of her parents would try to stop her if she set out on her own, even though they would much prefer her not to. But she liked New York well enough, enjoyed Rosie's company and above all, the freedom to wander at will around the city streets without fear of watching eyes. And the people she'd met in the Village were fun, particularly Jacob Hausman, who'd managed to get out of Germany several years ago, before the Nazi persecution of the Jews had become such a terrifying reality. Now, he had a studio in the Village and was gaining a reputation as a brilliant cartoonist and, what was more, considered that Lotte had the making of a similar talent.

'Come to me,' he'd advised. 'There is much that I can teach you.' And she had and was enjoying the experience greatly, although nothing could fill the gap left by leaving the art school in Montmartre. Sometimes, she felt more French than English, and certainly more so than German. How she hated what her father's country had become.

'Say, you have a light?' The voice that broke into her thoughts managed to sound both strident and suggestive.

Lotte stood up. It was time she was getting back, anyway. 'No,' she said, 'I'm afraid I don't. Sorry!' she added, suddenly feeling sorry for the down-and-out in his shabby parka and peaked baseball cap.

He watched her walk away. Silly of him to think he could stand

a chance with a classy bird like that. But worth a try for all that –
he had a weakness for redheads and this one sure was a beaut!

'Mam, its no use,' Mair Corben told her mother. 'Owen Griffiths
and I are not interested in each other and that's an end to it. We
never liked each other much when we were kids. Meantime, I'd
better be off or I'll be late for work.'

She kissed her mother, shouted goodbye to her father, busy
writing next Sunday's sermon in his study, and let herself out of
the back door of the Manse. Her bicycle was kept in the lean-to
that had housed the privy until a couple of years ago when indoor
sanitation had come to the valley. With the bus services now cut
to a minimum, cycling was the easiest way to cover the two miles
that lay between Llandeclan and the market town of Abercwm
where she worked as a post office telegraphist.

What her mother really wanted, she reflected as she pressed
down on the pedals so that her long black hair flew in the breeze,
was for her to marry Owen and become pregnant. Then there
would be no possibility of her call-up.

OK, she reasoned, hers was a reserved occupation at the
moment, but it might not always be so and if it ever did happen
that she could be released, you wouldn't see her for dust!

It wasn't patriotism that was the incentive – although no
doubt she'd have a bash at Hitler with the best of them – it was
the need to get away from sleepy little Llandeclan and the
inhibiting aura of 'the minister's daughter' that dogged her. Why
did people always expect her to be like her mother: kind, sweet
and long-suffering? She wasn't particularly kind (at least, only to
animals), hated to be referred to as 'sweet' and certainly wasn't
at all long-suffering. And she needed desperately to learn about
life outside this remote albeit beautiful corner of Wales, to overcome the inhibitions of a convent education in a small, Welsh
market town. It wasn't at all the right background for someone
who intended one day to be a world-famous writer! Apart from
a school trip to Stratford to see Donald Wolfit play Hamlet,
she'd never been outside the principality!

II

Although they saw the calling up of two million young men, the first few months of 1940 continued to justify Mat's assurance to Rosie that 'there simply isn't anything happening over here'.

At an aerodrome near Oxford, he was 'fined' half a crown for being sick in the cockpit of a Tiger Moth and thought he would die of shame.

In Wales, Mair sought some relief from her frustration by booking a seat at the local Gaumont for a performance of *Gone With the Wind*.

It was soon afterwards that the people of Kent saw the dense pall of smoke hanging over the French coast around Dunkirk and needed no second bidding to take to the boats. Within hours, the first of the British troops to be evacuated from the beaches were being ferried home in every type of vessel from paddle steamer and fishing trawler down to craft no bigger than dinghies. In Oxford, Mrs Moneymoon and her daughter-in-law made sandwiches and cakes and in company with many other women all over the country, took them to the railway station, there to press them upon the weary occupants of the troop trains passing through.

Inevitably, Paris was occupied and the French government fled to Bordeaux where Premier Reynaud resigned in favour of Marshal Pétain, who immediately sought an armistice which was signed on 22 June.

In New York, Lotte agonized over the fate of the artist friends she had left behind in Montmartre and prayed for their safety. At the same time, her fierce hatred of the Nazi regime hardened into a determination to join one of the British women's services as quickly as possible, and waiting only long enough to watch Rosie make her debut as Juliet in a drama school production of *Romeo and Juliet*, began her enquiries. When Winston Churchill assured the British people in a voice that made her blood run cold that this was 'their finest hour' and General de Gaulle declared that 'the flame of the Resistance must not go out', her anxiety to cross the Atlantic finally exploded into action.

At Moneymoon Manor, the professor sought out the shotgun he had used in the first, impecunious days of his marriage for potting rabbits and joined the Local Defence Volunteers. In Staffordshire, Mat's father, Robert, taking as his weapon the cutlass brought back from India by one of his soldier forebears, did the same. In August, the Battle of Britain began in earnest. 'Never in the field of human conflict', Mr Churchill told the nation, 'was so much owed by so many to so few.'

'Fighters, please!' Mat and Derek requested at their selection boards.

'Why,' asked the poker-faced Wren officer, 'did you decide to volunteer for the WRNS? Why not the air force or the army?'

It was a question Lotte had half expected. What she had not expected was that it would be put to her in German. And then she thought she understood and her pulse quickened. She was being tested for the skill in languages she had put on her application with an appointment to Intelligence in mind. As long as her reply was in fluent German, it probably didn't matter what reason she gave. For a brief moment, she considered telling the truth; that nothing would persuade her to wear the same uniform as the patronizing stuck-up Mathew Holker she remembered so well from childhood and that, anyway, khaki simply wasn't the colour for a redhead to wear while navy blue, on the other hand, was a perfect foil.

'The navy is the most senior service, ma'am,' she observed smoothly and in German. 'Also, there's a sea-faring tradition in

14

my mother's family. I believe there was an ancestor, Sir Richard Carstairs, who fought at Trafalgar.'

However, the battleaxe seemed unimpressed. She turned to the naval commander, who was the only other person present at the interview, clearly expecting him to say something. So far, he hadn't opened his mouth but merely fixed Lotte with a gaze so penetrating, she could almost feel his eyes boring into her skull. Now he spoke and his voice matched his gaze; cold, clipped and sarcastic. 'I'm afraid, Miss Schreiber, that your chances of emulating your illustrious ancestor are remote. Are you not aware that the WRNS, as yet, is not a fighting service?'

This time, the question was posed in French and again, Lotte guessed that it was only a method of testing her fluency and had no intrinsic purpose.

'Yes, sir, I had heard this was the situation at the moment.' In fact, she hadn't heard a word about it.

He nodded briefly, not at her but at the Wren officer. The rest of the interview was conducted mainly in English but with occasional unexpected sorties into either French or German. She told them about her education at schools in Germany, France and England, ending with her time in Montmartre and the few months she had spent in New York with Jacob Hausmann. The commander seemed to have heard of him, even managing a wintry smile and the observation that 'his cartoons are excellent'.

Abruptly, he pushed a piece of paper and a pencil across the table towards Lotte. 'Please make a rough sketch of the outside of the building we are in at the moment.'

She was confident that she drew it accurately: the centre turret and the two wings, the raised flower bed containing chrysanthemums in the middle of the courtyard. For good measure, she added the weathervane in the shape of a sailing ship that was fixed to the top of the turret. When she handed it back to the officer, he scrutinized it carefully but made no comment other than to nod briefly at the battleaxe, who made a few more notes on Lotte's application form. Then she glanced up.

'Thank you, Miss Schreiber. As you will appreciate, with your background certain formalities will have to be observed, certain Government departments consulted and this will take a little time. However, if all is in order, your appointment as a writer employed on general clerical duties should come through in a few weeks. Good day!'

Lotte got to her feet, said 'Thank you, ma'am! Thank you, sir!' and turned towards the door. But inside she was seething. General duties indeed! Perhaps she'd made a mistake after all. Perhaps the WAAF or the ATS would have been more appreciative of her talents.

Once she'd left the room, the officers exchanged glances. 'Worth watching, don't you think?' said the battleaxe. The commander nodded.

Outside, Lotte continued to seethe. *Now* what was she going to do? 'A few weeks,' the battleaxe had said. The thought of kicking her heels in her grandparents' huge house in Kent, cold as charity even in September, was anathema to her, especially with Grandpa, much as she loved him, telling her she should have joined the army. Sir Richard, in fact, had been at Waterloo, not Trafalgar!

And then, unexpectedly, one of her mother's parting remarks came into her head. 'If you have any time to spare in London, look up my old friend, Abbie Johnson. I knew her in the last war. She lives in the East End now and makes the most wonderful mutton pies. And her son, Charlie, must be nearly the same age as you.'

Why not? She'd go back to Kent now, put her grandparents in the picture, chop some more logs for the one fire they would allow themselves this winter and hold a few more skeins of khaki wool for her grandmother. But then she'd pop back to London, visit Abbie Johnson and give this Charlie the once-over. Although, come to think of it, if he was the same age as herself, he was probably in one of the services.

'It's not a particularly inspiring area,' her mother had told her, 'but the people are wonderful.'

16

She'd been right about the area, Lotte decided as she walked along a street of identical, terraced houses whose facades were grimed with soot and whose doors opened straight on to the pavement. Pasty-faced children were playing a game that involved hopping on one leg while trying to kick a stone from one flagstone to the next. One of the children, a boy, cannoned into her.

'Careful!' said Lotte, feeling bones like a bird's through the thin fabric of his jacket.

'Careful, yerself!' said the boy. 'Yer on our patch.'

'Well, I'm very sorry about that,' said Lotte, 'but what am I supposed to do? Walk in the gutter?' The boy considered the gutter then stared pointedly at Lotte's neatly shod feet. 'Yer ain't got the right boots on,' he accused.

'I won't quarrel with that,' she said. 'But tell me, what's this game you're playing?'

' 'Opscotch, a'course. Fancy 'er not knowin' that!' the boy declared to a little girl who could have been his sister and was wearing what was probably her father's discarded jacket, the hem brushing the ground and the sleeves completely hiding her hands. She nodded vigorously and gave an enormous, glutinous sniff.

'Wipe yer nose!' said the boy sharply. And she did – with the sleeve of her jacket. 'Ma's always tellin' 'er to wipe 'er nose,' the boy explained to Lotte. 'We call 'er Drip.'

Drip gave her a sudden, beatific smile that immediately transformed her from filthy street urchin into Botticelli cherub and Lotte yearned for pencil and paper. But this wasn't the moment; she was lost.

'Turn right, then left, then right again,' the helpful bus conductor had told her, 'and you'll see the Shoulder of Mutton straight ahead. Can't miss it!'

She could have sworn she'd done exactly as he'd said, but there was no sign of a public house. 'I'm looking for the Shoulder of Mutton pub,' she told the children. 'D'you know where it is?'

'A'course us knows where the old Scrag is,' said the boy. 'Don't us, Drip?'

17

Drip nodded. 'It's back the way yer come,' she explained kindly. 'Us'll show yer, won't us, Tom?'

'Won't your parents worry where you've got to?' Lotte asked, looking up at the house where, presumably, they lived.

They crowed with laughter at the suggestion. 'Ma ain't never back till gawn five,' Tom explained. 'An' Pa – well, 'e's prob'ly in the Scrag, anyway.'

There was no answer to that and Lotte meekly turned about and allowed herself to be led back the way she'd come.

'There!' said Tom, turning sharp left down a narrow alleyway that Lotte hadn't noticed. 'There's the ole Scrag!'

She saw a solid, turn-of-the-century public house with heavily engraved windows and bay trees in sawn-off barrels standing sentinel by the door. As she'd sat in the bus, she'd noticed several similar establishments except that their paintwork had begun to peel and the brasswork was dull and tarnished. The glass, paintwork and brasses of this one glistened in the mild sunshine and the bay trees would have done credit to any West End hotel; their drumheads neatly clipped, their leaves shining as if newly washed. Over the door, a brightly painted sign showed a very fat, very woolly sheep grazing in a flower-filled meadow; a meadow, Lotte reflected, such as Tom and Drip had probably never seen.

'Thank you,' said Lotte to the children and then pondered upon the question of recompense. Money, she instinctively rejected – how could she know what they'd spend it on or if some higher authority, like a parent, might not take it from them? She hadn't liked the sound of Pa.

And then she realized that both children were staring not at herself not at the Shoulder of Mutton but at the shop front next to it, and that thin streams of saliva were coursing down their chins. At the same moment, her nose twitched as she became aware of the tantalizing smell that always caused her grandfather to sniff the air like one of his spaniels and murmur, 'Glory be! Cook's mutton pie!'

Her own mouth began to water as she saw that the shop was the sister establishment of the 'Scrag', the same paintwork and

18

fittings but with only one enormous window on which the slogan 'Johnson's Celebrated Mutton Pies Fit For A King' had been engraved. Beyond the glass, she could see a counter where a woman of ample proportions swathed in a white overall and with an enormous bun of sandy hair skewered to the top of her head, was serving a young lad in a boiler suit. Clearly, it was a bulk order, for several pies were being removed from the glass shelves at the back of the shop and packed carefully into a cardboard box. Money changed hands and then the woman came from behind the counter to hold open the door for her customer.

' 'Bye, Alfie! Enjoy your pies!'

'As always, Mrs J!' And he strode off, giving Lotte a saucy wink as he passed. The woman saw her too.

'Did you want a pie, love? Because they're going fast today.' And then to the children, 'Hello, Tom! Hello, Drip!'

' 'Ello, missus! Any – any scraps?'

'There just might be,' conceded Mrs Johnson with a smile. 'I'll go and see.'

Lotte cleared her throat. At least the matter of recompense had been settled. 'I'd like three at least, Mrs Johnson, if I may. Mother always says she'd kill for one of your pies!'

Mrs Johnson, about to turn back into the shop, stopped abruptly and then moved forward to stand directly in front of Lotte. 'Bless my soul if it isn't young Lotte! I'd recognize that chin anywhere!' And then they were both laughing and hugging each other tightly. The children stared, open-mouthed.

'And how is your mother?' Abbie Johnson asked at last. 'It's ages since I've heard.'

'She's fine. And Papa. In New York now, as you probably know.'

'And living near Prissy and Hank. Oh, I'd love to see them all again. And dear Kate. Although I do see her from time to time. Always looks me up when she's in London. You've seen her too, I expect?'

'Not yet,' said Lotte. 'You're my first port of call. But I will be seeing her, if there's time. I'm waiting for my call-up to the

Wrens,' she added proudly.

'The Wrens, is it? My Jane can't wait to get into the ATS. But then that's because her brother's in the army.'

As they were talking, Abbie had taken Lotte by the arm and led her into the shop. Lotte turned back towards the children, now hovering uncertainly in the doorway. 'May they have their pies, Mrs Johnson? They've been very helpful.'

'Of course!' And two pies were taken from the shelves and handed to the children. 'No point in wrapping them,' said Abbie softly. 'They'll be gone in seconds.'

And they were, although Tom did manage to say 'Ta, miss!' before biting through the crust. Not so Drip, who consumed every crumb before licking her lips and giving another of her beautiful smiles. 'Ta, miss!'

'Mebbe see yer again sometime?' suggested Tom hopefully as he led his sister away.

Lotte watched them go. 'Shouldn't they be in school?'

Abbie nodded. 'Their mother does her best but she's out all day. Makes uniforms at a factory down the road. Earns good money but the father drinks it all if he gets half a chance. My Fred won't serve him more than half a pint but the other land-lords round here aren't so fussy. Now, come through and I'll put the kettle on. I'll hear the shop bell if anyone comes in.' And Lotte was led through a curtain at the back of the shop into a cosy living room where a fire burned in a black-leaded range she could have seen her face in, and a marmalade cat purred a welcome.

'Fred and I have our meal after the pub closes,' Abbie explained. 'Can you stay and join us? It's a bit special today because Charlie's home on leave.' And she glanced at the grand-father clock ticking steadily in the corner. 'Should be here any minute now.'

Lotte half rose from the chair she'd taken at the table in the centre of the room. 'But Mrs Johnson, I can't possibly intrude on a family reunion. I'll come back another day.'

'You'll do no such thing!' And Lotte was pushed unceremoni-ously back into her seat. 'Charlie will love to meet you. And anyway, you *are* family. Angie and I were like sisters. We all were. And by the way, call me Abbie. Everyone does.'

Just after she had bustled through to the kitchen to fill the kettle, the shop bell pinged. Lotte got up and went to take the kettle from her. 'I'll do this!'she said, and when Abbie made a movement of protest, added, 'Come on, you did say I was family!'

'All right, then! Put it on the gas. Quicker than the hob.'

Lotte had filled the kettle and was looking for matches when she heard footsteps in the living room. 'On the shelf by your right hand,' said a deep, male voice behind her.

She turned. A young man in khaki battledress with three stripes on his sleeve was standing behind her. 'Charlie?'

'That's me! And you're Lotte, Mum's just told me. She's got a customer at the moment but she won't be long. Here, let me!' And he took the kettle from her and lit one of the rings on the gas cooker then crossed to a cupboard and took out cups and saucers before moving swiftly on to another cupboard for a tea caddy and a sugar basin. Two paces took him into what must be a scullery and back with a jug of milk. 'There!' He stood in front of her and bowed from the waist, his dark eyes twinkling through lashes that any woman would have been proud of.

'I'm impressed,' said Lotte, hoping that the triviality of the remark would hide her surprise. Whatever else she had expected of Charlie Johnson, it hadn't been this smooth competence and the impression that whatever situation he found himself in, be it his mother's kitchen or a theatre of war, he would act with equal immediacy. Clearly, from the brevet on his sleeve, it was an opinion shared by others.

He grinned but there was a wry twist to his mouth. 'What else would you expect from a lad whose father's a publican and mother a cook? When I was a kid, I was either rolling barrels for my dad or peeling spuds for my mum. The East End's full of lads like me.'

Lotte felt her cheeks redden. 'Sorry! I'm not used to men being at home in the kitchen. I have no brothers and my father wouldn't raise a finger other than to pick up a paintbrush.'

'Not the sort my Uncle Bert uses over in Deptford, I'll wager!' And when Lotte nodded, he said, 'Mum's full of stories about the last war and how she mixed with the aristocracy.' And now there was a slight but undeniable curl to his lip.

Lotte bristled. 'If you mean my mother, then perhaps you didn't know she was conceived out of wedlock. And that *her* mother was a parlour maid. *Chief* parlour maid, mind you,' she added defiantly, as if that made the slightest difference.

He whistled softly. '*Chief* parlour maid, you say? She *did* have a long way to fall!' And then they were both laughing and it was on the wave of their merriment that Abbie came back.

'I knew you'd get on! Now, Charlie, after we've had something to eat, you must take Lotte for a walk down to the river.'

So it was that several hours later, she and Charlie were leaning over a railing and watching as a barge, moored below them, was loaded with crates. Dusk was already blurring the outlines of the buildings on the other side of the river and mist was rising from the water. Lotte shivered inside her thin jacket.

'Best be getting back,' said Charlie. 'Jane'll be home and Mum will be waiting to get tea.'

'*Tea?* My lunch hasn't gone down yet!'

'Ah, but you don't know Mum's jam sponge,' Charlie laughed. 'Light as a feather.'

It was at that precise moment that they heard the planes and looked up. Lotte was used to seeing dogfights in the skies over Kent but this was different. They were coming up-river in formation like a flock of giant, mechanical birds, their wings obliterating what light remained.

For a second they stood, frozen into silence. 'Christ!' Charlie shouted. 'They're Dorniers! Come on!' And then they were running, hand in hand, with Lotte's feet barely touching the ground and the wail of the siren that had started up almost obliterated by the roar of the planes. The dockers were running with them, all making for what looked like a hole in the wall that turned out to be a flight of steps leading down into a tunnel lit by a single, low-voltage bulb swinging on a piece of flex. Only when they reached another wall at the tunnel's far end did they

22

stop running. They stood there with Charlie's body protecting her from the press of people behind them.

'It's goodbye to Mum's sponge cake, I'm afraid!' said Charlie in her ear before all hell broke loose.

III

Kent
12 September 1940

Dear Rosie,

Well, I always said I wanted to be in the thick of things!
Dogfights over Kent and now the London blitz.

I'd gone to visit Mum's old friend, Abbie Johnson – she
who figures in the saga of the Intrepid VADs that we all
grew up on, not one of the main cast but a good supporting
role – at the pub and pie shop she and her husband run in
the East End. After we'd eaten an enormous meal, their son
Charlie – more of him later – and I went for a walk down
to the river. We arrived only minutes before the Luftwaffe.

Rosie, I can't begin to tell you how terrible it was. 'Hell
let loose' doesn't even begin to describe it. We made it to
some sort of shelter, along with goodness knows how many
others, dockers mostly, and I was seriously beginning to
wonder if death by bombing might not be preferable to
death by crushing. Academic, really, because Charlie would
never have let me go out into the inferno that was now
raging. The noise – not just of the aircraft and the bombs
but of an anti-aircraft battery that seemed to be just above
our heads – was terrifying. Then smoke began to drift in,
setting everyone coughing like old men. And if there was
smoke, there had to be fire and in between the shriek and
thump of the bombs, we could now hear the crackle of
flames. I really thought I'd had it as they say over here,

24

meaning in this case, the rest of my life.

I don't know how long we stayed there. I only know that the sweat was running into my eyes, my mouth was full of ash and my nostrils clogged with smoke when someone said, 'They've gone!' And I knew they must have because otherwise I would never have been able to hear him say it. So then we all began to peel ourselves off each other and stagger out into the open.

What we saw there was enough to make me seriously think about turning round and staggering back in again. You can't imagine it, Rosie. All around us, buildings were on fire, great tongues of flame shooting up into the night sky. Even the river seemed to be burning, barges had been hit and on the far bank, a wall of orange flame, mottled with smoke, was reflected in the water like a river from hell.

Everywhere, men with hoses were doing their best to dowse the flames. At least, being dockland, I supposed there weren't too many houses around and said as much to Charlie. But then we just stood there while the same dreadful thought came to us both. What had happened to his family – and the pub and the pie shop?

'Come on!' said Charlie and the next minute he'd crammed his tin hat on to my head and we were almost running up the road between the fire engines, ambulances and piles of smoking rubble.

I suppose it had taken us about twenty minutes to reach the river in the first place but it took us something like three or four hours to retrace our steps through the avenues of flame and smoke, not that we could, exactly, because time after time we'd turn into a street to find our way barred either by craters or by unexploded bombs that had been fenced off, or simply because the street wasn't there any more, but just a mass of tumbled masonry. But at last we rounded a corner and Charlie stopped dead in his tracks. 'Oh my God!' he said. We just stood and stared. What had been a thriving, well-cared-for family business, a monument to hard work and good management, was no longer there.

All that was left was a pile of rubble topped, incongruously, by a solitary bay tree in a tub.

Like a man in a dream, Charlie began to move forward, so slowly he could have had ton weights tied to his feet. And I followed. And then, when we were nearly on it, a group of men I hadn't even noticed turned from directing hoses on to some houses that were still smouldering and saw us. One of them started to pick his way towards us, calling out as he came: 'It's all right, Charlie! They were in the cellar. Nothing but shock and a few scratches. And Jane's with them. They're all in the church hall down the road.'

For a moment, I thought Charlie was going to keel over, but then he straightened up, clapped the man on the shoulder and said, 'Thanks, Jim!', in a funny, cracked sort of voice. And then, as we walked away, he called over his shoulder and said, 'I'll be back to help, Jim, just as soon as I've had a word.'

He was, too, once he'd made sure everyone was all right and he'd been forced to sit down and drink a cup of tea. I stayed in the hall and helped with the tea-making. And did my best to comfort a couple of kids who were there and whom I'd met earlier. Their mother had been killed as she was coming home from work, and their father was actually standing outside the pub waiting for it to open when the bomb came down.

Anyway, the upshot was that I persuaded them all to come back with me to Kent next morning. I doubt if Abbie and Fred will stay for long and Jane's got her job to go back to, but at least it's given them a break while they sort themselves out. But the kids are another matter. There don't seem to be any relations who'd take them and they can't really stay here. My grandparents have been wonderful but I know they don't really want to be saddled with a couple of snotty-nosed kids. And when I say snotty, I mean snotty! The little girl's actually called Drip!

In desperation, I rang your Aunt Kate and she was

wonderful, told me to bring them straight up to Staffordshire. She quite understood that I couldn't possibly have left them in the East End, especially now that the raids are continuing. Grandfather says he'll smooth it over with the authorities.

Sorry to have poured all this out on you, Rosie. I had to tell someone and it couldn't be my parents because they'd worry too much. I'm writing them a well expurgated account.

I promised I'd tell you more about Charlie but re-reading this letter, I think you will have got the picture. He's quite the bravest, most resourceful man I've ever met. And good company with it. Now I must go and separate Grandma and the kids. Until now, water has been something they either drank or boiled the 'taters' in. Certainly not something they washed their faces in!

Love Lotte

Rosie sighed deeply, wishing that she had Lotte's capacity for making immediate and clear-cut decisions, like taking those kids under her wing when she didn't have to. No one would have thought less of her if she'd just gone straight back to Kent on her own. If only she was like that: heroic, selfless, thinking only of others. She grinned suddenly. She could act it well enough! Even as the thought came into her head, she was composing her features into lines of suitable gravity, focusing her eyes upon a future that would inevitably bring pain and anguish, but lifting her chin and squaring her shoulders to show she would face it with courage and fortitude. A cross between Joan of Arc and Edith Cavell, no less! She grinned again. At least she was honest!

But one thing was crystal clear – this Charlie that Lotte seemed so keen on would never give her the time of day.

'No!' said Aunt Bella Holker firmly but, she hoped, kindly. 'That little lady you're holding is not a doll. She's a Dresden figurine. Put her back, please.'

But the description meant nothing to Drip. As far as she was concerned, anything within her reach was hers for the taking. However, there was something about this old lady who, she had been informed, lived with the man and woman she had been told to call Uncle Robert and Aunt Kate, a crispness in her voice, a steely glint in her eye that made her do what she was told. Besides, the old lady had been very kind when Drip and Tom had first arrived with the young lady who'd looked after them since Mum had died. It was a pity the young lady had had to go back to that awful place she'd first taken them to – just like the work-house Mum had always been threatening them with if they didn't behave. Drip's lower lip began to tremble. She missed her mother and still nurtured a faint hope she might yet turn up – like the bad penny her father had been. Drip didn't mind in the least about not seeing him again.

Aunt Bella saw that tears were threatening. 'Come and sit on my knee, child. It's not as bony as it looks.'

Drip considered the offer. If only Tom had been there to give her a lead, but he'd gone off somewhere with the man with the limp. Something to do with collecting eggs, which was just plain daft because eggs came from shops and had to be bought. You didn't just collect them.

She took a hesitant step towards the old lady, but there was nothing hesitant about her resounding sniff, and Aunt Bella winced ever so slightly. Drip saw it and instinctively drew back.

'Ouch!' Aunt Bella exclaimed with commendable ingenuity. 'My foot's gone to sleep. Do yours ever do that?'

'Ma's does – did. I 'ad to rub 'em for 'er.'

'D'you think . . . could you possibly rub mine?'

'Yer'll 'ave ter take yer boot orf.'

'Of course!' And bending down, Aunt Bella quickly removed one serviceable brogue. Drip crouched and began to massage her toes with surprisingly capable hands.

'That's really pleasant.' Aunt Bella was impressed. 'You're a very clever little girl, Drip.'

No one had ever called Drip a clever little girl before. Unable to cope with it, she scowled fiercely and yet again sniffed.

Aunt Bella took her handkerchief from her sleeve, leaned

forward and gently applied it to Drip's nose. Drip stopped massaging. Again she sniffed, but this time appreciatively. 'Lavender,' Aunt Bella explained.

'You can keep it if you like,' she said after a moment.

' 'onest?'

'Honest.'

Drip examined the wisp of fine cambric. Not only was it trimmed with lace and smelled delicious, there was a letter embroidered in one corner.

'What's it say?'

'It's a B – for Bella. That's my name. What's your name?' And when Drip didn't answer, 'You haven't always been called Drip, have you?'

'Oh, yus!' Drip was very sure about that. 'Never bin called nuthin' else.'

'What was your mother's name?'

'Ma. Jus' Ma. 'cept when Dad called 'er a silly ole cow or a fuckin'-'

'Quite so!' said Aunt Bella hurriedly. 'Have a sweet.' And she reached for the tin that was only opened on special occasions. Or in dire emergencies, she decided now.

'They need the company of other children,' Aunt Bella told Kate and Robert that evening when the children were in bed.

'So what did you have in mind?' Robert asked.

'I wondered about Moneymoon Manor, if your mother would be kind enough to have them, Kate. Polly and Stella are there. Of course, there must be no question that we're trying to get rid of them.'

'I'll ring in the morning,' Kate promised. 'Although I shall miss them.'

'I too,' Aunt Bella agreed. 'I really enjoy having my feet massaged.'

'She'll be too young for Guides,' the twins complained.

'There's Brownies,' their grandmother pointed out 'And the boy's round about your age.'

'We don't like boys.'

'Well, I don't expect he likes girls all that much.'

'Princess Elizabeth would expect you to look after them,' the twins' mother said with low cunning. Since her broadcast to the children of Britain on the wireless, Princess Elizabeth had been the twins' role model.

'OK!' the twins agreed immediately.

'But they're not having my picture of Katharine Hepburn,' Star added.

'Nor my Bing Crosby.'

IV

It wasn't what she'd expected. The commander at her first interview had been right, Lotte decided, to maintain that the WRNS was not a fighting service. In fact, it seemed more like a Girl Guides' jamboree or a Vicar's tea party.

The colour of her uniform suited her all right and on duty she was fairly satisfied with her appearance: a neat white shirt and a stiff collar – even though it rubbed her neck raw after the first few hours – went well with the short haircut she'd adopted. And Plymouth, where she'd been posted, was at least by the sea.

But the job she had dreamed of, although so ill defined in her imagination, was clearly not to be hers. Clerical duties of the most mundane nature were her lot. Even an interview with her senior officer, in which she had pointed out that the requisitioning of nuts and bolts meant a complete waste of her languages, had brought nothing more helpful than a brisk reminder that someone had to do the routine jobs and she should consider herself lucky she wasn't cleaning out the latrines! So much for trying to show initiative! she thought sourly.

'Right, girls!' said Mrs Moneymoon. 'Here are the carrots and potatoes and your mother's bringing the turnips.'

Stella checked the recipe for Woolton Pie that her grandmother had cut out of the newspaper. 'It says swedes as well.'

'I think there's a couple in the back kitchen. I'll go and see.'

'I'll go,' said Drip immediately, although greatly encumbered by the vast apron she was wearing over one of the twins' cast-off dresses.

31

'Don't run,' cautioned Mrs Moneymoon. But it was already too late. She was sprawled across the flagstones. Even before Mrs Moneymoon and the twins had reached her, she was howling like a little wolf.

Mrs Moneymoon scooped her up, then sat with her in the rocking chair by the fire while her sobs reverberated around the kitchen and the twins raised their eyes to heaven.

'I'll get the swedes,' said Polly.

'And I'll start on the carrots,' said Stella.

'Wanna 'elp!' shrieked Drip but making no attempt to leave the haven of Mrs Moneymoon's lap.

'And so you shall, my duck,' that lady answered. 'But let's blow your nose first,' and she felt for the square of old linen that ever since Drip's arrival she'd carried around in her pocket. 'The sooner we get your adenoids seen to, the better.'

'Don't want me ad'oids seen to,' said Drip, who had decided she rather enjoyed the attention now paid to her nose by all the people she'd met since the bombing, even though they were all such toffs.

'Don't no one talk like us no more?' she'd asked Tom after they'd arrived at Moneymoon Manor.

Tom had shaken his head. 'Reckon not.'

'Us'll go on talkin' like us do, though, won't us, Tom?'

'Reckon us won't be allowed to,' Tom had said. And then, a little while later, Drip had actually overheard him holding a painstaking conversation with the old man they'd been told to call Gramps.

'*Hon*estly, sir, Drip an' me ain't never – I mean, *haven't* never seen the sea.'

' 'onestly?' the old man had replied courteously and to Drip's complete bafflement. 'Well, I'm afraid you're further away from it now than you've ever been but one day, we'll take you there.' And Drip had drawn some small solace from the implication that she and Tom might be staying a while, for she was happy here, more even than at the last place. The old lady there had been kind, of course, but more than a little frightening.

June 1941

Dear Rosie, greetings!

Here I am in the bosom of the family for a few days while I wait for my posting to a squadron. At last I'm a fully fledged pilot with a pair of pristine wings on my chest to prove it. At the same time, I am very much aware that the most important lesson still has to be learned – what it's like to be actually engaging the enemy.

Derek and I have both opted for Spitfires and fortunately our choice coincided with that of our lords and masters at the Air Ministry. It's now just a question of where but the odds are we'll stay together.

Tomorrow, Mum and I intend to splurge some of my precious petrol coupons and go down to Oxford to see Gramma and Gramps.

I'm glad to hear your career is going so well. Unless Roosevelt decides to bring America into the war, I should stay where you are.

Dad has just appeared, wanting to know if I'd like to walk down to the pub for a drink before dinner – there's a rumour out that the landlord has a consignment of Scotch! So, goodnight, dear coz. If you're out on the town tonight, behave yourself!

Yours, Mat

Margaret Rose Potter – alias Drip – stared up at the tall figure in RAF uniform and let out her breath in a long ecstatic sigh. He was even better than the pin-ups Stella and Polly had plastered over their bedroom walls. And best of all, just for a moment at least, she had him all to herself. It was a Saturday so there was no school, a fact for which she was now supremely grateful.

It was her new grandfather who had consulted something called 'Records' and discovered she'd been christened Margaret Rose, presumably after the sister of the heir to the throne, and that she was five years old. With a handle like that, she'd told Tom – *he* was Thomas George Potter, aged eight – she might

33

even let them teach her to ride a pony; the height of poshness. That was where Stella and Polly were now, in their yellow polo necks and fawn jodhpurs.

When the red sports car crunched to a halt in front of her, she was sitting on the step of Moneymoon Manor wishing she had some chalk to mark out a hopscotch pitch, but this offered much better entertainment.

'Why, it's Drip!' said the lady who'd got out of the car at the same time as the man. Margaret Rose stiffened. Then she saw it was the nice lady she'd gone to live with soon after the bombing.

'I'm Margaret Rose now,' she explained, 'an' I don't drip no more. I got an 'ankie up me knicker leg, just in case, but I don't really need it now I've 'ad me ad'oids out.'

'I do beg your pardon,' said the nice lady, whom Margaret Rose now remembered as her Aunt Kate. She bent down and gave her a hug and over her shoulder Margaret Rose gazed solemnly at the young man.

'Margaret Rose,' he said slowly, seeming to roll each syllable around his tongue. 'That's a very nice name.'

'*I* think so,' said Margaret Rose with dignity. There was a move afoot to call her either Margaret or Rose but not both, but so far she had resisted it, even to the extent of pretending not to hear.

'I'm Mat,' the young man introduced himself.

She stared at him for a moment then grinned broadly. 'Pull the uvver one!' she invited.

'No, I'm serious. It's short for Matthew. But no one ever calls me Matthew unless they're cross with me. It's actually quite a good way of knowing if people are cross with you.'

Margaret Rose considered. He might have a point. 'Which one d'yer like best then?' she asked. 'Margaret or Rose?'

'Well, let's think.' He studied her carefully; the stubborn little chin and snub nose, the way she was standing with her feet apart and her arms akimbo. Her dress, probably an old one of Polly's or Stella's, was coming unstitched at the hem. Anyone less like her royal namesake he could hardly imagine. 'Actually,' he said, 'we've got one Rose in the family already – she lives in America. So how about Margaret and you could shorten it to Peggy if you wanted. Or Maggie? Maggie's a wizard name,' he added as Margaret Rose frowned in concentration.

'Is it? Cross yer 'eart?'

'Cross my heart,' he said gravely.

'More milk, Margaret Rose?' Mrs Moneymoon asked that evening at supper time. What was a name, after all, if it pleased the child? She'd been so well behaved today, she deserved to be rewarded.

'No, ta! An' I'm Maggie now, acksherly. Mat says it's a wizard name.'

'Does he now,' said Mrs Moneymoon, bending down to give her a goodnight kiss and to hide her smile. 'Up to bed, then, Maggie!'

'You can forget about sunning yourselves outside dispersal waiting for the controller to shout 'Scramble, chaps!' said Sandy, a quietly spoken Scot who was their flight commander. 'It's far more orderly here. Our job is to act as escort to the bomber boys so we know exactly when we're taking off and where we're going to. Tomorrow, it's Lille, take-off 1400 hours. You're flying with me, Mat, and Derek's with Nobby Clark. Don't worry,' as they exchanged glances, 'you'll fly together eventually.'

When we know what we're doing! Mat thought and tried not to think of gruesome tales of rookie pilots who hadn't survived their first op. He caught Derek's eye and guessed he was thinking much the same.

And now, it was tomorrow and walking out to his machine for take-off seemed to last for ever, his mind a jumble of random thoughts. Actually seeing his name chalked up on a blackboard in dispersal had come as a shock, even though he'd known it would be there. The months of training and, before that, the yearning to fly, no matter for what reason, lay behind him. Now, there was a reason – to shoot down the enemy and preferably to kill him in the process.

That thought led uncomfortably on to the knowledge that

young men in Germany would be thinking exactly the same and his mind veered away; to think of his parents and Aunt Bella, whose parting words to him – was it only yesterday? – had been 'Sock 'em for six, dear boy!' And then, to his surprise, he found himself remembering the little scrap he'd met at his grandparents' house the other day. If anyone deserved a future, it was she. And it was up to the likes of him to see that she got it.

End of pep talk! he thought. And by now, he'd reached his machine anyway and, cumbersome in his Mae West, was being helped into the cockpit by an airman.

'Everything ready, sir! Guns oiled and checked. Good luck, sir!'

Guns! For the first time he would be firing them in earnest. But what if he came back with his guns not fired? What would they say about him then, behind his back? 'He kept his distance, didn't he?' As if, when it came to the crunch, he hadn't had the guts.

Checking the controls, adjusting his helmet to make radio contact, he forgot about his guns. And then he was taxiing across the grass to where the squadron was lining up, ready for take-off with himself next to Sandy. On his other side, Taffy Williams and Des Carter, whom he'd met briefly in the mess, gave him a thumbs-up.

'OK, Mat?' Sandy's voice crackled inside his helmet.

'OK, Sandy!'

'Good! Stick by me!'

And then they were away, climbing up into the blue and heading for the Channel with gun buttons switched from 'safe' to 'fire'. Because you never knew, he'd been warned, when a pack of hungry Messerschmitts might swoop down on them.

'I'm not promising anything, Miss Corben,' said the postmaster. 'I'm just telling you to renew your application. That's if you still want to leave us.'

'Oh, yes!' said Mair fervently. 'I still want to. Nothing personal, of course,' she added hastily, for there was no point in antagonizing him. 'I've been very happy here.'

'You haven't gone yet!' the postmaster reminded her sharply. 'I'm merely telling you to renew your application. If I did let you go, your replacement would have to be found and trained.'

Even so, there must be something in the air, Mair thought triumphantly. A directive from above, perhaps. 'Yes, Mr Jones,' she said aloud. 'Thank you, Mr Jones.'

Outside his office, she punched the air in triumph. It wouldn't be long now!

Sweet coz,

Can you bear another letter so soon after the last? Its just that I've got to talk to someone or I'll bust! There's Derek, of course, but he's in a state of shock as well and all we've done so far is grin at each other like Cheshire cats and bash each other on the back. Maybe, after a jar or two in the mess tonight, we'll talk some more but somehow I doubt it. So, dear Rosie, it's your ear I'm bending. And your option to tear this up unread if you so wish. I'll never know!

The objective was Lille, seventy miles into France and an industrial centre that was bound to be well protected. Our job was to look after the bombers and we zoomed off over the Channel, stacked up around them like worker bees around the queen with us giving top cover. We met our first flak – and my first ever – as we crossed the French coast somewhere near Le Touquet so I didn't hang about trying to identify exactly where we all camped in that summer of '33. It took me all my time to manoeuvre and still stay near Sandy – he's my flight commander and a really good type.

It was when we were nearly over the target that we met the Messerschmitt 109s and I did lose Sandy. They came down on us from above and we broke to starboard. I must have made a sharper curve than the others because when I came out of it, I seemed to be alone in the sky with a bloody 109 screaming down on me. I kept turning, praying I wouldn't stall, and suddenly I was behind him and pressing my gun button, again for the first time. I didn't hit him – at least, I don't think I did – but he veered away. And then

37

Sandy seemed to pop up from nowhere and was yelling at me on the radio to drop in behind him.

After that it was like some crazy game of 'follow my leader' but at the same time keeping a sharp look-out for infiltrators. I was actually covering Sandy when he made a direct hit on an enemy plane – I *think* it was the same one I'd had a go at. I was so fascinated watching it spiral down to earth with this great plume of smoke pouring out of it, I nearly got jumped by his mate, out for vengeance. It was Taffy Williams, just above me, who warned me just in time.

We were reforming when we got the message from the controller at base that the bombers had dropped their cookies and were on the way back and we were to do the same. Almost immediately afterwards, the 109s had disappeared and we trundled home without further incident.

It's hard to put into words exactly how I feel now. Do you remember when we were kids – about ten, I suppose – and you insisted we went out with the local hunt and it turned out to be not at all what you'd expected? In fact, you shrieked at the master to 'bloody back off' when he tried to give you the brush. We decided we'd never do it again but at the same time admitted that the actual hunt – galloping hell for leather across the countryside – was one of the most exhilarating things we'd ever done. Well, I feel a bit like that now. I really enjoyed tumbling about the sky, pitting my wits against the chaps on the other side. Pressing the gun button was just part of the game – it was coincidental that if I'd aimed better I could have killed him.

I'm not at all sure this is how I should feel and doubt very much if this is how the other blokes react. Judging by the way Taffy and Des – the other oppos in my flight – reacted to Sandy's kill, it isn't! There'll be some serious celebrating tonight!

One thing was for sure, though – it was good to get back and find that Derek was still in one piece. Well, thanks for listening, Rosie – if you have!

Mat

Rosie groaned aloud. Why did everyone have to keep telling her about the grimness of war? First Lotte and now Mat. It was typical of dear old Mat to feel the way he did. Conventional English public school complicated by an inherited tendency to think for himself.

But he was still twisting the knife, albeit unknowingly. However, the way things were going with Roosevelt signing the Lease and Lend Bill and now telling the nation that the defeat of Hitler was not merely a sentimental hope but a vital necessity, it was surely only a question of time before America was in the war anyway, and then she'd know what she had to do. Meanwhile, she glanced at her watch. Her date would be calling for her in a matter of minutes.

V

At dawn on 22 June, Hitler's ambitions reached what many thought to be the height of madness when the German army invaded Russia. The front extended to an incredible 1,800 miles from Finland to the Black Sea; the greatest deployment of troops – about 100 divisions – the world had ever seen, Goebbels boasted over the German radio.

In July, twenty American Flying Fortress bombers were delivered to Britain under Lease Lend. 'What about the crews to go with them?' Sandy demanded of Mat, now considered to be an authority on Anglo-American relations since he'd put Rosie's photograph on his locker.

Over the airwaves, the oppressed peoples of occupied Europe heard the opening bars of Beethoven's Fifth Symphony broadcast for the first time as the symbol of victory over Nazi tyranny and Lotte wondered if the friends she'd left behind in Paris and Munich were listening.

Somewhere at sea, Churchill and Roosevelt met to draw up an eight-point declaration of their joint peace aims. 'How can he talk about peace when he's not even declared war yet?' Sandy grumbled but recovered his good humour when Mat shot down his first Junkers 88.

In September, the Nazis claimed the occupation of Kiev, capital of the Ukraine, and Moscow increased its defences.

In October, Leading Wren Schreiber was posted to Admiralty

HQ and Miss Mair Corben was told by her postmaster that she would be released to His Majesty's Forces early in the New Year. She immediately visited the local WAAF recruiting office.

In the same month, in Scotland, Sergeant Charlie Johnson complained bitterly when he was posted to the south of England as an instructor on a coastal assault course when all his mates were given overseas postings. 'The penalty of doing so well, I'm afraid, Sergeant!' said his CO, with a complete lack of sympathy.

Also in October, little Maggie Potter, under Professor Moneymoon's tuition, uttered, 'Hooray! Hooray! One hundred happy hikers have spent eight hundred happy holidays at Hastings,' without dropping a single aspirate and was rewarded with a bar of his chocolate ration.

On 7 December, bombers of the Japanese air force attacked United States naval bases in the Pacific and the United States was finally at war.

'About bloody time!' said Sandy.

'Britain, here I come!' said Rosie.

It was late when Mair arrived at the reception centre; too late for anything except a meal of Spam and bright yellow piccalilli and the last bed at the end of a long line in a corrugated-iron hut. Only seconds later, it seemed, the Tannoy system just above her head crackled into life. Eyes screwed up against the sudden glare from the naked bulbs dangling at intervals down the length of the hut, she fought with a desperate desire to go back to sleep or, preferably, home. Clearly, she'd been mad to volunteer!

Suddenly, she became aware that a stream of bleary-eyed, pallid-faced girls clutching towels and sponge bags was now trickling past her bed. Five minutes later, during which she must have nodded off again, they were back, rather brisker, pinker and now chattering away nineteen to the dozen.

'What d'you think you're playing at? Didn't you hear the Tannoy?'

A dark-haired girl, fully dressed in WAAF uniform and with

two stripes on her sleeve, stood at the end of the bed. Her boot-button eyes snapped with fury and patches of scarlet stood out on her cheekbones.

'Sorry,' Mair mumbled. 'Late in last night.'

'Sorry, Corporal! And that's no excuse! The ablutions are across the yard. And be quick about it! I'll be marching you all to breakfast in fifteen minutes.'

Mair seen to, she transferred her attentions to the next bed, also still occupied and yanked back the blankets. A tousled head of black curls lay on the pillow. And continued to lie. The corporal yanked further; bare shoulders and scarlet shoestring straps but no movement. More yanks and the whole of the long, shapely, scantily clad figure, only hinted at under the rough grey blankets, was revealed. For a second, even the corporal was silent. And then she put her hand on a shoulder and shook it violently. The head lifted and turned. Sooty black lashes fluttered open and enormous violet eyes tried to focus.

'Christ! Where am I?' asked a plaintive voice with a decidedly American accent.

The corporal told her. She was still telling her after Mair had donned dressing gown and slippers and collected her towel and sponge bag from her case under her bed. 'A disgrace to His Majesty's forces! Both of you!'

The spots of colour had now spread all over the corporal's face and down her neck. She consulted her watch. 'You now have exactly ten minutes before parade. And woe betide you if you're not ready.'

The vision on the bed put out her tongue at the retreating back. 'Corporal Fanny Fusspot!'

'All the same,' said Mair, 'she's the boss! Come on! Where's your towel and sponge bag?' They made it by the skin of their teeth, standing to attention at the foot of their beds, Mair in her sensible Harris tweed suit and sturdy brogues, Rosie – they'd exchanged Christian names while they washed – in an elegant black dress and coat and three-inch heels. The Corporal looked her up and down but forbore to comment. Instead, she told them all what would be happening after breakfast. First of all, there would be something called FFI.

'Know what it is, do you?' She paused in front of Rosie.

Rosie screwed up her face as if in deep thought. 'Fanny Fusspot Inc?' she suggested.

There was a startled gasp from the rest of the hut followed by an audible titter. Even though they didn't know it was the nickname Mair and Rosie had given the corporal, the suggestion was clearly out of order.

'Quiet!' The corporal glared at Rosie with obvious disgust. 'You may not be in uniform yet, but just remember I can still put you on a charge.'

Whether or not she really intended putting Rosie on one, they never knew, because at that moment a woman in sergeant's uniform put her head round the door. 'Ready, Corporal?'

'Just coming, Sergeant!' And soon they were slithering, hopelessly out of step, through the pale light of a January dawn towards the cookhouse.

It was while they were pushing an unappetizing concoction of pilchards and fried bread around their plates that they discovered the extraordinary coincidence of their meeting.

'What's your surname again?' Rosie enquired. 'It sounded like Corber the way Fanny spat it out.'

'Corben,' Mair corrected. 'Yours sounded like Sherton.'

'Shelton,' said Rosie.

They stopped eating and stared at each other, open-mouthed. 'Your mother's called Megan,' Rosie squeaked in her excitement, 'and you live in Wales.'

'And yours is Priscilla and you live in New York.'

'I don't believe it!'

By then, the whole table was listening.

'Our mothers,' Mair explained, 'knew each other in the last war. They were VADs.'

'And there were two others. My Aunt Kate and a woman called Angela.'

'Who married a German POW.'

'And had a daughter called Lotte. She's over here in the WRNS.'

43

Their audience was so enthralled that the corporal, coming back to collect them, had to shout twice before she got their attention. 'If your *mothers*,' she said tartly, 'were anything like you, it's a miracle we won the last war! Now, pay attention . . .'

VI

'It's lovely to see you,' Mrs Moneymoon said. 'Not,' she added, gazing at Mair, smart and trim in her "best blue", 'that I would have known you. It must be a good ten years since we met.'

'When we were staying at Long Wittenham,' Mair agreed.

'And you looked rather like a human humming top!' said Mrs Moneymoon with a smile as she led the way into the hall and then into the kitchen.

'Don't remind me.' Mair looked around the kitchen, cool and welcoming after the long hot slog into Oxford on her bicycle. Gratefully, she accepted the glass of lemonade Mrs Moneymoon brought out from a vast walk-in larder and took the proffered chair near an open window.

'I'm so glad you can stay the night,' Mrs Moneymoon continued. 'I still can't believe you're actually at Maybury, so near to Kate and Robert's cottage.'

'Well, I did ask to be posted there,' Mair admitted, 'but then so did Rosie and she's been sent to Lincolnshire! Of course, we're in different trades. I'm a teleprinter op and she's driving a three-ton truck.'

'Dear Rosie! She'd drive the Queen Mary if they let her!'

'I don't think I could have survived initial training if it hadn't been for her,' Mair said. 'Without her, it wouldn't have been half the fun.'

'She and Mat have always been very close,' Mrs Moneymoon confided. 'In fact, Kate and Prissy hope that something more might come of it one day. When this dreadful war is over.'

Mair was saved the necessity of commenting on a point of view she found vaguely disturbing by the appearance of a small child, bounding in to the kitchen from the garden and clutching a bunch of flowers already wilting in the heat.

'I've picked them for the lady, Gramma. Like you said!'

'Thank you, Maggie. Now come and meet the lady in person.' Mrs Moneymoon glanced at the propeller on Mair's sleeve. 'I'm afraid I don't know what rank you are, my dear.'

'Leading Aircraft Woman,' Mair explained. 'I was a teleprinter operator in civvy street, you see, and so I passed out of my course higher than most. But anyway,' she said, smiling encouragingly at the little girl, 'please call me Mair.'

Maggie had been studying her intently. 'You talk different,' she observed.

'That's because I come from Wales.'

Maggie nodded. 'I come from the East End and we talk different, too. But I don't any more. I talk posh now, don't I, Gramma?'

'*Very* posh!' that lady agreed gravely. 'Now would you like to show Mair to her bedroom before Stella and Polly get home? Maggie's school finishes before theirs,' she explained to Mair.

'Oh, yes!' Abandoning her flowers in a crumpled heap on the table, Maggie marched to the door. 'It's quite high up,' she informed Mair over her shoulder. 'So we'll need all our breath.'

But this didn't stop her giving a running commentary over her shoulder as Mair followed her up the wide oak staircase. 'I'm 'vacuated,' she explained. 'Me an' Tom. We was bombed – were bombed – an' our parents was – were – killed so now we're norphans. An' Gramma says we'll probably still live 'ere after the war. If we want to.'

'And will you want to?' Mair asked.

Maggie paused on the top landing to consider. 'I fink so. I missed me mum at first. But now I got a rabbit called Cuddles. An' I got Tom, acourse. An' Stella an' Polly. They go to a bigger school 'n me. An' they does 'omework. Tom 'as 'omework but he don't do it. I shall do mine when I 'ave it,' she added virtuously. 'Now this is where you're goin' to sleep. Shall I wait for you?' she asked, dumping herself down on the white linen counterpane that covered the bed. White muslin curtains, flecked with tiny yellow daisies, fluttered gently at the open window and a rag rug lay on the polished floorboards.

'I'm just across the landin',' Maggie told Mair. 'So if you gets lonely in the night, you can come an' get in wi' me.'

'Thank you,' said Mair gravely. 'I'll remember that. Do you ever get lonely in the night?'

'Not much now,' Maggie declared, lifting her chin. 'At first, I did. I went in wi' Tom once, but 'e kicked me out. He didn't mean to,' she added quickly. ' 'e just didn't know I was there. Auntie Mary – that's Stella an' Polly's mum – says I can always go in wiv 'er but she's on the next floor down.'

'Well, whenever I'm here,' said Mair, 'you can always come in with me. I'll leave the door open especially. Now, shall we go down and see if your gramma wants us and then, if she doesn't, perhaps you could show me around.'

Apart from collecting eggs – 'You know where to look, Maggie' – their services were not required so, hand in hand, they set off. Cuddles, dozing in his hutch in the shade of a huge oak tree, was duly stroked and admired and Strawberry and Cream – the roan and the palomino ponies belonging to Stella and Polly – were visited in their paddock at the side of the house.

Hours later, lying in bed with the scent of honeysuckle floating in through the window, Mair reviewed the evening; convivial talk in which each generation had been listened to with equal attention, a simple but satisfying meal, a bedtime story for Maggie, losing to Professor Moneymoon at chess, helping the twins' mother, back from some 'hush-hush' job in an Oxford college, to wash up. What fun they all were! Her own childhood had been happy enough but as an only child she realized now what she had missed.

'You're most welcome any time,' Mrs Moneymoon had assured her when she'd said goodnight, 'and don't forget the key to Kate's cottage is held by Mrs Dickson, the lady next door, and Kate's warned her you could turn up at any time.'

I'll take her up on that on my next day off, thought Mair

before turning on her side and drifting into a deep sleep, so deep she was unaware until the morning that a small child had crept into her bed sometime in the night and was now sticking to her like a postage stamp.

Mat sat on the edge of his bed in the room he'd shared with Derek since they'd joined the Squadron, and wondered how he was going to get through the next few hours, let alone the rest of his life. For Derek was dead, killed only an hour from home because of diving on a Junkers 88 he had presumably assumed to be separated from its fellows and making its solitary way back to base.

Mat, flying between Derek and Sandy, had seen it first, coming out of a bank of cloud about 300 feet below them to starboard and called out a warning on the radio.

'Mine, I think!' Derek had answered, peeling away.

'Leave it!' Sandy had shouted but Derek, concentrating upon lining up the Junkers in his ring sight, had probably never heard. The next moment, scarlet flame was shooting out of the Junkers' tank and it was spiralling to the ground. Derek had already begun to turn away in a half roll when another Junkers had appeared out of the cloud and closed on him, firing a stream of bullets into the exposed underbelly of his machine.

By then, Mat had been screaming down on them but he was too late. So horrified, he'd forgotten his own vulnerable position; powerless to help, he'd watched Derek's plane following the stricken Junkers down.

'Bale out, you fool! Bale out!' he'd yelled. But there was no heartening flutter of white to give him hope, only a gigantic ball of grey and orange as the Spitfire hit the ground. Only then did he realize that Sandy's voice was thundering in his ears. 'For God's sake, Mat, pull yourself together or you'll be with him.'

Between them they'd finished off the second Junkers. If necessary, I'd probably have flown straight into him like a Jap kamikaze pilot, Mat had thought later. And Sandy had realized it, too. And made no bones about telling him so once they'd landed. For a moment, Mat had felt like hitting him until he'd seen the pain in Sandy's eyes and known that he was suffering too.

Now, still sitting on the bed, he knew he must begin the task he most dreaded: collecting Derek's few possessions and writing to his parents. One day, perhaps, he'd go and see them, tell them what a wizard bloke their son had been – as if they wouldn't know that already.

A knock came at the door and Sandy came in. He sat down on Derek's bed and gazed at Mat. 'Sorry about the rocketing but I had to say it. Losing one good pilot was enough without making it two. There's no room for emotional attachments in this bloody war, Mat and you've got to realize it.'

'I know! I'm sorry!'

'You're due a forty-eight soon, aren't you?' Sandy asked.

'Next week.'

'Start it as of now,' Sandy said. 'I'll square it with the old man. And that's an order,' he added as Mat began to protest.

He stood up, touched Mat gently on the shoulder, and turned to go. But before he could reach the door, it was pushed open. On the threshold stood a young man clad in an immaculate uniform and with a pristine white brevet on his left breast. In his hand, he held a suitcase.

'Excuse me!' He glanced uncertainly from Sandy to Mat, then back to Sandy. 'Sir! I'm Ridgeway. Pilot Officer Andy Ridgeway. They said there was a bed here for me, but I must have got it wrong.'

But you're so bloody young! Mat thought as he forced himself to his feet. Aloud, he said, 'No, you haven't got it wrong, Andy.' He held out his hand. 'I'm Mat Holker, your room-mate, and this is our esteemed flight commander, Sandy McTavish. Just give me a moment and I'll clear out this locker for you.'

What had he expected, he thought savagely, as he collected Derek's books and magazines and photographs, that they'd wait at least a day or two before they put someone else in with him? There was a war on, for God's sake! Suddenly, he felt desperately tired. Sandy had been right – he needed that pass.

49

Mair turned the key in the lock and pushed open the door. A smell of beeswax and the lingering aroma of cigar smoke twitched at her nostrils. She walked into the narrow hallway and stood for a moment, getting her bearings. Sitting room to the right, dining room to the left with beyond it the kitchen and beyond that again, the conservatory. Stairs straight ahead, leading up to two large bedrooms at the front and two smaller ones at the back, one of which had been converted into a bathroom.

Leaving the front door on the latch, she went upstairs and put her overnight bag in the back bedroom then threw open the window. Just as she remembered them, the two gently rounded hills crowned with tall elms and separated by fields of corn, filled the skyline. Wittenham Clumps. This evening, when it was cooler, she'd walk up to the top of the nearest one.

Pulling an old cotton dress out of her bag, she peeled off her uniform, glad to be rid of the thick lisle stockings, the starched collar and the restricting tie.

Downstairs again, she went into the kitchen and found the tea caddy, noting the printed instruction stuck to it: DON'T DARE LEAVE EMPTY! She'd make a brew and take it out into the garden.

Grateful that he had his own key, that he didn't have to face Mrs Whatsit next door, Mat walked up the path between the two neat squares of grass and was disconcerted to find the door already on the latch. Mrs Whatsit must be doing one of her routine checks. He pushed open the door and went inside but could hear nothing – she must be out at the back. He'd just put his bag in the back bedroom where he always slept, then leave her to it. Walk up the Clumps, maybe.

He tiptoed up the stairs and pushed open the back bedroom door – then froze. There was no way Mrs Whatsit had joined the WAAF! And in any case, no way she could have crammed her ample girth in to the skirt and shirt thrown carelessly on to the bed.

And then the penny dropped. Rosie! Hadn't she said in her last letter that she was hoping for leave? What incredible luck to find her here! The one person with whom he could bear to be with at the moment, with whom he could cry his heart out if need be and know that she wouldn't swamp him with sympathy or utter trite, meaningless phrases that would serve only to trivialize Derek's death. And who, at the end of it, would pick him up, dust him down and send him back to the squadron if not a whole man, then as complete a one as he was likely to be for a while.

He turned and clattered back down the stairs, raced through the dining room and kitchen and burst out of the conservatory into the garden. If he knew his cousin, she'd be sunning herself under the cherry tree, half naked most like. And then, for a second time in as many minutes, he came to a grinding halt.

The girl under the cherry tree wasn't Rosie. Like her, she was dark haired, but her hair was long and straight, almost reaching her shoulders, her eyes were a dark, velvety brown and she was shorter, much shorter, than Rosie. As she scrambled to her feet, he could see that her body was slim and supple beneath the faded cotton dress – a garment that Rosie wouldn't have been seen dead in, coupons or no coupons!

His disappointment was so intense that, for a moment, it was almost like losing Derek again. He did his best to pull himself together – whoever she was, and there was a vaguely familiar look about her, her presence must surely be legitimate. But one thing was clear – he'd have to go. There was no way he could share the cottage with a stranger, attractive though he might have found her under different circumstances. He cleared his throat.

'I thought you were my cousin, Rosie,' he explained, 'but don't worry. I'll put up at the George in the village.'

'I'm sorry I'm not Rosie,' the girl said. 'I'm Mair Corben. We met years ago. Your mother gave me permission to stay but I can easily cycle back to camp. It's no distance.'

For as long as I live, Mair thought, I shall remember the look on his face when he realized I wasn't Rosie; as if, promised paradise, he'd been given purgatory instead. With a heavy heart, she

51

remembered Mrs Moneymoon's comments. 'They have always been close. In fact, Kate and Prissy hope that something more might come of it one day.' Here was confirmation, indeed, that they were right to be hopeful.

And then she looked at him more closely and saw the shadows like great purple bruises under his eyes and the flat deadness of those eyes and was reminded of the face of one of her father's parishioners when he'd heard of the death of his only son in a mining accident. This man, too, had been recently bereaved. She stopped being little Mair Corben, long-time worshipper-from-afar of the impossibly handsome boy who had grown into this impossibly handsome man, and became her father's daughter.

'Let's not either of us go anywhere for the moment,' she said gently. 'I've just made some tea. If you can bear tinned milk. And I've switched on the immersion heater. There'll be enough water for a bath in ten minutes.' He looked as if he could use one, and a shave, she thought, noticing the pale stubble on his chin.

'But not enough for two,' he reminded her. 'There never was, if you remember. When we were kids, it was a case of cleanest first, dirtiest last – and that was usually me.'

'Toss you for it,' she offered, leading the way into the house and grinning back at him over her shoulder. And he, to her great relief, grinned back.

In the event, Mat had the bath – with a cup of tea balanced on the edge of it while Mair sorted out the ingredients for a meal. Thank God for Mrs Dickson's hens, she thought, selecting four of the half-dozen eggs that lady had given her, along with some tomatoes from Mr Dickson's greenhouse. Added to the rashers of bacon she'd prevailed upon the girl in the cookhouse to give her for her evening meal, there were the makings of a good fry-up, with something left over for breakfast. For 'afters', there were the precious raspberries she'd found growing on some overgrown canes in the garden.

When Mat came downstairs, he was dressed in grey flannels and an open-necked shirt. 'I must have left them here last time I was over. And I've been thinking, if it's all right with you, neither of us need leave. The cottage is plenty big enough for two. Though I suspect,' he added, quirking an eyebrow, 'that your Queen Bee wouldn't approve.'

'I don't *think*' said Mair solemnly, 'that there's actually an Air Ministry regulation stating that an airwoman must not spend the night alone with an airman. Although come to think of it, it's definitely verboten for airwomen to fraternize with officers.'

'But only when in uniform,' he pointed out. He looked at the food that she'd arranged on the table, ready for cooking. 'That looks good. But how about a sprint up the Clumps before we eat? If only to find out if you're now capable of *walking* back down!'

So he'd remembered! Inordinately pleased, she grinned at him. 'I don't roll so easily these days!'

They walked up the Clumps with hardly a word exchanged but it was a companionable silence with one or other of them stopping occasionally to gaze around them at the unfolding countryside and the other strolling ahead. Mair was ahead at the top. Breasting the slope, idly slashing at the grass with the stick he'd picked up, Mat found her sitting on a fallen log, gazing down on the river as it meandered through the huddle of ancient houses that sprawled around the abbey. Beyond, across the fields, an aeroplane circled then landed on the runway of the airfield.

'I didn't realize you had Spitfires,' said Mat, coming to sit beside her.

'Yes,' said Mair. 'Photographic reconnaissance, as you probably know. They fly over Europe at about 30,000 feet, depending on their height and speed to keep them out of trouble. Not that they always manage it,' she added, 'and then we feel absolutely dreadful and, in a silly sort of way, responsible.'

She sensed the tension in him but he said nothing and continued to swipe at the grass with his stick. She waited.

'I know,' he said at last. 'My friend bought it the other day. And I feel guilty as hell.'

'But I doubt if you have any reason to,' she said carefully.

'If only I hadn't seen the bloody Junkers in the first place. Or if I'd just kept my bloody mouth shut.' Suddenly, he was telling her the whole story, leaving nothing out, knowing that he was

53

sometimes repeating himself over and over again but unable to stop.

'And then this sprog pilot, still wet behind the ears, strolls in and says he's my new room-mate. Just like that. As if old Derek was no more than a dog we'd had put down. Less, in fact, because we're all soppy as hell about dogs.'

He suddenly became aware that he was shaking uncontrollably. 'Sorry!' he blurted out. 'As you can see, I'm no hero.'

Mair put out a hand and covered his where it lay on his knee, clenched into a knuckle-whitening fist, and kept it there. Not only were words inadequate, she could no longer trust herself to speak. They sat in silence until his shaking had stopped and she'd collected herself.

'Sorry!' he said again.

She took away her hand. 'Don't be! I'm just glad you've talked about it because it doesn't help to keep things bottled up. I'll just say one thing, if I may. There's no way you were to blame. Your Derek led his own life and, in the end, died his own death. Really, it's almost presumptuous to assume anything else. Grieve for him, Mat, but don't feel guilty about him. Now,' she said, standing up, 'you need food and then you need sleep. Tomorrow, you'll feel better able to cope.'

He looked up at her. 'A sensible child has grown into a sensible woman!'

Sensible! That was the last thing she wanted him to say about her. But at least they would be easier with each other from now on.

'Race you to the bottom,' she said. 'And this time, I'm not falling over!' And was gone before he could get to his feet.

'Tell me about Rosie,' he said over supper, which they ate at the kitchen table, accompanied by the bottle of excellent claret he'd discovered in a cupboard.

So she regaled him with stories of those early days of 'rookiedom' and laughed so much in the telling, she could hardly finish them.

'We had no idea what we really looked like until we got to

Morecambe for square-bashing and then every plate-glass window in town had its line of WAAFs standing outside on the pavement, prinking and preening, Rosie looked wonderful of course, but I looked like the Michelin Man!' She paused to wipe her eyes. 'It was incredibly good luck that we met like that. As I expect you know, she wants us all to meet up somewhere soon. You and her and me and a Wren called Lotte whom I've never met.'

He made a face. 'Couldn't we keep it just you and me and Rosie? Lotte was a pain when we were kids. And hideous to look at – although that may have changed, of course,' he added hastily, remembering that Mair herself, had looked pretty hideous.

You certainly couldn't call her that now, he reflected, gazing at her across the table. Cheeks flushed with laughter and unaccustomed wine, eyes sparkling and with her hair swinging like a bell on to her shoulders, she was anything but hideous. He raised his glass. 'Thank you for being here today, Mair.'

She felt her cheeks grow even warmer. 'All part of the service!' she said lightly. 'Rosie would have made a better job of it, I'm sure.' And then, reverting to the safety of the previous topic, 'There's a bloke called Charlie.'

Mat misunderstood. 'I'm sure there is! Probably a Tom, Dick and Harry as well, if I know anything about my cousin.'

'No, not a boyfriend. A Charlie Johnson, Rosie says we must meet. He's in the army and part of the great VAD network we've all been raised on.'

'Conspiracy, more like!' Mat grumbled. 'Still,' and he raised his glass to her yet again, 'I'm not complaining when it brings me such delightful company.'

Steady! Mair told herself. He's drunk more than his fair share of the wine. In the morning, he won't even remember what he's said.

Soon afterwards, Mat suddenly gave an enormous yawn. 'Sorry, didn't get much sleep last night.'

'Bed!' said Mair firmly, although longing for him to stay.

'Can't leave you with all this washing up.'

'Two plates, two bowls, two wine glasses, one frying pan.' She made light of it.

He made no more objections but rose, a little unsteadily, planted a badly aimed kiss on her forehead and went. She listened until she heard him reach the top of the stairs and turn towards the back bedroom (she'd already moved her own stuff into one of the front rooms). Sleep should come easily to him tonight.

And it did. When she climbed the stairs a good hour later, she heard the sound of steady breathing through his open door. There was no blackout at her window and she undressed in the dark. Then, clad in her no-nonsense WAAF-issue pyjamas, she went to open the window. Below her, in the lane, Mr Dickson stood at his front gate, waiting while his dog sniffed along the verge. Oh Lord, the Dicksons! What would they make of Mat's arrival so soon after her own? Grinning to herself, she climbed into bed and was immediately asleep.

Sometime in the early hours, she awoke to the sound of sobbing. Propped on an elbow, she listened intently. What should she do? Try to comfort him or leave him to his grief? To cry could be the first step towards acceptance. Then there came a jumble of incomprehensible mutterings and she realized he was dreaming. And then the sobbing started again and she could bear it no longer.

Climbing out of bed, she tiptoed along the landing to Mat's door. He lay on his side, one hand over his face. As she stood looking down at him, wondering what she should do, he suddenly reared up and shouted.

'No, you bloody fool! No!' And then fell back on the pillows, muttering, 'Bloody, bloody fool!' And then the sobbing began again.

Mair didn't hesitate. As quietly as she could, she slid into the bed beside him and he, feeling the weight and warmth of her, half woke and turned towards her. 'Rosie, Rosie! Thank God you're here!' And he put his arms around her and held her close, falling instantly into a deep sleep, his head pillowed on her shoulder.

At first, she dared not move for fear of waking him but simply lay there, feeling his body against hers and wishing with all her heart that it had been her name he'd called out and not Rosie's. And there had been something else: his immediate instinctive reaction, even though half asleep, had seemed to indicate a familiarity with Rosie's presence in his bed. Oh well, she thought, easing her arm, she'd always known, compared with Rosie, she wouldn't stand a chance with any man, let alone one with whom Rosie had had such a head start. She'd been a fool to dream.

But dream she did, until dawn broke, making it easier to study and memorize his face as he lay, completely relaxed, beside her. And then she fell asleep herself, waking several hours later to find him standing by the bed, dressed and holding a tray on which two mugs of tea steamed invitingly. But his eyes were troubled.

'Mair, what happened? I thought we agreed . . .'

Blushing scarlet, she shot up in the bed like a jack in the box. He surely didn't think . . .

'You were crying in your sleep. I came to see if I could help. You thought I was Rosie.'

But he still looked worried. 'I didn't . . . didn't. . . ?'

At that, she burst out laughing. 'No, Mat! You didn't!' And what would she have done if he'd wanted to? she wondered, growing serious again. 'It just seemed the only way I could help,' she tried to explain. 'Human comfort, human warmth.'

'And it worked like a charm,' he told her. 'I feel tons better.' And he looked it, his eyes clearer, the skin no longer so taut over his cheekbones. 'And to prove it, I'm going to cook you a magnificent breakfast.'

'What time d'you have to be back?' she asked.

'This evening. Probably flying tomorrow.'

'Why not go over to see your grandmother, then? I've got to be back at camp at midday,' she added in case that influenced his decision.

'Oh, have you?' He sounded genuinely sorry. 'I thought we might have had time for a swim over at the hotel and then lunch.'

She shook her head. 'Sorry! On watch at 1300.'

'Can't be helped, then. Some other time, maybe.'

'Some other time,' she echoed.

'I'm so very sorry,' said Mrs Moneymoon after he had told her about Derek. They were drinking tea on a patch of grass at the side of the house that was surrounded by bushes of lavender, a relic of the days when lavender-scented linen had been a speciality of the high-class laundry Mrs Moneymoon had run. 'He was a lovely, lovely lad. Would you like me to write to his parents?'

'Oh, would you? They'd appreciate that. I'll be writing, of course.'

'And I'll tell your parents, if you like,' his grandmother offered.

'No, it's OK, Gramma. I won't let you do all the dirty work. I'll ring them later, if I may.' He felt so much more in control now, thanks to that wizard little WAAF. He remembered how she had cycled away from him that morning, taking the shorter, bumpier way over the fields, refusing his offer to tie the bike to his car in some way and give her a lift back to camp.

'Exercise is good for me,' she'd told him. 'I still need to watch my weight.'

'You're just right,' he'd said, hugging her hard out in the lane, neither of them caring about the twitching curtains in Mrs Dickson's front parlour. 'Nice and cuddly.'

'Look after yourself,' she'd called, wobbling away over the ruts.

'I met Mair Corben over at the cottage,' he told his grand-mother and then paused in astonishment at the sudden appearance of a small child, cartwheeling through the lavender and across the grass in a blaze of yellow.

'Look!' Coming to a halt in front of them, Maggie hoisted up her skirt to reveal a pair of bright yellow knickers. 'Aunt Mary made 'em out of old curtains. Stella's got blue an' Polly's got red but I like mine the best!'

'Yellow,' declared Mat solemnly, 'is definitely my favourite colour, too.'

'Really?'

'Really!'

Standing on one foot, she pondered. 'Is it yer favourite colour for anyfink, not jus' knickers?'

'Definitely.'

She put up a hand and pulled off the matching ribbon in her hair. 'You have this, then. An' I'll keep the knickers.'

'Oh, but . . .' He began to remonstrate but his grandmother put a hand on his arm.

'Maggie really wants you to have it, don't you, my love?'

' 'Course!'

'Then I'll keep it. And thank you, Maggie. I won't actually wear it because my CO wouldn't like it but I'll keep it in my pocket.' He patted his tunic pocket as he placed it inside. 'Next to my heart!'

Mair had been right to suggest him coming here.

VII

Rosie had decreed that they meet at Grosvenor House in Park Lane.

'Why not a canteen somewhere?' Mair, horrified, had protested over the phone.

'Because it's central and we can dance there if we want to.'

'Dance? I thought we were just going to talk. Have a meal maybe.'

'Well, of course we'll do that first but why not a bit of a knees-up afterwards?'

'You do realize there'll be five of us? So one of us won't have a partner.' And no prize for guessing who that'll be, Mair thought sourly.

'All taken care of, honey! Mat's bringing a friend – guy called Andy Ridgeway. So we'll have something to eat first and then trip the light fantastic. OK?'

'If you say so!'

'I'll book us in at a service hostel for the night so make sure you've got a pass.'

'Will do.' At least Rosie seemed to have no plans to spend the night with Mat.

She'd got there far too early, but the offer of a lift from a friend in MT who had to go and collect some bigwig from Whitehall was too good to miss. She was dropped at Hyde Park Corner a good hour before the midday rendezvous Rosie had arranged.

First she went to check on the exact position of Grosvenor

House and was grateful it wasn't the much larger Dorchester close by. But Grosvenor House was quite intimidating enough. From her vantage point on a bench in Hyde Park, she could see a steady coming and going of uniformed personnel and nearly all were commissioned. At least she'd had her best blue uniform cleaned and pressed and her buttons were dazzling in the late summer sunshine. And her hair under her cap was now styled in a 'liberty cut' – two and a half inches all over her head – and she knew it suited her.

If she kept her eyes skinned, she'd spot Rosie in time to join up with her outside, then she wouldn't have to brave the hotel foyer on her own. Unfortunately, when she did see her, she was climbing out of a taxi. Mair shot to her feet but by the time she'd waited for two buses and an army truck to pass, Rosie was having the door held open for her by an awe-inspiring commissionaire. Increasing her pace, wondering if she dare shout Rosie's name out loud, Mair cannoned sharply into two air force officers going in the same direction. Her nose came into painful, eye-watering contact with a tunic button and her cap fell off. Hideously embarrassed, she tried to straighten up.

'Well, if it isn't LACW Corben!' came Mat's voice somewhere above her head. Blushing furiously, she pushed herself upright then bent to pick up her cap but was forestalled by Mat's companion.

'Allow me! Although, if I may say so, you look much better without it!'

She had a brief impression of a laughing face with twinkling brown eyes as she crammed her cap back on her head.

'Andy, this is my old friend, Mair Corben. Mair, meet my oppo, Andy Ridgeway. I knew you'd get on,' he added smugly although, as far as Mair was concerned, entirely without foundation.

However, she was afterwards to realize the remark, whether deliberate or not, had put her neatly in her place as Andy's girl for the rest of the day, so that Mat could devote himself to Rosie. Not, strangely enough, that that was how it worked out in the end. Admittedly, they'd fallen into each other's arms when

they'd first met and Mat had kept his arm around her shoulders
as they'd found an empty table, but that had been before Lotte
and Charlie had arrived. From then on, it was a different ball
game entirely.

'I told you it wasn't a good idea to ask Lotte and this Charlie,'
Mat had grumbled to Rosie. 'They're half an hour late already.
And I'm starving. You chaps are, too, aren't you?'

Chaps indeed! In a moment, Mair thought, he'll be clapping
me on the back and asking me if I want a pint! She left it to Andy
to admit that he was 'a little peckish'.

'Five more minutes,' Mat said, 'then I for one am moving in to
the . . .' The words died on his lips, his attention absorbed
completely by a girl who'd just walked into the bar. Tall, slim and
wearing the uniform of the WRNS, she was certainly the most
beautiful girl he had ever seen and probably ever would. As he
gazed, all thoughts of lunch gone from his mind, she took off her
cap to release a mass of copper-red curls covering her head like
a cap. Her skin was like alabaster, without a single freckle to mar
the small, straight nose. Her eyes, he decided as she came nearer,
clearly searching for the lucky person she was meeting, were the
colour of jade.

And then he became aware that Rosie – dear, sweet Rosie
whom he adored and always would but not in the crazy, abandoned way he could love this girl – had risen to her feet and was
waving her arms above her head. 'Hi, Lotte! Over here!'

'I don't believe it,' he mumbled under his breath as he stum-
bled to his feet. 'I simply do not believe it.'

Then Rosie was making the introductions. 'Mat, of course, you
know.' But clearly she didn't because she was smiling in a distant
sort of way at young Andy and ignoring him completely. And
then, when Rosie had explained and she was looking at him, her
smile became even more remote.

'Of course,' she said, 'I should have known.' And he realized,
with a dreadful sinking feeling in his stomach, that her memories
of him had been as unpleasant as his of her. But there was
nothing he could do about it at the moment because she had

turned and was now introducing a very large, somewhat pugna-
cious-looking army sergeant – regimental sergeant major, he
amended, noticing the crown on his sleeve.

'Great to meet you, Charlie!' said Rosie, extending a
welcoming hand and drawing him into the circle. 'Lotte's told
me all about you.'

Mat's stomach gave another precipitous lurch. Surely this
ugly-looking 'brown job' wasn't her boyfriend!

The brown job's mouth relaxed ever so slightly. 'More likely
my ma's celebrated mutton pies she told you about!' It was an
innocent enough remark and they all laughed but there was
something about the tilt of his chin as he said it that made Mat
realize that, for some reason, he felt himself to be inferior to the
rest of them. A bit of a chip on his shoulder? he wondered and
immediately, and perversely, felt a need to reassure him. Clearly,
Rosie seemed to feel the same.

'I wish she'd passed on some of her expertise to my mom.
According to my pop, she can't even make corned beef hash
without supervision. But talking of food, how do you two feel?
Mat here says he's dying of hunger but don't let that put you off
having a drink first. He may be the most senior officer present
but he can't swing his rank on the army or the navy.'

'As if I'd try!' said Mat. 'But there's time for a quick half,
Charlie. What d'you say? I shouldn't mind another.'

'Great!' said Charlie, visibly relaxing, and Mat signalled to a
passing waiter.

Lotte having excused herself in order to go and 'freshen up', it
took only a couple of disingenuous remarks on Mat's part for him
to discover that Charlie wasn't her regular boyfriend. And anyway,
the fact that he and Rosie seemed, almost immediately, to establish
a rapport would soon have convinced him. He knew from experience that his cousin was like a chameleon, changing her voice, her
attitude, her personality even, to accommodate whatever company
she was in. And now, she was being sweet and funny, drawing
Charlie Johnson out from under his chip with effortless ease.
Visibly relaxing in his chair, he responded in kind, making her giggle
uncontrollably at some murmured comment. Good! thought Mat.

Throwing back his head to drain his glass, he glanced sideways and saw that Mair and young Andy also seemed to be getting along nicely. Including Andy in the party had been a wise move on his part. They were both such good mates of his; between them, they'd rescued him from the despair into which he could so easily have fallen after Derek was killed.

As if conscious of his gaze, Mair glanced up and flashed him a smile that, for a brief moment, made him almost jealous of Andy. It didn't last, of course. He only had to gaze at Lotte as she appeared to know that the affection Mair inspired in him bore no comparison with the passion that he devoutly hoped to share with Lotte. Even so, he returned Mair's smile and murmured 'Like the new hairstyle!' before turning his attention to the seating arrangements for lunch.

But he needn't have bothered. Without prior consultation, Rosie and Charlie took adjoining seats, as did Andy and Mair, and that left him free to pull out a chair for Lotte, then take the one next to her. So far, so very good!

'You've changed so much,' he told her over the soup.

She laughed. 'I must have been a gruesome child, insisting on my rights as a guest to play with your trains on Christmas morning! But when you have all the charm of a black widow spider, you have to stand up for yourself in whatever way you can. That brace took some getting over, I can tell you.'

'It certainly achieved its purpose,' he assured her. 'And what happened to all those freckles?'

'Oh, they're still there under the skin, ready to show if I'm out in the sun for too long.'

He was so eager to learn everything he possibly could about her, he couldn't decide where to begin. But one thing had to be cleared up first.

'I hope I've changed, too?' he said. 'And for the better?'

She took her time over replying. 'It's a bit too soon to tell,' she said at last. 'So I'll keep an open mind for the time being!' But he took heart from the gleam of laughter lurking in her eyes and at least the remark seemed to show a willingness to remain in his company.

'I shall do my best to convince you,' he told her. 'When do you have to be back in harbour – or whatever you call it in your set-up?'

'Quarters. And I've got a forty-eight-hour pass. I plan to go and see my grandparents in Kent.' He didn't dare ask if she planned to go later today or tomorrow. Nor to mention that he and Andy also had forty-eights.

'Are you happy in the Wrens?' he asked instead and glanced at the blue anchor on her sleeve. 'You seem to be doing well.'

She shrugged. 'No better than anyone else.'

'What do you do? Transport? Signals?'

Again, she shrugged. 'Just clerking. Boring stuff, really.' But there was something about the offhand way she said it, her immediate glance around the table as if seeking some other topic of conversation that made him wonder if there was more to it than 'just clerking'. He knew that she worked at the Admiralty and now he came to think about it, with her background she must be bilingual, if not tri. 'Clerking' could be another name for intelligence – codes and ciphers, perhaps. In any case, he wouldn't dream of pursuing such a delicate subject.

'How are your parents?' he asked instead. 'Are they settling in, in the States?'

She brought her gaze back to him. 'They're fine although I think my father longs to be back in Germany, but not under the present regime, of course. And my mother is happy to be wherever he is. How about yours?'

'Determined to look on the bright side.'

'I remember you had a wonderful great aunt of whom I was in great awe until the day she asked me if I'd go skating with her up at the Hall where the lake had frozen over. She said she was afraid of making a fool of herself in front of the residents.'

Mat raised his eyebrows. 'Aunt Bee was a wonderful skater. She'd never have made a fool of herself in a million years.' And then his cheeks reddened. 'She took pity on you, didn't she? Because we other kids were so beastly to you.' Briefly, he laid his hand over hers where it lay on the table. 'I've no doubt I was the ringleader. I'm so sorry!'

She grinned. 'Don't be! If I remember rightly, you followed us anyway, and ended up flat on your face trying to perform some difficult manoeuvre.'

He burst out laughing. 'Serves me right! Arrogant little sod that I was!'

'You were rather. But so was I. I used to shout at you in German and that really wound you up. You once called me a bloody Boche! And I retorted with lousy Limey!'

Then they were both laughing and Rosie, glancing up for a moment from an animated discussion with Charlie on the relative merits of Southend and Coney Island – heaven knew how they'd got on to the subject – gave a tiny nod of approval. She'd never forget Mat's face when Lotte had been introduced. Holy cow, but she was glad she'd never told him how Brunhilde had turned into Lorelei!

The reunion was turning out to be even more successful than she'd hoped. At first, she'd been a mite worried about Mair, afraid she'd taken a shine to Mat after their meeting at Wittenham, but now she seemed to be going great guns with Mat's friend, so perhaps she'd got it wrong. With a small sigh of satisfaction, she turned back to Charlie.

'We could always go there tomorrow,' he was saying.

'Go where?'

'Southend, of course. Coney Island will have to wait till we've settled Hitler's hash.'

'OK – you're on!' They'd already established that neither had to be back in camp until the following night.

There was no denying that they made a strikingly attractive couple, Mat's fair head only an inch or two above Lotte's chestnut curls as they swooped and twirled, chasséd and glided around the floor.

'As if they were joined at the hip,' said Andy enviously. 'Are you sure they've only just met?'

'As adults,' said Mair. 'They would have met while they were children, of course. Part of the charmed circle.' She despised herself for the hint of sarcasm in her voice but couldn't prevent it.

'But surely you were as well? Your mother was a VAD too, wasn't she?'

'Oh, yes. In fact, she shared a room with Lotte's mother in France but then she went off to Malta to nurse her wounded husband. He died but she stayed out there and eventually married my father and went to live in Wales. The rest you know.' For they'd already exchanged brief family histories. 'Mind you,' Mair continued, 'Mat's mother did invite us to use their country cottage whenever we wanted to. That's where I met Mat. When I was ten and fat as a pig!'

And that's probably where you first fell in love with him, Andy thought shrewdly. Aloud, he said, 'Would you like to dance? I should warn you, though, that I have two left feet.'

'Noble of you to ask but what I'd really like, if you wouldn't mind, is to get some fresh air. I've got the makings of a sizeable headache building up.'

'You do look a bit green around the gills. Not a migraine sufferer, I hope?'

'No, just a drop too much wine at lunch.'

Rosie, by now dancing with Charlie, saw them go. Charlie suddenly found himself being propelled at speed towards the edge of the floor.

'Hey! In this country, the man always leads. Didn't you know?'

But by then they'd come within discreet hailing distance of Andy and Mair. 'You OK?' Rosie checked.

Mair gave a thumbs-up. 'Just getting some air. Won't be long.'

Rosie relaxed back into Charlie's arms. 'I'm all yours, buddy!'

'You're playing with fire when you say that – honey!'

She laughed up at him. 'Hey! You're a fast learner! If this wasn't Grosvenor House, I'd teach you to boogie.' In fact, the band was actually playing 'Boogie Woogie Bugle Boy' but she doubted if Grosvenor House was ready yet for the real thing.

Charlie felt intoxicated by the rapport he could feel growing between them and he was pretty sure Rosie felt it too.

Rosie put back her head the better to study his face. 'You're so different from most of the guys I've met over here.'

'That's because I'm from the East End.' And this time he said it proudly and not as he so often did – as a prickly challenge. 'Straight for the jugular, that's us. No messing!'

She nestled more comfortably into his arms for the band were now playing "Whispering Grass". 'Suits me fine!'

'You know,' Mat whispered into Lotte's ear, 'if I hadn't known you already, I'd have thought of some way of getting to.' He wasn't at all sure that he'd phrased this very important statement correctly. 'I mean . . .'

'I know what you mean,' Lotte said. 'But like what?' This wasn't much better, grammatically speaking, but she was past caring about such niceties. Against all her better judgement, she could feel her body abandoning itself to the slow, sensual beat of the music, the feel of Mat's arms around her, the magical way her legs moved in unison with his. You weren't supposed to feel this way in wartime; at least, she wasn't supposed to. She had a job to do, old scores to settle, the fate of friends to discover. She'd been so pleased when she'd not only been posted to the Admiralty but also promoted. She mustn't throw it all away by starting some emotional involvement with an RAF pilot.

'I should have simply walked up to you and told you that you were the most beautiful girl I'd ever seen,' Mat declared.

'I would have looked the other way. Maybe slapped your face.'

'Would you? Really?'

No, she thought, I wouldn't. Because you are the most beautiful man I have ever seen. Not that she was ever going to tell him that, of course. 'Probably not,' she admitted.

'Good!' And his arm tightened even more firmly around her.

'Lotte,' he said a few moments later, 'do you have to visit your grandparents this time?'

She gave him a long look and he held his breath. Then her lips parted in a smile that made him seriously doubt if he could restrain himself much longer from kissing her in the middle of the dance floor.

'No, I don't have to,' she said, entirely against her better judgement.

'Wizard!' he said, because he could hardly shout out 'Excelsior' in the middle of the Grosvenor House ballroom.

VIII

'What now?' Mat asked as they stood in Park Lane. He knew what he wanted to do – tuck Lotte's arm into his, say goodbye to the others and lead her away. Annoyingly, it was Lotte who forestalled him. 'Does your mother still make those wonderful pies?' she asked Charlie.

'You bet! Why? Do you fancy one for your supper?'

'Now, that's an idea!' said Rosie, her face alight with eagerness. 'Let's all go to Charlie's place. How about it, Mat?'

'But wouldn't we be a bit of a crowd descending on your mother like that?' It was the last thing he wanted.

Charlie burst out laughing. 'When you run a pub, that's what it's all about. The more the merrier. And there are plenty of beds if we decide to stay the night, as well as plenty of pies.'

'Pies it is, then,' said Mat, knowing when he was defeated. 'All right with you, Mair? Andy?'

'Well, actually, Mat,' Andy said a little awkwardly, 'my parents are expecting me.'

'Oh, Lord!' said Mat, suddenly remembering. 'They're expecting me, too, aren't they?' For anticipating that Rosie's reunion might turn out to be a bit of a bore, he had accepted Andy's invitation to spend the night at his home.

'Don't worry,' said Andy. 'I just said one more RAF type. They won't mind in the least that it's a WAAF. That is,' he added gallantly, 'if Mair would do me the honour?'

'But—' Mat began then stopped abruptly. Who did he think he was – some eastern potentate with his harem? Just because he seemed to have this big brother thing about Mair – because she was such a nice little thing and had probably saved his sanity when Derek had bought it – didn't mean she shouldn't be allowed a life of her own. And, heaven knew, Andy was a great chap. And certainly if he wasn't coming on this pie expedition, it would make the party much neater if Mair didn't either. Anyway, she was now smiling up at Andy as if he were the fairy on top of the Christmas tree. 'If you're sure your parents won't mind,' she said, 'I'd love to.'

Abbie Johnson was beside herself with delight. 'Isn't this wonderful, Fred?' she kept saying and her husband nodded and smiled and agreed that it was, indeed, wonderful.

She seated them around a table in the pub's dining room. 'I don't do food on a Sunday night,' she explained, 'so you'll have the place to yourselves.'

'What's this if it's not doing food?' Mat protested.

'This is feeding an extended family,' she assured him. 'When Charlie said you were all meeting up, we sort of hoped – didn't we, Fred? – but we never thought you'd really come. What a pity Megan's little girl isn't with you – not that I ever met her mother. She'd left for Malta by the time I got to France. But I heard all about her, of course. I remember—'

'Later, Mum,' Charlie remonstrated, sliding an arm around her waist. 'Right now, you have four hungry people waiting to be fed.' It was suddenly desperately important to him that Rosie should see his parents in a good light. Lotte, he knew, loved them for what they were and Mat could lump it but Rosie – she was a different matter.

But he needn't have worried for Rosie was on her feet. 'Don't take any notice of Charlie, Mrs Johnson. But can I give you a hand? I want you to give me the low-down on my parents' wedding. Was there really a bombardment going on at the time? Pa always maintains they had to lip-read each other's vows, it was so noisy, and that they're probably not legally married at all.'

'Oh, it wasn't quite as bad as that. But . . .' Her voice died away as they disappeared in the direction of the kitchen.

She's a masterpiece, Charlie thought. She said she was an actress and I can quite believe it.

'Pints, gentlemen?' Fred Johnson enquired hospitably, and to Lotte, 'Your usual, my dear? White wine and soda?'

'Please!' Lotte smiled up at him.

As Fred went through to the bar, Mat, beginning to feel at a distinct disadvantage, murmured, 'You know them well?'

'I was actually visiting when London had its first big raid,' Lotte explained. 'Wasn't I, Charlie?' Charlie nodded.

'I remember now,' Mat said. 'My mother told me about it. It was the night you rescued Margaret Rose.'

'Who?' Lotte and Charlie asked in unison.

'Well, Maggie, as she is now.' And as they still continued to gaze at him, perplexed, 'You know! The little scrap my grandparents are looking after in Oxford.'

'Oh, you mean Drip!' Lotte said.

'No longer,' Mat assured her. 'Not since she had her adenoids out. And she really was christened Margaret Rose. My grandfather did some research. You should go and see her for yourself.'

'I know. I've been meaning to visit your grandparents ever since I came over.'

'That's it!' said Mat, thinking what an idiot he'd been not to think of it before. 'We could go tomorrow. All of us,' he added generously, looking at Charlie.

Charlie shook his head. 'Thanks. Some other time, maybe. Rosie and I have other plans for tomorrow. I'm going to show her Southend.'

'What about it?' Mat asked Lotte. 'Shall we go?'

She hesitated only for a second. After all, they would be with other people; it was being alone with Mat she must avoid. And she owed it to her mother to visit her old friends. 'I'd like that,' she said. 'I'd like that very much.'

'Sorry I haven't got my car,' said Mat next morning as they boarded the Oxford train at Paddington.

'More fun this way,' said Lotte, carefully choosing a compartment already occupied by three soldiers and a woman with a

72

small child. 'Anyway, this way you can read your newspaper.' For Mat had bought the *Manchester Guardian* on the station. 'And if you don't, I will.' She sat down next to one of the soldiers, took the newspaper from Mat and opened it in a determined fashion. Mat could do nothing else but sit on her other side.

'I see your lot have been busy,' she said, nodding at a column about the RAF's one-hundredth raid on Bremen.

'Stalingrad doesn't look too good, though,' observed the soldier sitting next to her and shamelessly reading over her shoulder. 'The Russians are taking some stick, by the look of it.'

'Poor sods!' said another soldier, sitting opposite. 'Let's hope winter comes early and catches the Jerries with their arses to the wind. If you'll pardon the expression, ma'am,' he added politely to the woman with the child. Lotte, being in uniform, presumably merited no such consideration!

From then on, the conversation became general and Mat resigned himself to being part of it. But once they reached Oxford, his spirits lifted. There was no rush to reach Moneymoon Manor.

'Lunch is a moveable feast these days,' his grandfather had told him when he'd telephoned that morning. 'Come any time.' Trusting this wasn't a purely masculine viewpoint, Mat had decided to take him at his word. Anyway, the odds against his grandfather remembering to pass on the message at all were pretty high.

'We'll walk,' he now told Lotte.

'Of course!' And she set off briskly down the Botley Road.

'Lotte,' he remonstrated, 'not only are you going in totally the wrong direction, Oxford isn't a place to gallop through at a rate of knots. It should be savoured slowly, sipped at delicately, rolled around the mouth like a . . .'

'Like a glass of vintage port?' she finished for him but slowing her pace nevertheless and allowing him to lead her in the right direction. 'Come on, Mat! I don't know who you're quoting but I bet you didn't savour Oxford slowly when you were here. I bet you whizzed around from party to party, doing the minimum of work.'

'Not quite like that,' he said. 'There was a war on after all and Derek and I couldn't wait to—' He paused, not at all sure that he could cope as yet with too many memories of Derek.

Lotte slackened her pace even more and glanced swiftly up at him, and then as swiftly away. She didn't know who Derek was but clearly this was a road he didn't want to go down. Tentatively, she tucked her hand into the crook of his arm, then remembered they were in uniform and quickly withdrew it. Immediately, Mat reached down and reclaimed it. 'I promise that in the unlikely event of our meeting an admiral in the Cornmarket, you can have it back!'

They didn't meet an admiral in the Cornmarket nor, in fact, anywhere at all as they walked down Beaumont Street and paused outside the Randolph Hotel while they pondered the merits of a mid-morning cup of coffee but, deciding the autumn sunshine was too good to waste, walked on. Crossing St Giles, they entered Broad Street, lingering briefly for Mat to tell Lotte that Brasenose was 'his' college.

'Isn't there anyone you want to visit there?' Lotte asked.

'No,' he replied, for he had no wish to share her company, 'but if you're agreeable, I'll show you where my parents used to sit and talk. And then I promise you, we'll nip on a bus.'

They walked on into the High Street and followed it down to Magdalen Bridge, where they crossed to enter the Botanical Gardens.

'There,' said Mat, drawing her to a halt beside a bench. 'Shall we sit for a few minutes? I think we deserve it.'

She wished she didn't feel so strongly that, for him, it wasn't so much an easing of tired feet as a nostalgic wish to repeat his parents' assignation. She was soon proved right.

'Mum's told me how they used to come here to talk after they'd delivered the laundry to the various colleges and before going back to Moneymoon Manor.'

In spite of herself, she was curious. 'But why was he helping her deliver laundry? Wasn't he an undergraduate here?'

'Oh yes, but the summer term had almost ended when they met. It was the only way he could get to see her. He was lucky it was a laundry business Gramma ran and not a coal merchant! Mind you, I think he'd still have been there, heaving sacks!'

'He must have . . .' Lotte left the sentence unfinished, unwilling to mention the word that could be her undoing. But Mat had no such scruples.

'Loved her very much? You're right. But then he went off to war and didn't see her again until it was all over.'

She grasped at the implication she chose to read into his statement. 'Presumably, your mother thought it sensible not to become emotionally involved with anyone until the war was over.'

'Sensible, my foot! Because of what she'd said, they didn't communicate for the entire war. She spent most of it regretting she hadn't thrown caution to the winds and married him before he went.'

There was no answer to that other than to glance down at her watch.

'Hold on a moment,' said Mat, 'and hear me out. I'll come straight to the point. I think – no, I *know* – that I could become very fond of you indeed. And that's putting it mildly. And I have a feeling – conceited, though it may be – that you're also attracted to me. No,' he said, as she made a movement of protest, 'let me finish. But I'm also pretty sure that for one reason or another, maybe because I'm likely to be shot to pieces by some passing Hun, perhaps because you may have a pretty important job to do, you don't want to get involved in any emotional entanglement. And I can understand all that. There are too many grieving widows dotted about the countryside without my adding to them. Even so, why should we deprive ourselves of the simple pleasures of meeting now and then, maybe in London if our jobs permit, maybe here in Oxford if Gramma and Gramps can bear it. No commitment for either of us. What do you say?'

For what seemed to Mat like an eternity, she said nothing. Her mind was racing. There was much sense in what Mat said. She *did* enjoy his company. Just because her mind was set so firmly on getting back to France didn't mean she had to live like a nun

PAT LACEY

in the meantime. Some relaxation could mean even greater concentration when it mattered. And how could she deprive a man who might be killed tomorrow or the next day of something that obviously meant a great deal to him?

She turned her face to his and put out a hand. 'Agreed!' she said. And he, his eyes alight, took her hand and repeated the word, not knowing that his parents had also used it to give face value, at least, to a similar lack of commitment.

'Sorry it's not quite as I remember,' Charlie told Rosie. They were sitting on a bench on Southend's promenade, eating fish and chips out of newspaper.

'Hardly your fault old Adolf bombed the pier,' Rosie observed.

'But I should have realized the beach would have anti-tank stakes all over it,' Charlie insisted. 'Incidentally, I was brought back here from Dunkirk.'

'I didn't know you came back from Dunkirk.' Rosie stared at him, a chip suspended halfway to her mouth.

'Me and 300,000 other blokes,' said Charlie, 'and we were the lucky ones. I came back on a fishing boat out of Leigh-on-Sea. Since then I can hardly look a herring in the face.'

'You tucked into those jellied eels we bought off that stall,' said Rosie.

'That's different. You can't come to Southend and not eat jellied eels.'

He grinned at her. What a girl she was turning out to be, clearly not caring in the least about the coating of fat that was now glistening on her fngers. Lotte, he reflected, would never happily eat fish and chips out of a newspaper although innate politeness would have made her go along with it, whereas Rosie had actually suggested it. Not, he was sure, that Rosie didn't have her own standards, just as high in their own way as Lotte's. He didn't know much about WAAF uniform but he was pretty sure those weren't service-issue stockings she was wearing, and her skirt seemed to have been pressed into a less sack-like shape than the norm. There was the way, too, that she'd got up early and helped his mother clean up the bar while he gave his father a hand out in the yard. She had seemed as at home doing that as she had been at Grosvenor House yesterday. Were all Americans like her? he wondered. And if they were, how did you know when they were being their true selves? Or, in other words, when the person they were with was really special to them? He wondered if he could frame the question in such a way that Rosie would understand what he was getting at but wouldn't think he was being too presumptuous.

'Are all Americans like you?' he asked as a preliminary.

'How d'you mean? Too much to say for themselves? Too brash and cocky?' He shook his head, for that was not at all what he meant. 'Too non-Brit? But I can assure you, old boy,' and now her voice acquired a pompous, upper-class English accent, 'I can be as British as the rest of 'em if I put my mind to it. Believe it or not, old boy, I've ridden to hounds. Just the once, mind you. That was enough.' And then, breaking into broad Cockney, 'I told the master wot 'e could do wiv 'is bloody brush an' no mistake!'

Charlie winced and looked away from her across the estuary, his face serious. 'I know one thing, Rosie. You're a bloody good actress. Too good, maybe.'

'How d'you mean?'

'Well, you're so good at pretending to be other people, but what's the real Rosie Shelton like? Does she ever stand up to be counted? And if so, would you let this poor, dim-witted Brit know when her next appearance will be?' He turned and looked at her directly. 'Because I'd really like to know, Rosie, before I let myself fall hook, line and sinker for you. At first, I felt as if we fitted together like . . . like a hand in a glove. And maybe that's true of Rosie Shelton as she was yesterday and today. But maybe not with the Rosie Shelton of tomorrow and the next day when she's with some other guy. Like Mat Holker, for instance. And that,' he added, switching his gaze back to the sea, 'is probably the longest and dumbest speech I've ever made in my entire life.'

To his surprise and consternation, Rosie said nothing but continued to eat her chips. I've blown it, he thought. She'll never want to see me again. And if that were to be the case, he knew he would be utterly devastated.

At last, when the silence had lasted longer than he could bear, he turned and looked at her and watched while she ate her last chip, then scrunched up the newspaper and threw it into the litter bin next to their bench. Then she turned to face him and he saw that she was frowning.

'I'm sorry, Rosie,' he began. 'I didn't mean—'

'No, Charlie, it's my turn now. You've been honest with me so I must be the same with you. The difficulty is knowing how to put it.'

He was sure, then, of what she was going to say.

'Without hurting my feelings, you mean? Rosie, I've got the message. Let's go.' And he got to his feet and picked up the strap of his respirator, ready to swing it on to his shoulder.

Rosie stood up too, and seized the strap. 'For Pete's sake, will you sit down! No – I've got a better idea!' And she put both hands behind his neck and pulled down his face until she could reach his mouth with hers and kissed him long and hard. When she eventually drew back and looked at him, she saw that his face had paled beneath his tan. 'Are you all right, Charlie?'

'Of course I'm not bloody well all right! I've just had a minor heart attack! Rosie, never, ever do that to me again unless you mean it. It's more than human flesh can bear. At least,' he said, managing a wry grin, 'than this human flesh can bear!'

'Oh, I meant it all right, Charlie! Have no fear on that score. If we were holed up in some hotel or other, I'd probably be in your bed before you knew what had hit you. But as it is, even I draw the line at a bench on Southend promenade in broad daylight. And before you ask, I don't make a habit of sleeping around, in beds or on benches – it's just the way I feel about you, Charlie Johnson. At the moment, that is.'

'At the moment?' Charlie sat down heavily on the bench, trying to make some sense of the last few minutes. There was now no doubt in his mind that Rosie cared for him so why 'at the moment'?

'No one else,' Rosie said, 'not even Mat, and he knows most things about me, has ever asked me the question before, Charlie, but it's one I ask myself almost daily. Who is the real Rosie Shelton?'

'Tell me,' Charlie suggested.

'I'll try.' She screwed up her face in concentration. 'It's as if I'm always standing outside myself, watching to see how I should behave. Should I be happy? Sad? Helpful? Dismissive? What do people expect of me? And, once I've decided, I do my best to oblige and to really *feel* the emotions they think I should have. Sometimes it's not easy. Sometimes, I take the coward's way out. Before America came into the war, I told myself every day that I should come over here and join up. After all, I was born here and have dual nationality. But then I'd kid myself that my duty was to stay with my parents for as long as I could. A silly butterfly, that's me, Charlie, flitting from flower to flower, never settling for long. Unlike Lotte, who always knows exactly what she wants to do and does it, no matter what. Mat seems to have taken a shine to her, which is great, but it's not going to be easy for him if he doesn't fit in to her scheme of things.'

But Charlie didn't want to even think about Mat or Lotte. 'And what about us? he asked. 'How do I fit into your scheme of things?'

She grinned ruefully. 'It's the classic situation, isn't it? Wartime, boy meets girl, boy may go overseas, girl may be killed in an air raid. It's a powerful part you've given me, Charlie, and I don't know how to play it yet. Does girl really love boy as much as he thinks he loves her? Or is she just reacting to the drama and romance of the situation? What if boy does come back from the war and girl doesn't get killed and they can't bear the sight of each other in the cold light of civvy street? Tell me that, Charlie, because I just don't know the answer.'

He put out a finger and traced the clean line of her jaw. 'All I know Rosie mine – and I'm going to call you that in spite of what you've just told me – is that I love you even more now than I did five minutes ago, if that's possible.' And it was true; her ruthless honesty was compelling. For such a girl, he would willingly wait – although he hoped to God he wouldn't have to for long.

'I'll wait,' he told her, 'but not happily. One day you'll wake up and know that Charlie Johnson is your man. Meanwhile, Rosie mine,' and once more he stood up and this time shouldered his respirator strap, 'let's go and have a drink.'

After their first obvious but hastily disguised astonishment that his 'friend' was a girl, Andy's parents couldn't have been more welcoming, even though Mair's unexpected arrival had entailed making up another bed in another room.

'Andy,' Mrs Ridgeway had scolded, 'you should have warned us you were bringing home your young lady. Not that it isn't very nice indeed to meet you, my dear.'

Uncertain how she should react, Mair glanced at Andy. He didn't fail her.

'Now don't embarrass the poor girl, Mum. We're just very good friends, united by a mutual lack of home comforts. Mair's home's in Wales so she has much further to go to sleep in a comfortable bed, wallow in a hot bath and enjoy some home cooking.'

'Oh, I can promise you all of that,' Mrs Ridgeway said confidently.

Much later, on the verge of sleep, Mair thought about Andy. She'd have to tread carefully there. Although he'd assured his mother they were no more than good friends, she doubted if that was the way he wanted it – any more than his mother did.

This belief was strengthened next morning when, after a late breakfast, Mrs Ridgeway despatched them both to the park, ostensibly to exercise Butch, the family's Labrador.

The park was beautiful, its trees already tinged by autumn colour but with roses still uncurling fragile petals among the spires of flamboyant blue and purple delphiniums.

'Let's sit for a few minutes,' Andy suggested. 'Old Butch could do with a rest.' And indeed, the Labrador flopped gratefully beside the bench they chose. 'Mum won't expect us back for ages.'

'She's been great,' Mair said. 'Not many women would have welcomed a stranger arriving practically in the middle of the night like she did.'

'She likes you,' said Andy. 'It's as simple as that. So do I,' he added after a moment, glancing down at her.

It's now or never, Mair thought and drew breath. 'And considerably more,' Andy continued quickly before she could utter anything. 'than you like me. I know that. No,' he said, as she tried to splutter out a protest, 'let me finish. I just want to say that you needn't worry. I'm not going to go all passionate on you. Although I might be tempted if it weren't for Mat Holker.'

Mair concentrated hard on a bee trying to negotiate the spur of a delphinium flower. 'Is it so obvious?' she asked, feeling her colour heighten.

'Only to one of my extreme sensitivity and perception,' said Andy with a grin. 'I doubt very much if anyone realized it yesterday. Certainly not Mat.'

That, at least, was something. 'I've always had a bit of a crush on him,' she admitted, trying to make light of it. 'It started when we were children.'

'Very understandable,' said Andy. 'He's a great guy. And I should know. Anyway . . .' He picked up one of her hands where it lay in her lap and squeezed it reassuringly. 'The secret's safe with me and I just wanted you to know that I do understand. All the same, I'd like to see you again, if I may.'

'Well, of course. I'd love to see you again, too. But Andy . . .' She looked up at him with a worried frown. 'Best not here, don't you think? I don't want your mother to . . . to . . .'

'Build up her hopes?' Andy finished for her. He bent and kissed her swiftly on the tip of her nose. 'Don't worry. I'll make sure she doesn't.'

'Well, the best way to do that,' Mair advised, 'is for you to take someone else home.'

'The next one in the queue, I promise you,' he assured her solemnly.

'Such modesty!'

He got to his feet and held out his hand. 'Best be getting back.'

IX

Rosie held open the door of the staff car.

'Thank you, Shelton, but I'll sit in the passenger seat if you've no objection,' said the station commander, sliding into it before she could offer any. Not that she would, of course. Group Captain Marshall was reputed to be a nice enough guy whose company she would probably have enjoyed under normal circumstances. She might even have conducted a mild flirtation with him because he wasn't *that* old and he'd obviously taken the trouble to check out her name beforehand. She would have allowed her 'Yank' voice to take over and he, as most people did, would have expressed an interest in her background and she could have made him laugh with her account of life in New York. With a bit of luck he would have suggested stopping for lunch before they reached the airfield to which she was taking him, and that would have meant avoiding the queue in the airwomen's mess, which was normally her fate on these staff jobs. But even the thought of a decent meal in a country pub didn't grab her today because she desperately wanted to switch off, as it were, and think about Charlie – and the letter she'd had from him that morning.

They reached the perimeter guardroom and she checked out the password of the day. Having the CO on board, the corporal on guard duty when they came back would be sure to insist on correct procedure.

Today, the password was 'pilchards'. Rosie let out an involuntary 'Ugh!' and the CO chuckled.

'Not your favourite dish, I gather?'

'No, sir! Not for breakfast, anyway.'

'They're supposed to be rich in vitamins,' he said.

'If you say so, sir! Personally, I prefer a good plate of corned beef hash.'

'Ah, that explains it – the accent, I mean,' he said predictably. 'What part of America?'

'New York, sir. Greenwich Village.'

'Know it well! My wife and I were in the States the summer before the war. Even thought about living there.'

'Why didn't you, sir?'

'Missed the cricket too much,' he said. 'Somehow, baseball was never quite the same!' He studied her profile for a moment before glancing around the flat Lincolnshire landscape. 'Very decent of you, Shelton, to come over and lend us a hand. I don't imagine you were drafted?'

'Oh no, sir! Actually, I'd been thinking about it for some time before Pearl Harbour. My mother's English, you see. Married a Yank during the last war.'

'So you probably have relations over here?'

'Oh yes, sir! Grandparents near Oxford and an aunt and uncle in Staffordshire.' And really, she thought guiltily, it's more than time I went to see them again. It was ages since the leave they'd all been given after 'square bashing' and she'd dutifully divided it between the two households, but not finding either quite the same without Mat. I wonder if Charlie would like to. . . ? She suddenly became aware that the group captain was gazing at her expectantly, clearly expecting an answer to something he'd asked. 'Sorry, sir! Just checking on the petrol.'

He glanced at the gauge. 'Looks all right to me. I was just saying you must have felt a bit homesick last week.'

'Last week, sir?'

'Thanksgiving Day, Shelton. You surely didn't forget it.'

'Oh no, sir! But Spam's not quite the same as turkey.'

'Never mind. We'll have to see what we can do for you on Christmas Day.'

'Oh. I'm sure Christmas Day will be fine, sir. Ours is a really good station. I'm very happy there.'

'I'm pleased to hear it, Shelton. Now – we're nearly there, I think.'

Jeez! So they were and actually driving down the main street of the little village on the edge of the airfield. So, no pub lunch. It would have to be the airwomen's mess after all.

It was at that moment that she heard the drone of approaching aircraft and coming from the direction of the sea. At the same time, an air-raid warning sounded from the airfield.

'Junkers!' said the CO gazing into the distance. 'It'll be the airfield they're after.'

Then she saw them; at least six, coming out of the cloud and diving fast.

'We'd better take cover,' rapped out the CO, 'by those bushes.' And he pointed to a line of laurels growing between a house and the road. It was providential that she was already out of the car and running when she saw the children. There were two of them – a girl of about five and a younger boy, hand in hand, as they stood uncertainly by a garden gate. Slightly ahead of the CO, she altered course and ran towards them just as the first bomb fell on the airfield. And then the next, and the next, and coming steadily nearer.

She reached the children just as the dark shape of the first Junkers loomed directly overhead and heard the whistle of a bomb above the roar of its engines as she threw herself down on top of them. And then gave an involuntary scream as she was struck forcibly in the small of her back by a heavy object that knocked the wind out of her.

'Sorry, Shelton,' said the CO in her ear as he lay spread-eagled across all three of them. 'And keep your head down. It's not over by a long chalk.'

It certainly wasn't. She had never been so terrified in her life as each aircraft – and there were six of them, she thought – tore down on the airfield and seemed to level out just above their heads. She found herself counting as each one dropped its stick of bombs until the last one was shrieking down and she heard herself cry out as the ground lifted beneath them and clods of earth rained down on top of them. Something sharp hit her on the forehead and she remembered her tin hat on the back seat of the car. She'd bet her bottom dollar, though, that the CO was wearing his. And then the children began to sob and she forgot her own fear as she murmured ridiculous, meaningless phrases.

'It's all right! Don't worry! It won't last much longer.' The last, at least, was true but it still seemed an eternity before the final Junkers turned and went back the way it had come.

The group captain rolled off her and staggered to his feet. His tin hat was tilted drunkenly over one eye and there was a smear of dirt across his face. 'All right, Shelton?' He put out a hand and hauled her upright.

'You've got a bit of a cut on your forehead. Painful?'

'Not at all, sir! Didn't know I had it!'

And now they were both helping the sobbing children to their feet. Fragments of soil and grass mingled with the tears coursing down their cheeks but clearly they were unharmed. Rosie sank to her knees and put her arms around them. 'It's all right, poppets. It's all over.'

'Bar the shouting!' The CO muttered, staring around him. The street was littered with debris and there were innumerable holes along it but the houses on either side seemed to be untouched.

So was their car. But there were great clouds of smoke billowing over the airfield. 'We'd best get down there,' the CO said, 'once we've done something about these children.'

'Shouldn't I . . . ?' Rosie began, but then a woman shot out of a house on the other side of the road and came running towards them.

'Shirley! Tommy! Are you all right?' And she, too, knelt and hugged them.

'They're all right!' both Rosie and the CO assured her. 'Just very shocked.'

The woman was crying now. 'I can't thank you enough. Won't you come in? A cup of tea, perhaps?'

Rosie could have killed for a cup but she guessed it was out of the question, and one look at the CO's face confirmed this view.

'We'd better be getting on,' he told the woman. 'See what we can do down there.' And he nodded in the direction of the airfield. As he turned to go back to the car, Rosie saw that the back of his coat was plastered with mud and earth. Clearly, both she and the children would have been in a considerably worse state if he hadn't been on top of them.

'Are *you* all right, sir?' she asked as they got back into the car.

'Fine, thank you, Shelton. Bit like being in a rugger scrum, I thought! Now, can you negotiate these potholes, d'you think?'

'No problem, sir! Bit like a slalom course on the level, don't you think?' And they both laughed.

'That's the spirit!' said the CO.

December 3rd 1942

Dearest Charlie,

Well, I've had my baptism of fire and emerged unscathed, I'm delighted to say, because suddenly life has become almost unbearably precious. It happened like this.

I had to drive our CO to an airfield near the coast and just before we got there, it was bombed by half a dozen Junkers. Another five minutes and we would have been in the thick of it. As it was, we took cover, sort of, and looked after a couple of children before carrying on to see if we could help.

Charlie, I've never seen such devastation. It was a bomber station, Wellingtons – or Wimpeys, as they're called – and as luck would have it, they were just back from a mission, lined up like sitting ducks on the tarmac. But at least there were no bombs on board. At least three of them had been hit; one of them was still burning when we got there.

There was a great chunk missing off the tower of Flying Control and the dispersal huts had collapsed like a pack of cards. Two hangars had had direct hits and the runways were pitted with craters. Ambulances and fire wagons were whizzing about all over the place and people were trooping out of air-raid shelters – the lucky ones, that is, the not so lucky ones were still in a barrack block that had had a direct hit. It was a WAAF barrack block where signal personnel were sleeping after night duty. I thought of how it could so easily have been Mair in there and joined in pulling the bricks and rubble away. (The CO had gone off to find his opposite number.) We had to go very carefully so as not to bring more stuff down on the people underneath.

At first, we didn't know if they were alive or dead but then someone heard a cry which spurred us all on. We got three out: one had a broken leg and cracked ribs, another a broken collarbone and the third seemed unhurt except for bruises and shock. But there was a fourth – and she was dead.

It was terrible, Charlie. At first there was this awful silence while they got her out and then one of the WAAFs who'd been helping began to cry and had to be led away by a very young section officer who looked as if she was pretty near to tears herself. Apparently, she – the WAAF who was crying – had been the dead girl's best friend and had changed duties with her because she had a date. No wonder she was so distraught.

After that, I reported to what was left of the MT section and the flight sergeant there gave me a shovel and told me to join a working party that had already begun to fill in the craters on the runways. That's where my CO found me when he was ready to go. Goodness knows what he had been up to but he had this dog in tow. It had belonged to a pilot who'd been at the controls of one of the Wellingtons that was hit and it went berserk after they'd got him out – dead, of course. Groupie seemed to be the only one who could calm it, so he'd decided to take it back with him.

Anyway, when we drove off – it was dark by then – the CO said, 'Shelton, stop at the first pub you come to. We both deserve a drink. And something to eat.'

So that's what we did and the landlord was brilliant. The pub was near enough to the airfield for him to have heard what had happened. He put us in a sort of snug with a roaring fire and let us bring the dog in, too. Then he brought us real ham sandwiches and a pint for Groupie and a shandy for me. I could have done with a triple Bourbon but thought it better not to ask as I wanted to get Groupie home in one piece!'

Rosie stopped writing and nibbled the end of her pen as she remembered the firelight winking on the brass fender, the spaniel stretched out at the COs feet and the way the landlord had fussed over them, not caring in the least that they were still plastered with mud. When at last he'd left them alone, Groupie had raised his eyebrows and commented, with a grin, 'Quite the blue-eyed boys, aren't we? But seriously, Shelton, you deserve a medal for what you've done today. You won't get one, of course, and nor will all the other airwomen who've done their bit. But they'll probably get a pat on the back from Bomber Command and I'll certainly make sure your Queen Bee, Squadron Officer Henshaw, hears about your actions.'

She'd grinned back at him. 'If I was a modest little Brit, I'd probably blush modestly and say it was nothing but as I'm a cocky little Yank, I'll say, "Thank you very much, sir!" '

But inside, she'd felt a warm glow of satisfaction, not because old Henny was probably going to be told she was the best thing since Lease Lend but because today she hadn't thought of herself once, hadn't once considered how her actions would affect the way other people thought about her. She'd just got on with the job. Now, to hear that the 'real Rosie Shelton', as Charlie had put it, deserved a medal was music to her ears. From now on, her life would never be quite the same. There was nothing like a brush with death, she reflected, to sharpen the senses and make you reconsider your priorities.

'By the way,' Groupie had added, giving her a quizzical glance, 'who's Charlie?'

Her mouth had dropped open, every bit of her normal sang-froid deserting her. 'How on earth. . . ?'

'I only ask,' the CO had said mildly, 'because every time a bomb dropped near us when we were with the children, you called out his name.'

'Did I really? Jeez!'

'For a cocky little Yank,' the CO had said, looking as if butter wouldn't melt in his mouth, 'you blush very nicely, Shelton! Have another sandwich!'

The CO's statement shouldn't really have surprised her because Charlie had been in her thoughts all day. She went back to her letter.

Anyway, dearest Charlie, the upshot of it all is – I love you! Not just for now but for ever and ever, amen. All during that dreadful day, you were always there at the back of my mind. I couldn't have got rid of you even if I'd wanted to.

So, I'm yours, Charlie boy, in whatever shape or form you want me. Wife? Lover? Fiancée? Camp follower? Although, on second thoughts, I don't think they're allowed any more. But rest assured I'll be down to see you as soon as I possibly can. Groupie says I deserve a medal – so maybe I'll get a thirty-six or a forty-eight instead!'

She signed the letter 'Yours, for ever and ever' and, for good measure, added a robin on a sprig of holly with 'I love Charlie' coming out of its beak.

Then she pulled another sheet of paper towards her and began, 'Dear coz . . .'

Surely Charlie wouldn't mind her telling Mat their glorious news? Since childhood, if had become second nature to confide in him just as, she hoped, he'd do with her. But she'd still take care to post his letter after she'd sent Charlie's. *He* must be the first to know how she felt. And then, of course, there was Mair. Lotte, too, but perhaps Mat would tell her.

'Rosie and Charlie have got a thing going,' Mat told Lotte when they next met; in London, this time. She was in civvies and wearing a dress of some floaty, gauzy material the colour of primroses that had made him catch his breath and go weak at the knees. If he didn't hold her in his arms very shortly, he'd probably explode.

At least if they danced, he'd be halfway there. In desperation, he'd suggested Quaglinos although it wasn't a place he normally went to. He would really have preferred somewhere less fashionable and less crowded but at least there would be dancing. Now, with the scent of her hair – was it verbena? – titillating his nostrils and a saxophone sobbing out 'We'll Meet Again', he was at least satisfying part of his desire.

She glanced up at him, one eyebrow raised. 'A thing?'

'Engagement? Affair? Liaison? Does it matter? They love each other.'

'Good! I'm glad. Rosie's a great person – and so's Charlie. Now I think about it, they're a perfect match. Rosie's completely mad and Charlie's inclined to take himself a shade too seriously at times. He needs to relax and she needs someone to . . . not to curb her high spirits exactly, but to point them in the right direction.' And then Lotte suddenly stopped dancing and stared up at Mat. 'Listen to me! Telling you about Rosie when you know her so much better than I! Sorry! Anyway, shall we sit down for a while? I'd quite like a drink.'

'Of course!' He fetched the drinks and Lotte raised her glass. 'To Rosie and Charlie!'

'Rosie and Charlie!' he echoed. And then, against his better judgement but because he couldn't help himself, added, 'And what about Lotte and Mat? Should we drink to them, too?'

'Why not!' She raised her glass again. 'To Mat!'

'To Lotte!' It wasn't how he'd meant it to be said but it was better than nothing.

Later, in the taxi taking them to her quarters, he held her in his arms and kissed her – and kissed her again and again. 'I'm not sure when I'll have leave again,' he murmured. 'Sandy's going on leave some time soon. Any chance of you coming down?'

Lotte hesitated, remembering the interview she'd had earlier in the day when her selection for 'special duties' in occupied France – and that was now the entire country – had finally been confirmed. 'Take some leave,' she'd been told. 'Put your affairs in order, tie up any loose ends. Training won't start until the end of January at the earliest.'

Now that she knew she was really on the way, that she'd achieved the first part of her objective, surely she could relax just a little? Mat wasn't exactly a 'loose end' but he deserved to be treated with love and respect. She remembered the commander's final recommendation: 'Let your hair down, Schreiber! Enjoy yourself! It may be your last opportunity for a while. And that's an order!' he'd added with a grin.

Who was she to disobey a senior officer?

'I think I should be able to manage a couple of days,' she told Mat.

X

The New Year began on a tremendous wave of optimism. Caught with their 'arses to the wind' and their bellies cramped with hunger, the Germans surrendered at Stalingrad. In the North African desert, Rommel's retreat continued and the Eighth Army entered Tunisia. At the end of January, Mosquito fighter bombers made the first daylight raids on Berlin with minimal opposition from the German defence, perhaps because attention was focused at the time upon Goering's impending broadcast to the nation to celebrate ten years of the Nazi regime. 'Very little opposition,' the crews reported on their return.

But such was not the case when Mat's flight took part in a daylight sweep over northern France and tangled with a formation of Focke-Wulfs. He was lucky but coming out of a sharp turn after firing his cannon into the underside of a Focke, he was appalled to see a Spitfire spiralling down in flames beneath him. Andy? Thick black smoke made identification impossible. But then, to his enormous relief, he heard Andy's voice over his radio.

'Break to starboard, Mat! Bastards right behind you!'

Automatically, he banked to starboard. Thank God Andy was OK! But if not Andy, then who?

He soon found out. When it was over and the Fockes – what remained of them – had turned for home, he waited with mounting fear for Sandy to 'round up his flock' as he always put it. It didn't happen.

He glanced at his petrol gauge: just about enough to get home.

He cleared his throat. 'Looks as though Skip's bought it, Andy.'
'You sure?'
'Near as dammit. Best be getting back.'
'Could he have bailed out?' they asked him at debriefing.
'Unlikely.'
It was an opinion shared by others in the squadron, who had seen the wounded Spitfire spiralling down. That evening, he and Andy got very drunk indeed.

Next morning, Mat was summoned to the group captain's office. As he'd half expected, he was to take Sandy's place. 'And Mat . . .' The grey-haired veteran of the First World War tilted back his chair, his hands clasped behind his head. 'Don't think you're just filling a dead man's shoes. You would have been recommended soon, anyway.'

'Thank you, sir!' But for all that the old man had said, it still didn't feel like that.

That evening, he rang Lotte and told her what had happened. 'Any chance of you coming down? It's difficult for me to get away at the moment.'

'Mat, I'm so sorry but I can't just now.' Clearly, this wasn't the moment to tell him she'd just been instructed to report to a remote country house in Surrey, where her selection – or de-selection – would begin.

'I see!' He made no attempt to sound other than desperately disappointed.

She thought furiously. Wasn't this, in fact, the perfect moment to see him, before she was caught up in a prolonged training process?

'Perhaps I could manage it. Just twenty-four hours.'
'That would be wonderful!'

Lotte put down the phone and stood, deep in thought. She'd certainly burned her boats now. It had been a crazy idea, right from the start, to think she could see so much of Mat and remain emotionally uninvolved. It would be her own fault if the way ahead was now doubly difficult.

He met her at the station. At first, in the early dusk of a February evening, he didn't recognize her for she wore a pre-war suit of smooth Donegal tweed and a black velvet beret pulled rakishly over one eye.

'You look so smart!' he told her after they'd hugged and kissed.

'I discovered the suit in a wardrobe at my grandparents'. I must have left it there ages ago.'

He led her out of the station to where his car was parked. 'Where are we going?' she asked.

'Believe it or not, I've been lent the CO's cottage. He's up at the Air Ministry for a few days and his missus has gone with him.'

The cottage, from what she could see of it when they arrived, was long and low and thatched. Inside, a log fire burned in an inglenook fireplace, shining on polished wood and leather. A bowl of white hyacinths stood on a coffee table in front of the fire. A Golden Retriever rose from the hearth rug and came ambling to meet them, tail wagging furiously.

'Heavens!' said Lotte, fielding the Retriever. 'Are you sure they've actually gone?'

'Drove them to the station myself just an hour ago,' said Mat. 'And part of the deal was looking after old Monty here. By the way,' he added, as he took her jacket, 'we're meeting Andy later for a meal at the pub. Is that all right? I didn't want to leave him on his own just now – so soon after Sandy.'

'That's fine by me.' Visibly she relaxed and Mat knew he had done the right thing. Although he longed to simply pick her up and carry her upstairs to the big feather bed that he knew awaited them in the guest bedroom, he knew instinctively that he mustn't rush her. A good meal, wine if they were lucky, then a relaxed nightcap in front of the fire. And then . . .

'I've had a wonderful evening,' said Lotte several hours later and meant it. Not only had the landlady of the Dying Duck, the airfield's nearest pub, excelled herself with a concoction of rabbit, swedes and potatoes, ladled straight from the pot into deep, earthenware bowls, there had been the fun of meeting not only Andy but several of Mat's other friends as well.

'Word's got about,' said the first one, called Digger or Dusty – or was it Nobby or Nails? – peering around the door of the little sitting room off the bar where she and Andy were eating.

'Fair's fair, share and share alike,' suggested another, joining him.

'Bugger off, the pair of you!' Mat had said cheerfully.

And they had, at least until the meal was finished. But when Mat had poked his head into the bar and called, 'We're off now, chaps. See you in the morning,' there had been howls of protest.

'Just for a minute or two, then,' Mat had compromised, helping Lotte up on to a stool and taking up position by her side – like a nursemaid with her charge, she had thought with amusement.

But the minutes had lengthened to an hour and more and it was closing time when they'd eventually left, coming out to find a sky thick with stars and with puffballs of white cloud sailing across it like an armada of galleons in full sail.

'Blast!' Mat had said, looking up. 'Just what I didn't want,' But he'd said no more and Lotte hadn't pressed him. Both he and Andy, she'd remembered, had drunk only in moderation.

Now, with Monty snoring contentedly between them, they sat either side of the dying fire. 'I can't tell you how wonderful it is to have you here,' said Mat. And now there was a purposefulness about him, a sort of urgency that Lotte was beginning to share. He moved and sat on the arm of her chair, then put his arm around her shoulders and bent to kiss her.

And Lotte kissed him back, long and hard. Why not snatch a few hours of happiness before they went their separate and dangerous ways? The art of living from day to day was something Mat already knew about and she would soon learn. Sarah had. Sarah was the new friend she'd met while they were waiting for their final interview.

Sarah's fiancé had been killed at Dunkirk and since then she'd ceased to care about the future. A short life and a gay one was her philosophy now and it was one Lotte was doing her best to share.

Now, she returned Mat's kiss with an abandon that delighted him. Breathing in the scent of her hair, feeling the smoothness of her skin as he slid his hand inside her blouse and pulled down the narrow straps of whatever garment she was wearing beneath before finally cupping the firm roundness of her breasts, he was in an agony of longing.

'Oh, Lotte. Darling Lotte! I love you so much.' And now his hands were fumbling desperately with the fastening of her skirt, pulling, yanking . . .

At that precise moment, the telephone rang. Mat drew in his breath in a great shuddering sigh. 'Oh, God! Not now! I can't bear it!'

For several seconds, they sat there, letting it ring where it stood on a carved oak chest beneath the blacked-out window, willing it to stop.

'Perhaps,' said Lotte at last, 'it's your CO ringing to see if everything's all right here.'

'No,' said Mat, 'it'll be the ops room.' He walked across and picked up the receiver. 'Holker!' Then he listened intently. 'Yes, I understand. Yes, right away.' He put down the phone and came back to Lotte. 'I was afraid this might happen. The weather's improved and there's a raid on Essen tonight We've got to give cover.'

'Oh, Mat!' Lotte didn't try to hide the depth of her disappointment. 'Can't someone else go?' And then she gave a half-laugh at the absurdity of the suggestion.

He put his arms around her bare shoulders and she shivered at his touch. 'What time d'you have to leave in the morning?'

'About nine. I shall have to go.'

'Of course, but I should be back long before that.' And he bent and kissed her. 'I love you, Lotte.'

'I love you, too, Mat.' It was a relief to say it, to know that whatever happened . . . But she mustn't go down that road.

Two minutes later, he was driving away.

As she got ready for bed, Lotte listened intently but there was no roar of aircraft overhead, only a sort of muted, continuous grumbling in the distance, which eventually died away. She wondered how long it would be before she could reasonably expect him back. Even when the planes returned, there would be debriefing.

She lay back on the pillows and closed her eyes, although there was no way she was going to sleep. But the seductive warmth of the feather mattress enveloped her like a cocoon and she'd slept badly the night before. When she awoke, there was a rim of greyish light around the blackout curtains and she peered at the luminous dial of her little travelling clock on the bedside table. Seven o'clock! But, she tried to reassure herself, there was no need to worry – not yet. Mat hadn't given her a specific time to expect him. Now that he was a flight commander, there could be all sorts of procedures he must follow.

She lay there for a few moments longer, willing herself to stay calm. And then, below her in the living room, the telephone began to ring.

Fumbling her way down the stairs and across the blacked-out room, bumping into furniture, only just avoiding Monty where he lay in front of the cold hearth, she thought she would never reach it. When she finally picked it up, she was trembling uncontrollably.

'Hello?' Was that strangled whisper really hers?

'Lotte? It's Andy. Not good news, I'm afraid.'

'He's dead?'

'We simply don't know yet. He came down over the sea. No sightings as yet but Air Sea Rescue are out looking. Anyway, I'll be with you in half an hour. I'll borrow Mat's car.'

'Thank you, Andy. No matter what, I've simply got to catch my train.'

'I understand.'

She replaced the phone, then sank down on to the chest. 'Borrow', Andy had said. One didn't borrow from someone who was dead. There must be hope.

Kate put down the telephone. She had to use two hands because her whole body was trembling uncontrollably. 'That was . . . that was . . . Andy, Mat's friend.'

The next moment she was in Robert's arms. Thank God I'm here for her, he thought. Whatever the news, and clearly it's bad, we can take it together. He led her to a chair then crouched at her feet while great sobs wracked her body. At last, she drew breath – a shuddering sigh that ended on a ridiculous hiccup. She looked at Robert and tried to smile.

'It's not as bad as it could be.'

'He's not dead?'

She shook her head. 'Just terribly burned but otherwise only superficial injuries. He's . . lucky to be alive.'

I just hope that's the way he'll see it, Robert thought, remembering some of the burn casualties he'd seen in the last war. But, he reminded himself, they could do so much more for them these days. Aloud, he said, 'So there's hope. Can we go and see him?'

Kate nodded. 'Andy said it was all right for close relatives.'

'Lotte? They've found him. He's alive.'

'Oh, Andy!' She gave a great sob of relief. 'Thank God for that! How is he?'

'Impossible to say yet. But you know Mat, he's a fighter. But he's very badly burned. His face . . .'

'I see.' She cradled the receiver, trying to come to terms with this new development; to grasp the implications of what Andy had told her or, even worse, not told her. But at the back of her mind was a growing but as yet unidentifiable horror. And then she remembered. Hans Moser! Suddenly, she felt violently sick and reached out a leg to hook her ankle around the leg of a nearby chair and drag it towards her. Sitting down, she put her head between her knees but still managed to hold on to the telephone, trying to make sense of what Andy was saying.

But her mind was racing. Hans Moser had been a boy in her class in junior school who had had a very bad harelip so that he was unable to speak properly. Worst of all, he had had a violent crush on her. She could still remember her revulsion when, in a secluded corner of the playground one afternoon, he had tried to kiss her, pinning her up against a wall with his body while his grotesque lips had sought hers and his sweaty hands had pawed at her breasts. His breath had stunk of stale garlic.

He hadn't kissed her; her best friend had come looking for her and he had drawn back before running away in the opposite direction. Lotte had tried to make a joke of it to her friend but that night she'd had a terrible nightmare in which Hans had not only kissed her, forcing his tongue down the back of her throat, but had wrestled her to the ground before trying to tear off her clothes. For several years afterwards, the nightmare had recurred.

Mat, she told herself now, was nothing like Hans Moser. But his face, a small clear voice persisted, could be infinitely worse to look at.

'I don't know if they'll let me see him,' Andy was saying. 'But I'll ask when I next visit. They're allowing me in but otherwise it's relatives only at the moment. We could always say you're his fiancée—'

'No!' she heard herself say before she could even think it through. 'There's no way they'll give me leave just now. Sorry, Andy, but he'll understand how it is.'

'Yes, of course. I see.' She doubted if he did but she was past caring. 'I'll ring you again, shall I?' he suggested. 'Let you know how—'

'No, that could be difficult at the moment. I'll ring you, Andy. Promise. And please give him my love.'

'Will do.' And Andy rang off.

Later that same day, after he'd rung the hospital and been told Mat was 'comfortable' – whatever that meant – Robert Holker rang Rosie.

'Rosie? Uncle Robert here. Not good news, I'm afraid, love, but could be worse. Mat's been shot down. Badly burned but otherwise minor injuries. We're going to see him . . Rosie, are you all right?'

But Rosie clearly was not. There had come a sort of strangled scream followed by a silence that was even more disturbing.

'Rosie! I should have told you to sit down or to go and find a friend. Is there anyone. . . ?'

'It's all right, Uncle Robert! I am sitting down now.' In fact, she had slid down against the wall of the draughty corridor in which she'd been standing and was now sitting with her back against it. 'Just tell me where he is and I'll go and see him straight away.'

'Rosie, hold your horses! He's still in a very bad way. Heavily sedated. Only close relatives are allowed to see him at the moment. Much better that you wait.'

'But I'm his cousin, for God's sake! I've known him for . . . for ever!'

'I know, Rosie. And I'm sure there's no one he'd rather see. But that's the whole point. He can't see. Not at the moment.'

'Uncle Robert, just *tell* me! Where is he?'

'Rosie, I'm not going to tell you. I know you too well. You'll go AWOL at the drop of a hat. But I'll ring you tomorrow, I promise, and let you know how he is.'

'Oh, Uncle Robert, I give in! Don't worry!' And she put down the receiver.

Robert frowned. When Rosie gave in like that, suddenly, like a pricked balloon, alarm bells sounded. But what more could he do? At least he hadn't told her where Mat was.

Andy wished Mair would cry. Anything rather than sit there, stony-faced and tight-lipped. But he was still glad he'd driven over to tell her rather than telephone. Now, they were sitting in a corner of the lounge of Maybury's only hotel, a tray of coffee in front of them.

'It's really good of you to come and tell me face to face,' Mair said at last.

'I wanted to see you anyway. There's something else I want to talk to you about. But it can wait.' He leaned forward to pour her a cup of coffee and added a liberal spoonful of sugar although he knew she didn't normally take it. 'Here, drink this.'

Obediently, she took a sip, then grimaced. 'Drink it,' Andy said. 'And that's an order!'

She gave him a wan smile. 'Tell me exactly what happened, Andy, every little detail. If you can bear it,' she added quickly, noticing the pallor of his skin, the dark circles under his eyes and feeling suddenly guilty. He was really going through the mill.

'We met this posse of Fockes over the Channel. Quite what

happened I don't know yet but Mat was probably trying to look after the new chap we had with us. Anyway, I saw him go and I thought that's it because I didn't see him bale out. However, Air Sea Rescue were alerted and they found him. He'd not only baled out but managed to pull the toggle on his Mae West jacket before passing out. He wasn't conscious when they picked him up,' he added quickly, noticing how Mair was now holding her coffee cup as if it were a nut she was trying to crack. 'And in a way, of course, the sea was by far the best place for him to end up, like lying in an enormous bath of saline solution. They can do wonderful things with burns now, you know, and of course they're controlling the pain with morphine.' He broke off, wondering if he should try and take the cup from her before she broke off its handle.

'Will I be able to see him?' she asked.

'Not yet,' he told her gently. 'His parents will be with him now but it's only close relatives for the moment.'

'Rosie? Lotte?'

'I just don't know. Rosie rang me last night. Mat's father had told her but clean forgot to tell her which hospital Mat's in. So I was able to tell her. And Lotte – well, I rang her but there's no way she can get away at the moment.' He didn't tell her that Lotte had been with Mat only hours before his crash. What was the point? It would only add to the anguish she was already feeling.

Mair glanced at her watch. 'I'd better be getting back, Andy. On watch in an hour. Will you let me know how. . . ?'

'Of course!'

'And thank you again for coming.'

They walked outside to where Andy had parked Mat's car and Mair had left her bike.

'Oh!' Mair paused. 'You said there was something else you wanted to tell me?'

Andy paused. 'Plenty of time for that. It'll keep.' But would it? he wondered as he watched her ride away. His unexpected posting to Canada on a goodwill recruiting campaign would be within the month. He'd had mixed feelings about it at first but now that Mat was out of it – probably for the duration – the prospect had a definite appeal. Leaving Mair would be a hell of a wrench but clearly there was no future for him in that direction; not while old Mat was around. Her reaction just now had given him conclusive proof, if he'd needed it.

Interesting, he thought, as he drove out on to the Oxford road – he'd just pop in to Moneymoon Manor while he was down here. Mat's grandparents knew about the crash but they'd still be worried sick – how Mat's various popsies had taken the news. All had been devastated but obviously Lotte had felt a certain reluctance to see him, Rosie clearly couldn't get there fast enough and Mair had shown the patience and common sense he would have expected. For sheer endurance and fortitude, he'd back her against Lotte every time. It was just a shame that Mat was too besotted with Lotte to see it.

'Is 'e goin' ter die?' Elocution abandoned, Maggie stared out at Andy from the haven of Mrs Moneymoon's arms where she sat in the kitchen rocker. Behind them, Professor Moneymoon leaned heavily upon the back of the chair. All three were now silent, awaiting Andy's reply.

'No,' he said gently, 'he's not going to die, Maggie, but he may not be quite so . . so good-looking as he was before.'

Visibly, all three relaxed. 'We didn't like to pester Kate with too many questions when she rang us,' Mrs Moneymoon explained. 'But we hardly slept a wink last night, worrying.'

'I can imagine,' Andy sympathized. 'But you'll be able to see him when he's a bit more . . presentable,' he added, addressing the child. What on earth would she make of Mat's inevitably changed appearance?

'Wot's p'sentable?' Maggie asked.

'Not quite so pretty,' Mrs Moneymoon tried to explain.

'Like Mr Golly?' Maggie asked. Mr Golly was the disreputable old golliwog the twins had passed on to her and whom Maggie insisted upon taking to bed with her every night. Mrs Moneymoon thought of its black face, its torn ear and its thick blubbery lips and tried to suppress a sob.

'A bit like that,' she answered and suddenly bent her head over Maggie's tousled curls to hide her tears.

'That's orlright, then,' said Maggie, 'cos that means I'll love 'im even more'n I do now.'

'We all will,' said the Professor, his voice rough with emotion.

XI

'Sit down!' ordered the nursing sister, pushing up a chair so that the edge caught Rosie behind the knees and she had no alternative but to do as she was told. The trouble was, she'd had no idea what to expect, certainly not this mummy of swathed bandages lying not on the bed but above it, suspended on some sort of cradle system operated by pulleys. The head resting against the pillows had two slits cut in the bandages for eyes, a hole where the nose should be and a slash for the mouth, like some grotesque mask for Halloween. It could be anyone lying there; she only had the sister's word it was Mat. She cleared her throat.

'Can he hear me?' she asked.

'I should think so,' said the sister, 'but in a muzzy sort of way, I expect. He's sedated, of course, but he is conscious.'

'Rosie?' a voice croaked from the pillow. 'Is that you?'

'Who . . . who else?' Her own voice was no more than a whisper.

'I'll leave you,' said the sister, 'but only for two minutes, mind. It's only because you're his sister that you're allowed in at all.'

'Thank you!' And Rosie gave the sister one of her most brilliant smiles.

'Pop into my office on your way out,' said the sister and walked away.

'Did you say sister?' came from the pillow after a few seconds.

'Well, I'm as good as, aren't I? And I certainly wasn't going to come all this way and then be told they wouldn't let me in!' She looked for his hand to hold and was faced with two great paws

104

of bandages. 'I can't even hold your bloody hand,' she said.

'What . . . ever . . . you do, don't make me . . . laugh,' pleaded the voice.

'You're not supposed to talk, either,' said Rosie. 'I only dropped in to offer cousinly support and to say it's so wonderful you're still alive, even if you do look like Tutankhamen. And I'll come again as soon as I can,' she added quickly, thoroughly alarmed when a sort of strangled snuffle, halfway between a laugh and a sob, came from the pillow. But she knew if she didn't wisecrack she'd cry and that would be worse, much worse. Best if she went now; at least he'd know she'd been.

'Love you, Mat!' she said.

'Love you too, Rosie!'

'Hang on in there!'

'Will do!'

She left him then, making a kissing noise just above where she guessed his left ear to be, then tiptoed away down the ward, looking neither to right nor left, because she couldn't bear to catch sight of the other mummies that she knew were lying there.

'Come in!' called the sister through the open door of her cubbyhole of an office. 'I've got a cup of tea here for you. And cry as much as you want,' she added kindly. 'Your parents were here this morning and I thought your mother would never stop.'

'My? Oh, yes! Mom – Mum's always been a bit . . . emotional.' She made her voice as 'cut-glass' as she could manage. 'Dad's very stiff upper lip, of course. How long before they take off my brother's bandages?' she asked, steering the conversation into what she hoped were safer channels.

'Well, it depends upon how quickly he heals, of course, but they like to start surgery – plastic surgery, that is – after a couple of months. So' – she shrugged – 'a few weeks, I expect. They'll start with the eyelids, probably.'

'He'll be able to see then?'

'Oh, yes! In many respects, your brother's been very lucky. Where are you stationed, by the way?'

'Lincolnshire.'

'So you've come a fair distance.'

'Mmm. And I'd better be thinking of getting back.'

'Would you like me to see if I can get your pass extended?'

'Oh, no! Thanks all the same.' Rosie got to her feet and picked up her cap, shouldered her respirator and turned to go. 'Thanks for the tea.'

They sat in the buffet at Waterloo station and sipped undrinkable tea from thick white cups.

'Well,' said Lotte, 'we've survived so far. More tea?'

Sarah glanced at her watch. 'Actually, I should be going. My parents are expecting me.'

'Just a few more minutes,' Lotte coaxed.

'You're trying to put it off, aren't you?' Sarah accused. 'Visiting Mat?'

'Is it so obvious?' Sarah nodded. 'The trouble is, I don't know what to expect. The last time I spoke to Andy – that's his friend – he just said it was too soon to start skin grafting and that he was still swathed in bandages.'

'So at least you won't have to look at anything too gruesome,' Sarah tried to comfort her.

'But I shall guess at what's there, under the bandages.'

Sarah gazed at her reflectively over the rim of her cup. Was this Lotte's Achilles heel? The inability to look at a torn and mangled body and not show her distaste? 'Where we're going,' Sarah lowered her voice, 'you might see worse – much worse.'

'Oh, I know! And I'd have to cope. But could I love someone like that? Could I spend the rest of my life with him?'

'That's a bit of a hypothetical question at the moment, isn't it?'

'I doubt if that's the way Mat's going to see it. He's going to need reassurance, the knowledge that people love him no matter what.'

'You couldn't just pretend?' Sarah suggested. 'You're a damn good bluffer. The course has shown me that.'

'I couldn't pull the wool over Mat's eyes. Anyway, he deserves better.'

It wouldn't have been so bad, she decided later, if she'd been able to reach Mat's bed without walking down that interminably long corridor. Or even if she could have forced herself to stare straight ahead, instead of glancing to right and left, catching glimpses of wards where the beds held not people but mummies. They weren't all in bed; some, incongruously, were mobile mummies in wheelchairs or walking with the aid of sticks. Some even held a book or magazine, so presumably they could see through those holes in the bandages. And some were clearly talking to each other through the wider slits of their mouths.

And then, straight in front of her, a man in pyjamas and a dressing gown came out of what must be Sister's office because the man had his head turned and was talking over his shoulder.

'OK, Sister! Back to bed like a good little boy. You joining me later, after lights out?' And then he turned his head and Lotte found herself gazing at a hideous travesty of a human face; there was no nose, only two little black holes above a mouth whose huge bloated lips reminded her of the painted gash of a circus clown. One eye was wide and staring and very blue but the other was invisible beneath a bandage that gave the face an almost piratical look. Above the 'good' eye, the remains of a black eyebrow sprouted like an old toothbrush.

It's pure Picasso, Lotte though wildly. What if Mat. . . ? But the man was talking again – this time, to her.

'A Wren, by Jove! And a beautiful one at that! Can I help you, madam? Pipe you aboard? Splice the main brace? Sister, do we have a tot of rum for our nautical visitor?'

'That's enough, Fergus!' Sister had joined them in a flurry of starched skirts. 'Behave! And back to your bed at once!'

'Yes, Nanny!' And he went, the lid of his visible eye flickering in an incongruous wink.

The sister looked at Lotte. 'Come and sit down for a moment. It can be a bit of a shaker at first. Who is it you've come to see?'

Lotte, her heart pounding, sank down gratefully into the chair beside the sister's desk. 'Flight Lieutenant Holker. Mat.'

'Ah well. Nothing to alarm you there. He's still under wraps, as it were. And you are. . . ?'

PAT LACEY

'Lotte Schreiber. I'm not a relative. Just a . . . very close family friend.' Traitor! she thought. That's not the way Mat would describe you. She suddenly realized the sister was gazing at her curiously.

'Lotte? It must have been you, then, that he was calling for when he was brought in and hadn't regained consciousness. They often do that at first, before the morphia starts working. But in Mat's case, we couldn't make out who, exactly, he was calling for.' She smiled apologetically. 'Lotte's not a familiar English name.'

'My father's German and I was born in Germany,' Lotte explained. 'I was christened Charlotte after my maternal grand-mother but naturally it was abbreviated to Lotte when I went to school.' She was feeling calmer now and able to ask the questions that she badly needed answers to. 'Is Mat badly burned?'

'Yes, I'm afraid so. I doubt if there'll be any question of him flying again. His hands will never— Well, let me say that holding a knife and fork will present difficulties, let alone the operation of the controls of an aeroplane.'

'And his face?'

'Not unlike Fergus's, I'm afraid. But you won't recognize *him* after a few months. He's just had an upper lid grafted on to his left eye, then it'll be the lower lid and after that he'll be able to close his eyes. He can't at the moment, you see.'

'And . . . his nose?'

'Oh, he'll definitely have one – of sorts. He pretends he can't decide what shape to have. Short and straight? Roman? Retrousse? In fact, he won't have any say in the matter and it will probably be more like a button than anything else. He knows that, of course, but according to Fergus, it's a crime to take life seriously. It's his way of coping. And I think,' she said gently, 'that your Mat will find his own particular way of living with himself. But he'll need all the love and understanding he can get. Fortunately, his family are being very supportive. Parents, sister, grandparents . . .'

'Sister?' Lotte queried.

'Yes, Rosie, I think she said her name was.'

'Ah yes, of course, Rosie!' Lotte suppressed a smile. Trust Rosie to wangle her way in!

'I'll take you along to see him now, shall I?' the sister suggested, getting to her feet.

'Thank you.' She couldn't put it off any longer.

'Just ten minutes this time, please. He's not long had his dressings changed and that always takes it out of him.'

She turned off the corridor into a small ward with only four beds and with a window at the far end. Here, three of the beds held recumbent figures but in the fourth, a man, swathed in bandages, leaned back against a mound of pillows.

'Visitor for you, Mat,' the sister said, swishing the bed curtains along so that he and Lotte were hidden from view but still had the window in sight. Then she turned and left them.

Lotte walked to the head of the bed, forcing herself to smile. 'Hello, Mat!'

His eyes, peering out from the bandages, were disconcertingly as she remembered them, their gaze made even more penetrating by the absence of lashes. As he looked up at her, they softened and she guessed that beneath the bandages, he was trying to smile.

'Great to see you!' He spoke slowly as if it was an effort to form the words.

'You, too!' She smiled again and felt her mouth begin to stiffen into a sort of grinning rictus. She pulled up a chair and sat down.

'Can you . . . move a bit nearer?' Mat asked. 'Can't see you properly with the light behind you.'

She hitched up her chair. 'Nearer!' Mat commanded.

Now she was sitting right beside him. 'Take off that silly hat!' She did as he asked. 'As beautiful as ever!' he said.

She felt tears gathering behind her eyes because 'beautiful' was certainly not the word to describe Mat now.

'Don't cry!' he said. 'I'm doing well. Bandages off next week, the docs say, and then they can really start to go to town on me.'

'That's good!' She forced back the tears but now the rictus was back.

'How's the course going?' he asked.

109

'OK. In fact, they seem quite pleased with me – so far, that is.'

'So there'll be more to come?'

She nodded. 'Quite a bit more. The next part's in Scotland.'

'Scotland?' His eyes clouded.

'Only for a few weeks,' Lotte said hurriedly. Her mind felt like a battlefield as compassion fought with the knowledge that she could not – must not – offer him any hope. She lowered her gaze. 'I'll be able to come again, at least once before . . .' She left the sentence unfinished.

'You go away for good?' he finished for her.

'Something like that. I'm sorry, Mat. But you did know it was a possibility. Or at least, you had a rough idea.'

'I know! Just because my own war's over, I mustn't expect other people . . .' His voice trailed away.

'How – how are your parents?' Lotte asked. 'And Rosie? I hear she's your sister now!'

Once more, his eyes softened. 'Good old Rosie! Ever resourceful!' And then the smile left his eyes. 'Lotte?'

'Yes?'

'Lotte it's an unfair question but I have to ask it. After the war . . . will you. . . ? Is there any chance. . . ?'

It was as she had feared. He needed to know – one way or the other. That, at the very least, she owed him. She forced herself to meet his gaze. But the words wouldn't come. Dumbly, she shook her head, saw the raw pain in his eyes and lowered her own, then watched in horror as she saw her tears begin to fall on the bandages swathing his hands. 'I'm so sorry, Mat! So very sorry, darling!'

A minute later, the sister looked up from her desk, frowning at the sound of footsteps running down the corridor. Didn't her nurses know by now that she wouldn't countenance such haste, no matter what the emergency? And what on earth could have happened to cause such undisciplined speed? She got to her feet – then stared in astonishment as Lotte ran down the corridor, looking neither to right nor left and with a handkerchief pressed to her face.

Strange! She would have thought she was the last person to give in to grief with such abandon. However, she shrugged, you never could tell. She'd best go along and see if Mat was all right.

Mair knew that her initial reaction would be important, not only in helping to sustain Mat's confidence in himself but also in laying the foundation of any relationship they might share in the future. Clearly, pity was out of the question, but surely not sympathy? To pretend that nothing had happened, that he was still as attractive as he'd ever been, would be an insult to his intelligence.

'A shade tetchy, at the moment,' Andy had said when he'd come over to say goodbye before sailing for Canada. 'He hasn't said so in so many words but I gather that Lotte's visit wasn't exactly an outstanding success.' He'd been watching carefully when he'd delivered this last piece of information and any hopes he may have fostered about a shared future with Mair were immediately dashed when he saw the flicker of hope that momentarily shone in her eyes.

'Where's Lotte stationed now?' Mair asked carefully.

'Scotland, I gather,' said Andy and left it at that. By now, he had a pretty shrewd inkling of what Lotte was up to and the less anyone, even Mair, knew about it, the better.

'Is he allowed visitors now?' Mair asked. 'I mean, other than family?'

'I'm not sure.' Andy admitted. 'They let me in because they reckon I boost his morale but I shan't be going again before I sail. Just a couple of days with the family and then I'm off.'

'I shall miss you,' Mair told him.

'And I you.' That was an understatement if ever there was one. Would he ever forget that pointed little face with its frame of dark hair, those huge brown eyes that normally showed her feelings so easily but were now guarded and withdrawn.'According to Rosie,' Mair said with a sudden, impish grin, 'Canadian girls are quite something. Although not as attractive as the American variety, of course!'

'I'll let you know!' Anything to give him an excuse for writing.

'By the way,' he added, 'why not go and see Mat with his grand-parents and then you'd be sure of getting in?'

And that was what she had done. Now, all three were walking towards the man sitting up in bed with a mountain of pillows behind him whom she had been told was Mat. It could be anyone, she thought, in a flurry of panic. A perfect stranger whom she'd never met before? perhaps that was how it would be from now on.

Mrs Moneymoon, hesitant until now, suddenly quickened her pace. The next moment, she was bending over the man who had now turned his head towards them.

'My dearest boy!' she said, leaning over him. 'It's so wonderful to see you sitting up like this.' Mat's eyes softened. 'Wonderful to see you, too, Gramma. And Gramps,' as the old gentleman joined his wife.

'And we've brought Mair.' Mrs Moneymoon waved Mair forward.

His eyes widened. 'Mair! Lovely surprise!' And suddenly, everything was all right. She smiled back at him then went to look for chairs but found only two.

'Sit here!' he told her, nodding towards the side of the bed. So his grandparents sat on one side and she on the other. 'How's things?' he continued. 'What's happening in the outside world? Are the daffies out in the orchard yet? And how are Maggie and the twins and Tom?'

'Well, we've turned the front lawn into a vegetable garden,' Mrs Moneymoon told him. 'And Stella and Polly are growing carrots and Maggie and Tom parsnips. And the daffs are just coming into bud. We'll bring some next time we come. And Mair's been over to the cottage – haven't you, dear?'

'And Mr and Mrs Dickson send their kindest regards along with some eggs,' said Mair. 'I've left them with a nurse.'

'And I'm trying to teach Tom to play cricket,' said the professor, 'but it's an uphill struggle. I could really do with you there, Mat, to bowl him a few of your googlies.' And then he stopped abruptly as his wife kicked him hard on the ankle.

'That might not be for a while yet,' said Mat lightly.

Mair decided to take the bull by the horns. After all, if he'd just broken his leg, they'd all be asking about it without hesitation. 'What's the prognosis?' she asked, nodding at his hands.

'Early days to tell,' said Mat. 'But in fact, Gramps, bowling cricket balls could be part of the treatment, so tell Tom to hang on. And as for the rest of me, well . . .' His shoulders lifted in an attempt at a shrug. 'I'm certainly not going to break any female hearts, that's for sure.'

Only mine! thought Mair. And perhaps Lotte's? But that was forbidden territory.

Soon after, a nurse arrived to change Mat's dressings and they rose to go.

'We'll come again soon,' Mrs Moneymoon promised.

'Me too,' said Mair, 'if that's all right with you.' She must be careful not to intrude on a family gathering.

'Of course!' said Mat. And then, as she smiled down at him, 'Sorry about Andy going. You'll miss him.'

So she was still Andy's girl.

XII

'This is all right,' said Rosie, casting a critical eye around the hotel lounge. True, the flowered chintz covering the easy chairs and sofas was a little shabby and faded, the carpet a little worn, but that was only to be expected after three years of war.

Charlie was on embarkation leave. 'D'you mind,' he'd written, 'if we meet in some place other than home? It's partly because I want you to myself and partly because Mum wouldn't approve. She loves you to bits, Rosie, but in her book, the wedding ring should come first.'

And of course she hadn't minded. In fact, she infinitely preferred it this way but understood his mother's point of view. In her book, she and Charlie didn't need the ritual of a marriage service to prove their love. They'd go through with the ceremony one day, if they survived the war, if only to please their families, but for now this was strictly between herself and Charlie.

They'd arrived at the hotel, deep in the Cotswolds, soon after midday and were now drinking coffee in the otherwise deserted lounge. 'Was it difficult for you to get away?' Rosie asked. 'What did you tell your parents?'

'The truth – but not the whole truth,' Charlie said. 'I told them it was important that I saw you and Mum got quite dewy-eyed about that and asked why you weren't coming to stay. So then I explained that you couldn't get away, so I was going up to stay near your airfield for a couple of days. I don't think Dad believed me altogether but he didn't say anything.'

Charlie stopped talking and picked up Rosie's hand then

turned it over and kissed the palm. 'What shall we do now?' he asked.

'Go for a walk? Have a game of shove ha'penny?' Rosie teased. And then, seeing the look of disbelief on his face, she relented. 'What would *you* like to do?'

Charlie got up and pulled her to her feet. 'I think we should go and unpack.'

Rosie thought of their minute overnight bags containing, in her case at least, a clean shirt and change of underwear, and giggled. 'Suits me!'

She lay under the quilt that Charlie had solicitously wrapped around her before falling into a deep sleep, his head pillowed on her bare shoulder, and grinned to herself. So that was what all the fuss was about! The big deal that her mother had told her was the most important thing a woman had to offer a man, and that it was worth waiting for until the right one came along. Well, she had been right about that; it *had* been worth waiting for and she sure was glad that Charlie had been the one to initiate her, that it had been his hands that had explored her body with such tenderness, that had awakened it to such a pitch of frenzy she had actually cried out to him that enough was enough and please to get on with it. True, it had been a bit painful after that but nothing she couldn't handle and Charlie, after he had subsided beside her, had assured her it would be even better next time.

Next time! For a minute or two, she revelled in the thought of the next two days. They'd have to do other things now and then, of course, maybe actually take a walk or two and even play shove ha'penny with the locals in some ancient, half-timbered pub but always with the knowledge that this wonderful, luxurious bed she was lying on was waiting for her to sink into with Charlie beside her. God! She was happy!

Charlie stood on deck as the troop ship nosed out into the Clyde. In a little while he'd have to go below and make sure his blokes had settled in before going to claim his corner of the cabin he was to share with five other sergeants for the next month or so. He wondered how long it would be before he was home again – if, perish the thought, he came home at all. But the possibility had to be faced even though it sounded as if everything, bar the shouting, was over in North Africa. There was still the little matter of Europe to consider, especially Italy, which was probably where his lot would end up.

His thoughts dwelt on the two wonderful days he and Rosie had spent together, cramming more happiness into them than the rest of their lives put together; at least, that was certainly the way it had been with him and he was pretty sure it had been the same with Rosie. He just hoped . . .

He frowned as he remembered how they'd thrown caution to the wind. But Rosie had insisted. She'd hated the thought of using any form of contraception.

'If it happens, it happens,' she'd declared, 'and I'd be the happiest girl alive if it did.'

Fighting talk! But he doubted if she'd really thought it through. Neither of them had. He shrugged his shoulders. No point in thinking about something that might never happen.

Lotte rested on her oars, head bent over her knees, then realized it had been a mistake; much better to have carried on even though every muscle in her body protested and the blisters on the palms of her hands must be the size of grapes than to stop for an admittedly blissful minute then have the agony of starting afresh.

A sudden, savage squall caused the dinghy to rock violently and sent a flurry of stinging rain into her eyes. Time to get going. Once round the bloody island that must be very close to her now and she could head for shore.

'And no cheating,' the sergeant instructor had barked. 'All the way round!'

'How will you know if we don't?' Sarah had dared to enquire.

'*I'll* know!' the sergeant had replied. 'Just you wait and see!'

And now, as Lotte settled once more into a sort of agonizing rhythm, looking over her shoulder for the rocks surrounding the island then feathering one oar as she steered herself around them, she understood what he had meant.

A beacon, set on a tiny promontory on the far side, was sending out its continuing message in a series of short and long flashes. Lotte's knowledge of the Morse code was still elementary and she had to watch it several times round before she got the message. 'Hamish says hurry! Bar open for one hour when you get back!'

She burst out laughing. Thank God for the British sense of humour! And for Hamish!

She was tempted to stay there until the next boat appeared through the gloom, just to share the joke, but guessed she'd be penalized if there was the merest hint of collaboration and she wouldn't put it past Sarge to have posted someone up on the rocks to check. So, once more, she bent to her oars, the pain easing magically on the homeward stretch.

In this happier, almost euphoric mood, she allowed herself at last to think about Mat. That their relationship was over, she had no doubt, and she had no doubt, either, that it was her fault. Without flinching, she faced the fact that there was something lacking in her personality that prevented her from feeling what she was pretty sure most women would have felt in her circumstances; an overwhelming compassion for humankind in general and for Mat in particular, that would cause her to love him even more deeply now that he was maimed and his life virtually in shreds. Pity she had in plenty; a terrible, searing pity that would do no one any good, least of all Mat. And with pity, there was also revulsion, the more so because she would always remember how moved she had been by his beauty.

But none of this helped Mat. She could but hope that he would see her as she really was and cease to love her. And certainly, there was nothing she could do to help him now; it would have to be Rosie. Dear, generous Rosie whom she'd once seen weep genuine tears over a butterfly with an injured wing that would never fly again.

XIII

'Congratulations!' said Rosie. She and Mair were sitting in the little café they'd discovered not far from Mat's hospital. Visiting him together, they had decided, would be more fun for Mat. Mair was now sporting a very new pair of corporal's stripes on her arm.

'Thanks!' she said. 'It was only because I could do the job before I joined. Anyway,' she added, '*you* look great.'

The comment was fully justified. Not only was Rosie's skin glowing with health, her eyes sparkling and her hair an exuberant mass of curls, she seemed to be exuding a sort of inner radiance that she was having difficulty in controlling.

'Love?' suggested Mair, one eyebrow raised. 'Can I put it all down to Charlie or do you know something I don't – like his convoy's turned around and is steaming home?'

'That,' said Rosie, 'is the only fly in the otherwise perfect ointment. Charlie doesn't know yet.'

'Know *what*, for heaven's sake?'

'That I'm pregnant. There, I've said it. Isn't it wonderful?' And Rosie sat back in her chair and gave Mair an enormous grin, clearly expecting her to share her delight.

'You're – you're sure?' If there wasn't delight, there was certainly astonishment, even incredulity, written on Mair's face.

'Oh, yes! I haven't reported sick yet because I don't want to set the official wheels in motion until I've decided where to go but I've missed two periods now, and I've had the dreaded morning sickness. But now that's behind me. I feel so well. I've

118

written to Charlie, of course. But heaven knows when he'll get the letter. He'll be over the moon, too.'

'You're sure about that?'

'Holy cow, of course! And his parents will be, too, when I get around to telling them. They love kids.'

'And your parents?'

The faintest shadow flitted briefly across Rosie's face. 'Fingers crossed there, for the moment. Mom's always been a stickler for not leaping into bed before the marriage ceremony. Folk over here tend to think anything goes in the States but it's not true, And Mom is English, remember.'

'So are Charlie's parents,' Mair pointed out gently. 'Sorry,' she added quickly, 'I don't mean to be a wet blanket. If *you're* pleased, then of course I am, too. But I'm just trying to be realistic. *My* parents would die of shame if it happened to me.'

'That's because your father's a man of God,' Rosie said. 'Charlie's parents are East Enders and they have a reputation for being big-hearted and generous. Anyway, it will be their first grandchild.'

'Yes, I see that,' Mair agreed. No point, after all, in spoiling Rosie's obvious happiness. But she just hoped Rosie was right. 'Are you going to tell Mat?' she asked.

'I'll play it by ear. Depends how he's feeling. What I can't decide,' Rosie continued, 'is whether to say anything about his face. Make light of it or just not comment.'

'We'll have a better idea when we see him and know how he's reacting. I've heard they don't have mirrors in the wards but at the same time, they can't stop looking at each other.'

In the event, it wasn't his face Mat was concerned about, it was his hands, and these he could see. One was still swathed in bandages but the other was claw-like and with strips of newly grafted skin, the whole encased in a sort of wire frame. But examination of this came later; first had come what they feared would be the ordeal of greeting him.

At least, they saw with relief, he was now out of bed and sitting in an armchair in the company of two other patients. All wore dressing gowns over pyjamas. Mat's face was now a criss-cross of bandages with patches of healthy-looking skin showing and one eye exactly as it had always been, the other padded with dressings. The good eye brightened as they walked towards him.

'What a sight for sore eyes! Well, one sore, one OK. Chaps, may I introduce my cousin Rosie and my good friend Mair. These two ne'er-do-wells are Johnny Dixon and Woody Morgan. And you can bugger off, the pair of you, once you've said hallo!'

'Well, some things haven't changed! Still as rude as ever!' said Rosie. Mair heard the relief in her voice and felt her own spirits lift.

'We were going anyway,' said Johnny Dixon, 'but nice to meet you, girls.'

'Likewise,' said Woody.

Mat watched them go. 'They're a grand pair. It's touch and go if Woody will lose his sight but whatever happens, he'll only have peripheral vision. Makes me realize just how lucky I am. Don't know what I look like but I hope it's not too terrifying.'

'Not horrifying at all,' Rosie assured him and looked around for chairs.

'Sit on the bed,' said Mat, 'then I can see you both. I knew Rosie would turn up like the bad penny she is, but it's good of you to come, Mair.'

'Try keeping me away!' said Mair while Rosie pretended to punch Mat in his good eye. 'Are they pleased with your progress?'

'I think so. They've just put a new eyelid on my gammy eye. Grafted on a piece of skin from the inside of my arm. The surgeon's a real wizard at the job. But the really good news is that I've still got most of my nose and my upper lip. The lower lip isn't so good, so I'll probably end up with a pout like Mae West's. And one cheek will look sort of crumpled and creased but the other won't be too bad. It's the hands that will be the real problem. It's goodbye to flying, I'm afraid.'

'There'll be other things you can do,' said Rosie.

'I can't think what, at the moment, but I'm sure you're right. Now, what's your news? Apart from Mair now being the cuddliest corporal I know!'

'Would you like to hear my news?' asked Rosie.

'Don't tell me! Let me guess!' teased Mat. 'I can't believe you're going to be made up to corporal, too, so what else is there? I know! You're leaving our air force and are transferring to the Yankees? Or you're leaving the services altogether and going to entertain the troops? Show Vera Lynn how to do it? Am I right?'

'Only in one respect.' Rosie was grinning from ear to ear. 'I will be leaving the air force before too long. That's for sure. But not for the reason you think.'

'There's nothing the matter with Aunt Priss or Uncle Hank, is there? You're not getting a compassionate discharge? No – it can't be that or you wouldn't be looking so cheerful. And anyway, Mum would have said.'

'You're getting warmer!' Rosie chuckled. 'But more of a *passionate* discharge!'

'More of a. . . ?' Mat was clearly puzzled. And then he stared at Rosie and Mair guessed that, as much as his injured face could register emotion, it was now complete disbelief. 'You can't mean you're *pregnant*, Rosie?'

Her hands did a slow handclap. 'Well done, that man! You've got it at last! Isn't it wonderful? You're the first relative to know so consider yourself privileged. And by the way, would you like to be its godfather? I'm sure Charlie would approve.'

'Now, hold your horses! I'm still trying to get my head round it. Did you know?' he asked, turning to Mair.

She glanced at her watch. 'Not until one hour ten minutes ago, to be exact.'

'And what do you think about it?'

'If Rosie's pleased then I'm pleased too,' said Mair staunchly.

'And Rosie's obviously over the moon,' said Mat slowly, 'so I guess I'll have to be too.'

'Of course you are!' said Rosie.

'Does Charlie know?'

'Not yet. At least, not unless he's got my letter by now.'

Mat gazed at her, his mind a jumble of confused thoughts. Obviously the fellow hadn't taken precautions but knowing his

121

tempestuous cousin, as he did, that might have been difficult. And would he, if it had come to the crunch, with Lotte? Suddenly, he was engulfed in a wave of intense longing for her. If only there hadn't been an operation that night. If only . . . But that train of thought would get him nowhere. And certainly it wasn't going to help Rosie now. And she, poor kid, though she didn't seem to realize it yet, was going to need all the help she could get.

Charlie was in a sober mood. He had just attended a service of thanksgiving in Tunis; thanksgiving that, between them, the 1st and 8th armies had driven the Germans and Italians out of North Africa. He had felt a bit of a hypocrite, standing there with his blokes, for they had played no part in it although their turn would soon come. Italy was still under Axis domination and while no one thought much of the Italians as fighters, their German panzer divisions were another matter. And there was also the little matter of Sicily to be overcome first, although the air force was already having a go at it.

Now, he sat outside his tent on a discarded petrol can, thrust out still pathetically white knees to the sun and opened the letter from Rosie that he'd just received.

Dearest Charlie,
How I miss you! Every second of every minute of every hour of every day! I spend my time either in abject misery because you're not with me or a state of utter bliss when I remember those wonderful days we spent together and how much I love you.

Great stuff! Thought Charlie. More of the same, please!

And I know that you love me and just for a little while, that's enough, until the next wave of despair hits me. But now, everything's going to be different. I shall have a purpose in life. Because – wait for it, Charlie – I'm carrying our baby! Isn't that the most exciting thing that ever

happened? *Our* baby, Charlie! Can you believe it? I can't –
and then I have to let my skirt out a notch and I know that
it's true. Thank goodness for battledress, say I! Because I
haven't reported sick yet.

I'm going to tell Mair and Mat when Mair and I visit him
in hospital and I've written to Mom and Dad. The next
thing I must do is to visit your parents. After that, I'll make
it official and get my discharge and go and live with them.
That's what you would want me to do, isn't it? At least
there'll be plenty of room and I know they'll welcome me
with open arms. Their first grandchild!

All my love, sweetheart,

Rosie

Charlie read the letter through again as he tried to marshal the
thoughts that were tumbling about in his mind. Above all, was
the realization that Rosie hadn't a clue about his parents' reaction to her news.

Treat her like you would your sister, he remembered his
mother telling him when he'd first asked a girl out and she'd got
to hear about it. Pure as the driven snow a girl should be when
she was led to the altar, according to his mother.

Meanwhile, what was the best thing for him to do? If only he
were still in England and could simply apply for a compassionate
forty-eight and marry Rosie straight away! But he'd write to his
parents tonight and do what he could to smooth things over. And
surely Rosie's grandparents in this manor place would help if
necessary. Mat, poor sod, wouldn't be of much help to anyone
just now, but his parents might be. Gradually, his panic subsided
and he read the letter again. This time, a sense of wonderment
gripped him and a slow grin spread across his face. He, Charlie
Johnson, was going to be a dad!

Charlie had been wrong in one respect. Mat was the greatest
help although it was Mair who took the brunt of Rosie's distress.

They had already arranged to meet up at the café before going on to visit Mat and now Mair was appalled to see the change in her friend.

'Rosie, what's up?' For all the inner radiance that had shone out from her like a beacon was now gone and her eyes were red-rimmed and deeply shadowed. 'Is it the baby?'

Rosie shook her head. 'No, the baby's fine, thank goodness. I've reported sick and been given the once-over and everything's normal. It's . . it's Charlie's parents that are the problem. They . . . they . . .' Her voice wobbled and she gave a great gulp while tears began to trickle down her cheeks. 'Oh, Mair! I couldn't believe his mother could say such hurtful things. According to her, it's all my fault and I've led her precious first-born astray.'

'Do I take it she gave you the "never darken my doors again" routine?' Mair asked.

'Well, no! That's the most sickening part of it. When she'd finished telling me what she thought of me, she said she'd get a couple of rooms ready and I could have those until Charlie came home and made an honest woman of me. But can you imagine what it would be like living with someone who thought you were Jezebel reincarnated and lost no opportunity to tell you so? I couldn't face it, Mair.'

'I do see what you mean.' And Mair could. Her own mother would be just as condemnatory, never able to forget that her daughter had brought shame on to the family. 'What's Charlie's dad like?' she asked.

Rosie gave a sudden grin. 'He's OK. When I was leaving, he saw me to the door, gave me a quick hug and said, "Don't worry, love. She doesn't mean the half of it." All the same, I'm not risking it.'

'Are you going to tell Mat what's happened?' Mair asked.

'He'll probably get it out of me anyway,' said Rosie. 'He's got two good eyes now, so Aunt Kate says.'

It would be difficult to describe them as two *good* eyes, exactly, Mair decided when they found Mat immersed in a game of chess with Johnny Dixon, who moved the pieces for both of them. As she and Rosie walked down the ward, Mat looked up and she saw the papery whiteness of his new upper lid and its lack of eyelashes. Almost, Mair thought, like a piece of sticking plaster he'd forgotten to peel off. There were still dressings over the cheek below the eye.

Mat, however, was inordinately proud of his new acquisition. 'I can close both my eyes now,' he boasted after Johnny had wheeled himself away, promising to finish the game at a later date. And he slowly lowered, then raised, both the old and the new lids. 'It means I can now actually close my eyes when I go to sleep. The next big job will be my mouth and parts of my cheek. Then the second hand. After that, heaven be praised, I should have some leave.'

They sat, once again, on Mat's bed. 'Let me just look at you both,' he said. 'You've no idea how wonderful it is to look at you properly.' And then, fixing his gaze upon Rosie. 'What's the matter, coz? Nothing wrong with the baby, is there?'

'Oh, Mat!' Rosie gave an enormous sniff and Mair began to get to her feet.

'I'll just go and . . .' Quite where she intended to go she had no idea but she felt instinctively that the cousins would want to be alone. But Rosie put out a detaining hand and Mat shook his head.

'Please don't go, Mair,' he said. 'You count as one of the family. Go on, Rosie. Spill the beans.'

And she did, but this time managing to restrain her tears.

'You poor kid!' said Mat when she'd finished. 'But don't you worry. We'll sort something out. Mum's due to visit me tomorrow – she's bringing Aunt Bella with her this time – and I'm sure she'd love to have you.'

'D'you really think she would?' It was clear from Rosie's unsurprised reaction that she'd been hoping for something like this.

'Of course. She'd be horrified to think of you going anywhere else. Except possibly to Gramma's and I suppose she's got a pretty full house already.'

'There's the cottage too,' Mair suggested hesitantly, not wishing to presume too much on Mat's heart-warming assertion that she was one of the family. 'I could pop over and see you most days.'

'So, what with one thing and another,' declared Mat jubilantly, 'you've nothing to worry about. Anyway,' he added, 'just wait until the baby's born. Charlie's parents will be fighting to get their hands on him then.'

'*Him?*' queried Rosie and Mair in unison.

'Well, OK then! But I bet it's a boy!'

XIV

'Well, we've made it!' Sarah was exuberant as she and Lotte wandered through the grounds of the country house where they'd completed their training.

'Don't relax too much,' Lotte said. 'They can always change their minds.'

'That's why I thought it would be safer to talk out here. I'm pretty sure they've bugged our rooms.'

The path had taken them towards a small lake and now they scrambled down a grassy bank to the water's edge. A pair of mallards, ever vigilant, came paddling towards them, hopeful for food. Bullrushes stirred in a gentle breeze and from somewhere amongst them, a moorhen called to its young.

'Wouldn't put it past them to bug the bullrushes,' said Sarah.

Lotte chuckled. 'I doubt if even they would go that far. But if you like' – she pointed along the lake shore to where a rowing boat rocked at a tiny landing stage – 'we could take that out to the middle of the lake. Yes, I know,' she added, as Sarah opened her mouth, 'the boat could be bugged, too! Come on – we're getting paranoid.'

They untied the boat's mooring rope and clambered in. Lotte picked up the oars while Sarah lay back, her face tipped to the sun. Lotte rowed out to the middle of the lake, then rested on her oars and gazed back at the house. Chimneys soared into the azure sky and from this distance, the now unkempt flower beds merged easily into the gently sloping terraces of grass, cropped short by a small flock of sheep. Just above the lake where the ground would be damp and soft, creamy meadowsweet blended with the purple tufts of thistles.

It was a scene of tranquil beauty and even though so much of her life had been spent in Germany and France, Lotte was sufficiently English to be moved by it. This was partly what the war was all about, she reflected: the preservation of such beauty and the leisured, orderly lifestyle that went with it.

'Lotte,' said Sarah, opening an eye, 'where are you going for your leave?'

'My grandparents', I expect, down in Kent.'

'Why not come home with me for a few days?' Sarah suggested. 'My parents would love to have you.' Although Lotte hadn't gone into any great detail, Sarah knew that she had no intention of seeing Mat again.

'Sarah, I'd really like that. Thank you. Just for a few days.'

'I know I shouldn't be asking you this,' said Sarah's mother, dead-heading a rose with a brisk click of her secateurs and transferring the shrivelled flower to the trug Lotte was carrying for her, 'but if it's at all possible for you to keep an eye on Sarah while you're . . . er . . . away, I should be eternally grateful. I do have a rough idea,' she added quickly, noticing how Lotte's face had suddenly become inscrutable, 'of what's going to happen to you both. Terence is in the War Office, remember.'

'I know,' said Lotte, 'and believe me, if it's at all possible, I'll do as you ask. But it's not very likely, you know, that we'll end up in the same place.'

'I'm afraid I clutch at every straw these days,' confessed the older woman.

Two days later, both Lotte and Sarah received instructions to report to the same London office on the same day at the same time.

'It isn't usual,' said the grey-haired man in a dark suit who sat opposite them on the other side of the desk, 'to brief more than one agent at a time but your mission is, perhaps, a little unusual, even for a set-up like ours.' He paused for a moment as if collecting his thoughts. 'It's unusual in the sense that neither of you are being asked to do anything specific during the next few months other than to integrate quietly into the communities you will be living among. And to go on doing so over the coming winter. You are to become as familiar to any Germans who may be stationed there as you will be to the local population. You will lead uneventful, possibly even boring, lives and you will probably long to take on the tasks that many of your colleagues are required to perform. But, without going into any great detail, your turn will come. There are great plans afoot but the less you know about them at this stage the better and, indeed, they are by no means finalized and will probably be altered many times before reaching fruition. But when they do, then I can promise you both all the action you want.

'Now, the destination for you both is to be the Vercors region of France. As you probably know already, it largely consists of a huge plateau about 3,000 feet high, thirty miles long and lies twelve miles south-west of Grenoble. It is part of the French Alps and contains many spectacular caves and chasms. The roads can be blocked by snow for long periods in the winter and it is, you might say, an area almost purpose-built for creating ambushes for unsuspecting Germans.

'There is already an active Resistance movement there, of which you will be told in greater detail, but you will not, as yet, be an active part of it although they will know of your arrival in the area. Contact will be kept to the minimum until the time comes for more positive action.

'Although you are both to be parachuted into the Vercors, it will be on separate occasions and you will not know of each other's exact whereabouts. But it is possible that you will meet, or at least see each other, during the time you are there and you must be prepared for this so that you show no sign of recognition.

'This is by way of a preliminary briefing. You will each receive your individual instructions during the next few days. So, for now, thank you and good luck.'

Five minutes later, they were outside in the sunshine, surrounded by the bustling activity of a busy London street.

'Regent's Park?' Lotte suggested. 'That's the nearest place we can talk in peace.'

'Fine! Let's go!'

They sat on the grass away from any paths and where they knew no one could overhear them. Even so, they found they were keeping their voices low.

'D'you know the area we're going to?' Sarah asked.

'I went skiing there one winter. You?'

'Grenoble is the nearest I've been to it.'

'It's like he said, full of caves and with huge areas of forest,' Lotte said. She fell silent as she remembered the happy time she'd spent there with other students from the art school, the long treks they'd made across the high plateau, staying overnight in primitive mountain huts, not caring about the hard wooden bunks they'd slept in after gargantuan fry-ups washed down by cheap red wine.

'How do you feel,' Sarah broke into her thoughts, 'now that it's actually going to happen?'

'A certain anti-climax, I suppose,' Lotte admitted, 'now that we know there's going to be no immediate action. But that will bring its own dangers, I suppose. Difficult to remain entirely passive if there are many Germans there.'

'Depends where they put us, I imagine.' Sarah said. 'Anyway, one thing's for sure – I shall miss you.'

'Me, too. And perhaps being on one's own will be the hardest part. But there's no turning back now.'

'How are things with Charlie's parents now?' Mat asked Rosie. His discharge from hospital had coincided with hers from the WAAF and he had decided to stay with her at the cottage where she was to spend the months prior to the baby's birth.

'Well, I think I detect a slight softening. Charlie wrote to them, taking all the blame, but I think I'll always be a Jezebel in his mother's book.'

They were sitting in the tiny cottage garden, enjoying the evening coolness after a hot day. The scent of roses and the musky fragrance from the bed of pinks that Kate had planted under the kitchen window filled the air.

'How is Mair?' Mat asked. 'Does she know I'm staying here?'

'You bet! She'll be over for supper later.'

'Great!'

When Mair arrived, it was to find Rosie peeling potatoes and Mat doing his best to lay the table. As she'd wobbled precariously across the fields on her bike, her mind had been occupied with the thorny problem of whether or not she should give Mat a friendly hug and a peck or offer a hand in comradely fashion. What were the ground rules for someone with a face that must still be raw and sensitive?

However, the problem went clean out of her mind when she came into the kitchen. Mat looked up from the plate he was carrying, lost his concentration and dropped it on the tiled floor. 'Bugger!' he said loudly.

Stepping carefully over the fragments of china, Mair walked towards him. 'Sorry, that was my fault. I should have knocked or shouted out.' And she leaned forward and put her face close to his, at the same time fluttering her eyelashes so that they brushed his cheek. 'That's what my mother calls a butterfly kiss.'

By now, Mat had recovered his poise. Clumsily, he put his arms around Mair's shoulders. 'At least I can give a girl a hug, even if I can't be trusted with the best china!'

What did she smell of? Some pre-war, hoarded perfume, perhaps. Roses? Gardenias?

He meant only to hold her briefly but found he was enjoying the feel of her body pressed, ever so lightly, against his own and didn't immediately release her. It was the first time, he realized, that he'd held a girl since . . . And suddenly, as happened still, in spite of all his resolutions, memories of Lotte swept over him and he was filled with an almost unbearable longing for her. Would he never be rid of her? Was he to spend the rest of his life tortured by a yearning that could never be appeased?

'When you two have quite finished drooling over each other,' Rosie's voice cut into his thoughts, 'the dustpan and brush are under the sink.'

'Of course!' said Mair, immediately going on her knees and

131

grateful for the opportunity of hiding a face that must show, all too clearly, just how moved she'd been by the feel of Mat's arms around her.

Returning from Dorchester one morning soon after his arrival at the cottage, Mat was horrified to find Rosie sitting at the kitchen table, her face ashen and with tears cascading down her cheeks. On the table in front of her was a single sheet of writing paper.

'Rosie, love, what is it?' He crossed to her and crouched down beside her, trying to take her hands in his.

'It's – it's Charlie. He's missing, believed killed. Here – read it!' She pushed the sheet of paper towards him.

It was from Charlie's father and it was very brief. 'Just heard Charlie missing at the battle of Salerno, believed killed. Will write more when we know more but thought you should know.'

'Oh, my poor love!' He knelt beside her, cradling her as best he could.

'If only – if only I knew what happened. Why do they only *believe* he was killed? Surely, they know. Oh, Mat – I must find out. I've *got* to know.' She was becoming hysterical and he gave her a little shake.

'Now listen, Rosie. You've got to be grown up about this. Think about Junior. You *will* find out in time. I'm a bit vague about procedure in the army, but I'm pretty sure Charlie's CO will be writing to his parents telling them exactly what happened. Meanwhile—' He paused, thinking frantically. Wasn't his Uncle Dan something high up in Intelligence? Surely he could pull a few strings. Find out just what happened. He'd go over to Moneymoon Manor as soon as Rosie was a bit calmer. Thank God Mair would be along soon.

XV

Her field name, by which she would be known to the Vercors network, was Claire and her cover name, for 'everday use', as her briefing officer put it, was Denise Lebrun. Her cover story was that she had lived in Nice with a great aunt for most of her life – her parents had died in a car crash when she was eighteen months old – and had worked in a florists in Nice until the war had put an end to such a luxury trade. She had come to the small town – little more than a large village – St Tomas-en-Vercors at the foot of the western flank of the Veymont ridge that traversed the plateau, to help her cousin, Claudette Fouquet, with her young family. Claudette's husband, Pierre, was a farmer.

'Claudette and Pierre have four children,' her briefing officer told her. 'Twins of four, Celeste and Brigitte, and Sophie who is six. The baby, Jean, is three months old.'

Lotte was given a day to study and memorize her life history. After her 'test' – which she passed with no trouble – she was taken to another building to be 'kitted out' and to write the cards which would be sent to her family at regular, if infrequent, intervals telling them that she was well but busy – and would, presumably, she thought grimly, stop if that should cease to be the case.

Now, wearing a thick, serviceable skirt, jacket, woollen blouse and hand-knitted cardigan, woollen stockings and stout shoes – all made by French machinists and with French labels sewn in where appropriate – she waited for the car that was to take her to the airfield from which, weather permitting, she would fly that night. Her mouth was still sore from the manipulations of the dentist when her one English filling had been replaced by a heavier French mixture. She should be grateful, she supposed, that such minute attention to detail was being observed.

At the airfield, she had been told, she would be served with sandwiches and coffee – or tea, if she would prefer a last cup of authentic English brew – since it was advisable to have 'something inside you' before the flight. If only to dispose of during the nerve-wracking moments of her parachute descent! she thought. Any qualms she might be feeling about her actual landing in a German-occupied country were negligible by comparison with those she experienced when thinking about jumping from a moving aircraft. She never had liked that part of her training.

He was halfway to Oxford – in an RAF staff car from Maybury whose solitary occupant had been delighted to have his company – before Mat realized he would soon be seeing Maggie. And that, more importantly, Maggie would be seeing him. But there was nothing he could do about it now. The coincidence of Uncle Dan being at home for a few days was too great an opportunity to miss.

Dropped in St Giles and refusing the offer of a quick drink at the Randolph – he wasn't ready for crowded bars at yet – he decided to walk the rest of the way to Moneymoon Manor. Strolling up the Banbury Road under trees already beginning to shed their leaves, he remembered the autumn day four years ago when he and Derek had followed the same route. What carefree, irresponsible youngsters they had been, their only objectives to learn to fly and to kill Germans. The thought of death or maiming simply hadn't occurred to them. He squared his shoulders. Well, he'd come back when this filthy war was over and finish his studies – disfigured face or not. And then what? He'd have to think seriously about what he wanted to do. Meanwhile, there was Rosie to sort out. It looked as if both of them, particularly Rosie, were facing a bleak future, but at least they had each other.

Maggie, Tom and the twins, he discovered, were all still at school, for which reprieve he was truly grateful. He could come back looking like Dracula and he knew his grandparents would welcome him as would his uncle and aunt. And the twins were old enough to cope with whatever reaction they might have and, whatever it might be, they would have each other for support. Tom, he guessed, would have no problem; in fact, the more horrific Mat's injuries, the more he would probably boast of them to his peers. But the relationship he had forged with the little Cockney waif, who was not nearly as tough as she made out to be, was very precious to him and, he believed, to her.

So he was glad to settle down for a while over a cup of coffee in his grandmother's little sitting room while he talked to his uncle about the Salerno invasion.

'After your phone call,' said Dan, 'I made a few enquiries. In hindsight, as is so often the case, mistakes were made. To begin with, the troops were informed, while still at sea approaching Salerno, that Italy had surrendered to the Allies. Good news, of course, but in effect, it was too good. The troops relaxed; confident, presumably, that the opposition would now be nothing like as great as they had expected. But the Germans, of course, were still there and made even more determined, perhaps, by the surrender of their erstwhile ally. The reception they gave to the Allied landing was formidable, to say the least.

'The landing area where Charlie's division went in was code-named UNCLE and was divided into two sectors. In theory, rocket landing-craft were to blast a way through the minefields laid by the Germans and the British assault troops would then land on the cleared beach. Unfortunately, the rockets missed their target and cleared a path that caused Charlie's lot to land on that part of the beach designated for another British division. The result was not only total confusion but also meant that part of the German defence system was left untouched and was able to provide heavy artillery fire. From what my contact was able to tell me – and they're still trying to sort it all out it's probable that Charlie and his blokes were pretty thoroughly strafed. Very few, if any, would have come out alive or, at least, badly wounded. And as I'm sure you can imagine, it's often impossible to identify particular victims. "Blown to smithereens" can be an apt description. However, the official verdict has to be "missing, believed killed".' Dan sighed, then took a long drink from his cup. 'I'm afraid that's all I can tell you, Mat. How much you decide to tell Rosie is up to you, of course. If it's of any consolation – and I doubt if it will be – the general opinion seems to be that the assault achieved as much as could be expected; at least, it gave us a toe-hold in Europe.'

He looked across at his nephew, now carefully lifting his cup to his lips and saw the tiny dribbles of coffee at the side of his mouth. Poor devil! Maybe Charlie Johnson, if he was in smithereens, had been dealt the better deal of the two. 'Sorry I can't be of any more help,' he added.

Mat returned his cup to its saucer with a tiny clatter then wiped his mouth with a handkerchief. 'You've been of enormous help, Uncle Dan. I really appreciate it and I'm sure Rosie will, too. It seems cruel to say so, but it will help her to accept the fact that Charlie really is dead. And once she's done that, she can start to rebuild her life. The baby should help.'

'And how about you, Mat?' Dan asked gently. 'Are *you* beginning to rebuild your life?'

'Oh, I'm getting there! Don't you worry! And having Rosie to look after is helping. Takes my mind off my own problems.'

A door suddenly banged somewhere in the house and there came the brisk patter of small feet across flagstones. And then the sitting-room door burst open. Mat, who had been sitting with his back to it, rose to his feet and slowly turned around.

Maggie bounced into the room then stopped dead, staring intently at Mat. He held his breath while their eyes locked for what seemed an eternity. And then she gave a sort of chortle of laughter and came towards him. 'I wasn't sure if it was someone else. But it isn't, it's you!'

'It's me all right,' he said shakily. 'But I must look very different now.'

She cocked her head to one side. 'Your mouth's a bit bigger an' your nose is a bit crooked an' your face is pinker an' a bit wobbly – like the blancmange we had at school today. But your eyes are the same.'

She came nearer and he sat down and she leaned against his knee.

'Gramma said I prob'ly shouldn't kiss you, cos your face might be a bit sore. Is it?'

'Just a bit. The doctors are still working on it.'

At this point, Dan, who had been watching and listening almost as anxiously as Mat, got to his feet.

'Tom will be home soon and I promised him a bit of soccer practice. He's dead keen. Come and join us if you feel like it, Mat. And you, too, of course, Trouble!' And he gave Maggie's curls an affectionate rumple.

'Thanks, Uncle Dan. Perhaps I will. And thank you for all the gen you've given me on Charlie. I know Rosie will appreciate it no end.'

'I just wish it wasn't all so gloomy.'

'Now,' said Mat once he and Maggie were alone, 'tell me what you've been up to since I saw you last.'

Maggie screwed up her face. 'That's ages ago. How is Lotte?' she asked. And then, before Mat could answer, 'Gramma said I shouldn't ask but if I don't ask, I won't know. An' I liked her. You did, too, didn't you?'

'Yes, I liked her a lot.'

'So why did she go away?'

'She had to because of the war. A lot of people have to go away in wartime.'

'But she'll write to you, won't she? Gramps says we're winnin' the war an' when we have, she can come home, can't she?'

'Yes, but not to me. You see, it wasn't just the war.' He thought for a moment, struggling to find the words. 'More than anything, I think it was because she didn't like my new, wobbly face.'

He'd said it! Actually put into words, albeit to a child, the fact that he'd refused to face up to until now even though he had seen revulsion in her eyes so clearly.

'But faces aren't that important,' said Maggie. 'Gramma says it's what's inside a person that counts.'

Mat bent and gave her a quick hug. 'And Gramma's right, my cherub. And don't you ever forget it. And now,' he stood up, 'should we go and play soccer, d'you think?'

'OK.' And Maggie put her hand into one of his claws. 'Where's Mair?' she asked as they walked down the lane at the side of the house towards the field where the soccer practice was taking place. 'She hasn't gone away, too, has she?'

'No, but she's busy looking after someone called Rosie. Rosie's my cousin and she's having a baby.'

'I like babies,' said Maggie. 'An' Mair wouldn't mind about your face,' she added, suddenly letting go of his hand and doing a little inconsequential hop, skip and a jump around a rowan tree growing at the side of the lane. 'I always do that,' she said. 'Gramma says rowan trees are lucky.'

'I'll do it too, then,' said Mat. 'Except that I won't skip, if you don't mind.' And he walked solemnly around the tree.

But it wasn't the rowan tree that made him feel suddenly so light-hearted, he reflected moments later as he discovered he could still kick a ball. Not only had Maggie accepted him for what he was, he knew that he had, at last, begun to recover from Lotte.

She was here at last, lying in what seemed like the middle of a huge tract of open country and still shaking from the shock of the impact, even though she'd managed to remember the drill – knees bent, legs together. It was all behind her now; the steady drone of the Whitley's engines as they'd crossed the Channel and then turned south-east towards the Vercors, a drone that had eventually lulled her into a fitful doze that lasted until an RAF sergeant shook her awake to inform her that their target would be reached in a few minutes. Those were the minutes in which she'd discovered that the bare, bleak interior of the aircraft had suddenly become a haven of peace and security and the gentle cadence of English voices the most precious sound she would ever hear.

The sergeant had pulled back the cover from the drop-hole behind the cockpit and peered down into the roaring blackness before giving a reassuring thumbs-up and pushing her suitcase, parachute attached, out into space. Then he had come back to guide her towards the hole where she had sat with her feet dangling into the abyss, heart thumping, mouth parched and tongue like a piece of old flannel. Dimly, she had made out the three flickering lights far, far below and tried to be reassured that at least she was expected. But as she gazed, the distance between herself and the ground seemed to become greater. There was no way she was going to land anywhere near the dropping zone. Then the sergeant nudged her and pointed upward to the red light on the side of the fuselage. Within seconds, it had turned to green and Lotte knew that this was the moment she had been dreading.

'Good luck!' the sergeant called and shoved her out into the blackness. There were seconds of pure terror as she seemed to be buffeted hither and thither about the sky like a paper bag caught in a wayward gust of wind. Then, like a miracle, she felt the reassuring tug of the parachute's straps as it billowed out above her head and knew that she was safe.

For several seconds after she hit the ground, she stayed there, struggling to get her breath back, and then she heard the sound of running feet and sat up. Friend or foe? But then a tall, dark figure was bending over her, his fingers searching for the fastening that would release her parachute straps and urging her to 'Hurry, mam'selle!' She was with friends.

'You and Rosie have always been close,' said Mrs Moneymoon, easing herself down into the kitchen rocking chair. She and Mat were alone and enjoying a mug of cocoa before bed. Knowing that Mair had an overnight pass and would be keeping Rosie company, Mat had readily accepted his grandmother's invitation to stay to supper and spend the night.

Supper at Moneymoon Manor, he'd decided, looking around the table, could easily be classified as 'getting back into the normal rhythm of everyday life', as the shrink had advised him to do when leaving hospital; although he wasn't at all sure that a combination of Moneymoons and Holkers could ever be considered 'normal'. There was his full-bearded grandfather, wearing the knitted tea cosy that he had originally put on his head to make Maggie laugh on the day one of her rabbits had gone 'walkabout' and had worn ever since because he said it kept his ears warm; there was his grandmother, looking rather like an inebriated duchess with her silver hair piled high into a sort of beehive and held there, slightly askew, by an elaborate arrangement of meat skewers; there were Polly and Stella and Maggie, all wearing the 'play dresses' that had been fashioned by his Aunt Mary's clever fingers out of blackout material but saved from uniformity by glueing on felt cut-outs of the animals of their choice. Polly and Stella had, predictably, plumped for ponies and Maggie, to no one's surprise, a rabbit. One of its ears, Mat noticed, had come unstuck and was threatening to flop into her plate of rabbit stew. No one, of course, dared to call it rabbit stew in front of Maggie, so it was tactfully referred to in the family as 'Gramma's special hotpot'.

Perhaps, after all, he thought, this ingenuity was typical of the average British household in wartime trying to cope with rationing. Typical or not, he'd felt an enormous affection for them all as he'd glanced around the table. Even for Tom, who was sitting opposite him and barely able to take his eyes off his face, no doubt memorizing every detail for passing on to his school friends next day.

But Tom aside, no one else seemed to be in the least bit interested. Perhaps he should have brought Rosie with him so that she, too, could have had the benefit of their support and affection. What would Rosie do after her child was born? he wondered. How difficult was life going to be for her and the child without Charlie? What reaction would there be in the States if she went back there after the war with a child that bore the same name as her own so that his illegitimacy was clear to all? Americans were probably the same as the English in their attitude towards bastards. And what about the child's birth certificate? Would the poor little sod carry the stigma of illegitimacy for the rest of its life? He had welcomed the opportunity of talking to his grandmother about his fears.

He nodded now, in agreement with his grandmother's statement. 'We always seemed to have the same ideas at the same time – to be on the same wavelength. And then, of course, we'd egg each other on.'

'Your mothers always hoped something would come out of it when you were older.'

He stared at her in astonishment. 'You mean get married?' She nodded. 'But that would have been like marrying my sister. And I'm sure Rosie would feel the same.'

Mrs Moneymoon shrugged. 'It does happen in some families, you know. Cousins marrying each other.'

He thought about it; tried to imagine feeling about Rosie as he had about Lotte and knew that it was impossible. But would he ever feel the same about *anyone* as he had about Lotte? And in the event that he did, how could he expect any woman to love him in his present state – a state that was not likely to improve dramatically?

'I'm not worried about Rosie in any physical sense,' he told his grandmother. 'She's as strong as a horse and she'll have the baby at the Dower House under Mum's auspices, as it were. And financially, I'm sure Aunt Priss and Uncle Hank will look after her. It's the child growing up without a father that worries me, most particularly if it's a boy.'

His grandmother gave him a shrewd glance. 'Well, perhaps a caring uncle could be as good as a natural father. Although, of course, he'd have to be on the same side of the Atlantic!'

He was on his way back to Dorchester next day – conventionally, this time, on a bus – when the idea hit him. Why not suggest to Rosie that they marry before the child was born? It would be in name only, of course. And if Rosie ever wanted to marry someone else – and after Charlie that might not be for a long time yet – then the marriage could be annulled. He had only the vaguest idea of divorce proceedings but he was pretty sure that non-consummation of the marriage was sufficient grounds. He'd give Rosie a couple of days to take in what Uncle Dan had told him about Charlie's probable fate and then he'd see what she thought of the idea.

XVI

It was almost uncanny how she slipped back into the French way of life with hardly a hiccup, automatically glancing left instead of right at road crossings and using francs and centimes as if pounds, shillings and pence had never existed. She had even survived an inspection of her papers by the 'Milice'.

They're only Frenchmen, after all, she had thought, even if they are now policemen, probably forced into working with the Germans when Vichy was taken over. The inspection had happened while she was on the bus she'd caught at Die in order to give credence to her cover story that she'd travelled up from Nice although, in fact, the dropping zone they'd used had only been about five kilometres from the Fouquet farm.

'St Tomas is not a big village,' Victor had explained on that first night, 'and your coming will not go unnoticed so you must arrive in a conventional manner for all to see. Claudette has already spoken of you to her friends and how much she is looking forward to seeing you.' Victor was the leader of the cell to which she had been allocated. Victor wasn't his real name just as hers wasn't Claire.

The conversation had taken place in the kitchen of the farm-house to which she had been taken on that first night and where she had been offered a bowl of soup from the big black pot simmering on the stove. She had accepted it more from polite-ness than hunger but it had tasted so good that she had drunk it all, even mopping up the final drops with a piece of bread. Then there had been coffee or what must now pass for coffee in

France, its bitter taste of chicory almost disguised by the generous splash of brandy Victor had put into it.

'As you have probably been told,' he said, 'there will be little for you to do at the moment. But do not think that nothing is happening. Our numbers grow daily as the *réfractaires* join us. They are the young men who are on the run from the Germans because they want to conscript them to work in their labour camps in Germany. They would rather join the Maquis even if it means living rough in the forest. Training them without arms is difficult but we persevere and we are beginning to get drops, mostly of Sten guns but some grenades and explosives.'

'Wouldn't I be of more use helping to train them?' she had suggested. 'I am qualified to instruct.'

'I'm sure that you are, mam'selle, and I don't doubt your ability for a moment. But we need contacts in the villages, people who will keep their eyes and ears open.'

Next day, she had been taken to Die hidden in the back of a van owned by a man called Philippe, who 'does many odd jobs, the odder the better!', Victor had told her. And from there she had caught a bus to St Tomas.

As she'd been told, Claudette was waiting for her when the bus drove in to the market square at St Tomas and wearing the brightly coloured headscarf that identified her. Lotte walked quickly towards her over the cobblestones, then put down her suitcase as Claudette ran towards her, arms outstretched. They embraced fondly.

'I have been told,' Claudette whispered in her ear, 'that I must take you into the café and show you off before we go home. Pierre will be here in a little while to pick us up,' she added in a normal voice as she drew back, holding Lotte by the arms as she looked into her face and smiling as she did so.

'And the children?' Lotte asked as Claudette picked up her suitcase and they walked together across the square towards the café.

'They are with my mother,' Claudette told her, 'and looking forward to meeting their aunt.'

There weren't many people in the café but Claudette made a

point of greeting an elderly woman with eyes like black boot buttons embedded in a criss-cross of tiny wrinkles 'Madame Olivier, how are you? May I introduce you to my cousin Denise whom I told you about.'

The old woman put out a foot and pushed away the chair on the other side of the table so there would be room for Lotte to sit. 'Sit down, mam'selle!'

Lotte glanced at Claudette, who nodded her approval, so she sat opposite the old woman, trying not to wince when a waft of garlic came over the table at her.

Claudette ordered coffee and pulled out another chair. 'I understand you have come up from Nice, mam'selle?' Madame Olivier interrogated.

'Yes, madame,' Lotte agreed.

'A town of great wickedness, I understand. Full of people who have more money than sense. I have no wish to go there. How long will you be staying in St Tomas, mam'selle?'

'As long as my cousin needs me, madame.' Lotte turned to Claudette. 'How are the children, Claudette? Fully recovered from the chickenpox, I hope?' She had been well briefed by Victor.

'Quite well now, I'm relieved to say. They—' She stopped abruptly as a German army lorry drew up outside and half a dozen soldiers, led by a corporal, jumped down and clattered into the café.

It hadn't been exactly noisy before but now, Lotte thought, you could have heard the proverbial pin drop. The silence was broken by Madame Olivier. 'Bloody Boche!' she said in a loud voice.

If she'd suddenly stood up and started divesting herself of every garment she wore, she couldn't have caused a greater stir. Lotte felt an almost hysterical urge to laugh. There came an audible gasp – whether of horror or simply astonishment, she couldn't decide, from the other customers, and then the proprietor of the café hurried forward.

'Now, Madame Olivier, there is no need to be so offensive.' He turned towards the corporal. 'She is an old woman, you understand.'

But Lotte had the impression that the soldiers had already been briefed in conciliatory tactics. 'Think nothing of it, m'sieur,' said the corporal. 'We understand.' And to Madame Olivier, 'I'm sorry, madame, to inflict our presence upon you but I'm afraid you will just have to put up with us. And for a very long time.'

'Never!' said Madame Olivier stoutly. 'You killed my man in the last war and I shall never forget it.'

Claudette leaned towards her. 'There, there, madame! I understand how you feel but these men are only carrying out their orders.' She flashed a weak smile in the general direction of the corporal then immersed her face in her coffee cup.

'Speak for yourself, Claudette Fouquet!' thundered Madame Olivier and, with the aid of her stick, rose from the table and hobbled towards the door. The corporal sprang forward and opened it for her. For a second, Lotte thought she was going to spit in his face but a diversion came with the arrival of a man who, Lotte saw, had parked an ancient Citroen outside the café behind the lorry. 'And you, Pierre Fouquet,' Madame Olivier shouted, 'are probably no better than your wife!' And she went on her way, brandishing her stick at the children who had gathered like bees around the German vehicle.

Pierre came in and glanced across the café at the soldiers who were now sitting around a table and being served by the proprietor.

'They're the advance guard,' he said softly as he bent to kiss Lotte on both cheeks and then sat on the chair that Madame Olivier had vacated. 'I've been hearing about it at the forge. They're taking over the mairie. So, they'll be looking for *billets*. Don't worry,' he added, as Claudette looked at him in alarm, 'we're too far out. Besides, we have no room now that Cousin Denise has come to stay,' And he smiled at Lotte. 'Everything is ready for you, Cousin.' He turned to his wife. 'Have you finished your shopping, *chérie*?'

Charlotte nodded. 'All done, but I have bags to pick up from the bakers and the grocers.'

'I'll go and collect them while you two finish your coffee. It's not often that we can spare the petrol to bring the car into town,' he explained to Lotte, 'so we make the most of it.'

Fifteen minutes later, Lotte was ensconced on the back seat of the old car, surrounded by bags overflowing with packets of flour, sugar, dried fruit and baby food. She had arrived!

'And that's all he could tell you?' Clearly, Rosie was disappointed in what Mat had been able to tell her about Charlie's part in the Salerno landings.

'It was too soon for any specific details,' Mat tried to explain. 'When things are sorted out a bit . . .'

'You mean when they've found all the bodies, assuming that they ever find them?'

'Something like that,' Mat agreed miserably. 'Sorry, Rosie.'

'I'm sorry, too, Mat,' said Rosie, suddenly contrite. 'It's just that I keep imagining. But there's no reason for taking it out on you.'

'When's Mair coming over again?' he asked.

'This afternoon. But she's got to go back for a night watch. I don't know what I would do without her at the moment. Nor *you*, either, Mat!' And she gave him an affectionate hug.

'We must have a serious talk very soon, Rosie. About the future.' At least he could start the ball rolling.

'I know,' she said. 'Aunt Kate will want to know when to expect me.'

And with that, he had to be content. Perhaps he'd walk across the fields after lunch to meet Mair. See what she thought of his idea.

He saw Mair when she was halfway across the river meadows, wobbling precariously on her bike along the rutted path. He waved and then waited until she'd reached him and dismounted.

'Hello!' He bent and kissed her lightly on the cheek before taking the bike from her.

'How did you get on in Oxford?' she asked, falling into step beside him.

He gave her a brief summary of what Dan had told him.

'Which isn't exactly what Rosie wanted to hear,' Mair said when he'd finished.

'No, but at least it may help her to accept the probability that he's dead,' Mat pointed out.

'But her future's pretty bleak.'

'For the time being, anyway. But I've been thinking. Mair . . .'

They were approaching Day's Lock by this time and he stopped under a nearby tree, leaned the bike against its trunk and said, 'Shall we sit down for a minute? I'd like to ask you what you think of an idea I've had. Rosie doesn't know about it yet.'

He sat down on the grass with his back against the tree and Mair, clearly mystified, sat beside him. A barge, coming up river from Oxford, approached the lock gates and sounded its hooter.

Mat came directly to the point. 'I thought I'd ask her to marry me,' he said baldly. As he spoke he turned and looked directly at Mair, wanting to gauge her reactions. However, she seemed to be far more interested in what was going on at the lock, watching intently while the lock keeper came out of his cottage and walked down his garden path to open the gates. Was it because of the shade cast by the tree that made her face seem suddenly very pale and drawn or was she just tired? Poor kid! Helping Rosie through the last few days couldn't have been easy for her. But then she spoke, although she was still staring fixedly at the river where the gates were now fully open and the barge was easing its way into the lock.

'*Marry*, did you say?' she asked in a strange sort of voice.

'I know,' he said quickly. 'It's the last thing you'd expect. And probably the last thing she'd expect. But think about it, Mair. It makes sense. I can give the child a name. I can stop the gossip, or most of it, and most important of all, I can look after them both.'

'But what if – if Charlie should turn up? It does happen, you know.'

'I know. But the baby's due in a few weeks. So I shall have to put it to her before too long.'

She was silent, still staring at the river where the gates had been closed snugly behind the barge.

148

'Do I take it,' he asked at last, 'that you don't approve?'

'It's not that exactly. You see . . .' She turned towards him now, her cheeks slightly flushed. 'Before I met you but after I'd met Rosie, I used to think you and she might marry. You were so close and you obviously went back a long way. And something Mrs Moneymoon said to me once seemed to confirm it. And then, after we all met up in London and you and – and Lotte, and Rosie and Charlie, paired up together, I knew I'd got it wrong so . . .' She gave a little shrug. 'I'm just, well, surprised, I suppose. Not,' she added quickly, 'that it's any of my business.'

'It's my fault for involving you,' he told her. 'I'm using you as a sort of sounding board, I suppose. But going back to your first impressions – they were wrong, of course. Rosie and I are devoted to each other but only in a cousinly way. So I wouldn't be suggesting marriage in a conventional sense but only to legitimize the birth of the baby, if that's the right expression. After that, it would be up to Rosie. I like to think I'd bow out gracefully if she wanted me to.'

Mair went back to her contemplation of the river, grateful that the shock of Mat's announcement was now abating slightly. There should be time enough later to think of how it would affect her. For now, she must try and consider things from Mat's point of view. And Rosie's, of course.

'I should leave it a couple of days,' she said. 'And then be as casual as you can about it. If I know Rosie,' she added, 'she'll say no first off. But then she'll think about it. And then' – she gave him a sudden, wry grin – 'if she's got any sense, she'll say yes!'

In a sudden rush of gratitude for her wisdom, he put his arm around her shoulders and pulled her close. 'You're the tops, Mair, d'you know that?'

'Mat, are you out of your mind?' Rosie faced him across the breakfast table, as prosaic a place and situation as he could think of for his proposal. What he was proposing, he'd explained, was a sensible, no-nonsense sort of arrangement with no strings. Clearly, however, she didn't see it that way.

'Rosie, don't condemn it out of hand. As I said, it would be no more than a – a face-saver, if you like!'

But that seemed to be the worst thing he could have said. 'I don't need a face-saver, as you put it. I'm *proud* that I'm having Charlie's baby. Especially now. I don't care what other people think. Can't you understand that?'

'Of course I do! But think about the baby, Rosie. All he's—'

'Or she,' she interrupted automatically.

'All he or she's going to know is that he or she is growing up without a father. Missing out when all the other kids have someone to take them fishing or – or playing football or whatever you do out in the States.'

'Baseball. You mean,' and now she was even more disbelieving, 'you'd come and live in the States with me?'

'If necessary, yes,' he said doggedly. 'Maybe stay in Oxford until I'd got my degree, but after that we'd have to see. Although,' he added thoughtfully, 'I'd rather like him to go to my old school. Holkers have gone there since my great-grandfather's day.'

'Will you stop assuming it's going to be a boy,' Rosie flashed back at him. 'And anyway, we've got some darned fine schools in the States.' And then she stopped abruptly, suddenly conscious of what her comment might imply. 'Not that I'm accepting your ridiculous offer,' she added lamely.

Mat grinned at her. 'But you will think about it?'

She allowed him a brief nod. 'All right! I'll think about it. And Mat,' she said as he shot out a hand as if to seal some sort of business deal, 'thank you! I really appreciate the offer.' And she put her hand into his.

Later that day, he climbed up the steep slope at the back of the cottage and sat for a while under the elm trees. Up there, exposed to the wind, their branches were stripped of leaves but below him, along the banks of the river and far beyond, behind the airfield, the trees were a mosaic of vibrant autumn colour.

Here he was, he reflected, on the brink of marriage. And to Rosie. Briefly, he allowed himself to think of Lotte, the girl who, only a few months ago, he would have given his eye teeth to marry. Well, he thought wryly, in the end he'd given considerably more than his eye teeth but it hadn't given him Lotte; in fact, it had had the reverse effect. He wondered where and how she was. Somewhere in France by now, he supposed. He wished her well.

XVII

Lotte was cycling to the village, a basket on the handlebars and a shopping list in the basket to give credence to the expedition should she be stopped.

In spite of Pierre's opinion to the contrary, the farmhouse had been visited by the Germans in their search for billets. That, at least, had been the reason offered by the officer in the uniform of the Abwehr who had presented himself, courteous to a point but clearly not prepared to brook any argument should his orders be resisted. However, as far as the farmhouse was concerned, it was clear that all the rooms were fully occupied by the Fouquet family.

Half an hour after he had gone, Victor had cycled into the yard, a string of onions on his handlebars and another around his neck.

'It's happening all over the Vercors,' he told them, 'and there have been reconnaissance planes about just lately. Now that North Africa has fallen to the Allies, they fear a landing in the south of the country, just as there has been in Italy. And if that happens, then the valley of the Rhône will be the obvious route for the Allies to take. And it is then, my friends, that the Vercors Maquis will come into its own, snapping like terriers at the heel of the German army while the Allies advance. But meanwhile,' he said shrugging, 'we must be vigilant.' He turned to Lotte. 'Claire, see what you can find out in the village about the number of Germans drafted into the area. Is there any sign of Gestapo presence? That, indeed, would be something to pass on to London. So far, it is only the Abwehr, the German intelligence, that is here. Sit in the café with your ears and your eyes open. You are in a unique position, able to understand what the gossip is among the men without their knowing.'

So here she was, free-wheeling down the long, sloping road to St Tomas with the wind in her hair and trying not to think of the long trudge back with her bicycle laden with purchases.

Her shopping took her an hour. At the end of it, her basket was full. Pushing open the door of the café with her bottom, she edged her way inside and glanced around. There was one empty table near the window. She moved towards it, at the same time catching the eye of the patron behind the counter and mouthing a request for coffee.

Gazing out into the square, occasionally leaning forward as if to see better whatever was going on out there, she had ears only for the conversation going on between the German soldiers who were sitting at the table behind her.

They had, she gathered, been moved down from Paris where one of them had apparently begun a liaison with a Parisian hairdresser.

'You won't manage anything like that down here,' one of the others told him. 'Strictly no fraternizing we've been told.'

'Unless we hear something that might be helpful to the German cause. And then we must inform the Sturmbannführer,' said another, somewhat pompously.

Lotte, gazing through the window at old Madame Olivier, who had just appeared on the other side of the square and was walking slowly across the cobbles in the direction of the café felt the nerves on the back of her neck begin to tingle. Sturmbannführer was a rank in the SS. Victor had been right. Clearly, the Germans saw the Vercors as a region of great potential danger.

Sipping her coffee, she strained to hear more but the conversation had now deteriorated into the sort of bawdy exchange typical of most soldiers, whatever their allegiance. And then, one of them, the pompous one, she thought, suddenly said, 'Talk of the devil!' and an immediate silence fell on the little group as

153

they all peered out into the square.

A German staff car had drawn up outside the mairie and an officer had alighted; an officer in a black uniform. The colour of the uniform and the white piping clearly visible around the peak of his cap denoted that he was an officer in the SS, as did the aluminium cords on his jacket. Those, Lotte knew, would denote his rank and although, from where she sat, it was impossible to see what that was, she guessed it must be the Sturmbannführer the soldier had mentioned. His back was towards her but Madame Olivier, who had altered course towards him and quickened her pace, shouted something that caused him to turn as he was about to mount the steps of the mairie so that Lotte was able to see his face.

Afterwards, she was to wonder how she had managed to go on sitting there, outwardly unmoved, giving no indication other than a quick, momentary intake of breath, that she had just received the biggest shock of her life.

She knew him! Knew that arrogant face with the beak of a nose, the deep-set eyes and thin-lipped, cruel mouth. The last time she had seen it had also been in the Vercors but high in the mountains and his anger had been directed against a little Swiss girl whose clumsy movement had caused a line of 'parked' skis to clatter from the café wall against which they had been leaning, on to the ground. The string of abuse he had shouted had been out of all proportion to the extent of the mishap and the girl had been reduced to tears. Lotte had leapt to her defence.

Really, she had thought afterwards, it had been a mistake to let Karl Bluthner come on the trip. Not one of her fellow students had really liked him. In fact, when he had turned up like a bad penny in the coach that had been hired to bring them down from Paris, no one had admitted to inviting him. He had been an excellent skier, Lotte remembered now, usually setting the pace for their cross-country runs but not caring in the least that it invariably exceeded that of most of the party.

Watching him now, as he listened disdainfully to whatever Madame Olivier was shouting at him, before shrugging dismissively and indicating some course of action to his driver, then turning on his heel and disappearing into the mairie, Lotte knew that he had not changed. But why should he? The Nazi regime must suit him perfectly and he it.

Sick at heart, she watched while the driver unceremoniously took Madame Olivier by the shoulders and shook her, causing her to drop her stick and nearly fall. Then he, too, turned and hurried up the steps of the mairie behind his master.

Just as she had gone to the aid of the Swiss girl, Lotte's instinct was to dash out of the café, run across the square and put a protective arm around the old woman. But this time, she knew that she dared not. She must leave the village as quickly and as unobtrusively as possible, return to the farm and then get a message to Victor. What would happen to her then, she could only guess at. But one thing was certain, she could no longer stay where she was. She'd had no difficulty in recognizing Karl and he, no doubt, would remember her with equal ease.

It was a very simple affair, just Rosie and Mat with their grandparents for witnesses; Mair, to everyone's disappointment, had been unable to come.

'There's this bug around camp,' she'd explained. 'So we're desperately undermanned but I'll be thinking of you.' That part, at least, had been true.

Far away, in a tiny fisherman's cottage south of Salerno, Maria Benvenito poured water between the parched lips of the soldier she had found spreadeagled on the rocks below the cottage. How he had got there and how long he had been there, she had no idea. At first she had thought he was dead but a tiny moan of pain when she had tried to lift him had changed her mind. But for how much longer would he live?

She had gone to fetch her father and between them, they had managed to carry him up to the cottage. Maria's father had been in favour of handing him over to the Germans to take his chances as a prisoner of war but Maria wouldn't hear of it. Since the Italian army had capitulated – and about time, too, Maria had privately thought – the Germans had changed dramatically in their attitude to the local people, treating them now as their enemies where, only hours previously, they had been their friends. Maria certainly did not trust them to observe any sort of code of practice for their prisoners, be they British or American.

How the battle was faring now she had no way of telling and she had no intention of trying to find out. She would keep her head down, pray that the Germans were in retreat and do her best to keep 'her' soldier alive until she could hand him over to his compatriots.

'He won't last long,' said her father who had served in the last war and thought he knew a dying man when he saw one.

But his daughter had an obstinate streak in her. Besides, she liked the look of the soldier, even in the poor state he was in at the moment. All she could be sure about was that he was not a German. All that he wore was camouflage trousers and a singlet but she knew that they were not of German make. She knew, too, that soldiers usually wore identification tags around their necks but he had none. She thought it likely that he had been stripped by a local man down on his luck – and who wasn't during these dreadful days? – for even his boots were gone. Perhaps, she reasoned, if she managed to nurse him back to health he would be so grateful he would take her back to England – or to America. She would like that.

'We shall have to tell London,' Victor told Lotte.

'They may decide to recall me,' she said.

'Is that what you want?'

Lotte bristled. 'Of course not!'

'So what do you suggest should be done with you?'

Her reply was immediate and was the fruit of the long, sleepless hours of the previous night when she had tossed and turned, unable to accept that the months of preparation could end in an ignominious return home. Now, as she and Victor leaned with their backs against the gate that led into the Fouquet farmyard so that they could keep a watchful eye on the road that led up from St Tomas, she asked, 'D'you remember my suggestion that I might be of more use to you in the field, possibly helping to train the *réfractaires*? Well, why shouldn't I do that now?'

'It is no life for a woman,' said Victor.

'In peacetime, perhaps not. But you don't need me to remind you, Victor, that we are at war. Why not suggest it to London? They will know better than you what I am capable of. They will know that I can strip and reassemble a Bren in the dark faster than many men. And I am tough, Victor, believe you me. I wouldn't stand any nonsense.'

Victor allowed his mouth to curl upwards, ever so slightly, at the corners. It was the nearest to a smile that he would permit himself. 'All right, I'll put it to London. But first, I must speak to Jacques. No matter what I or London might say, that would be it. Jacques is not a man to be trifled with.'

'Is he a native of this area? What is his history?'

Victor's lips curled again, but this time the direction was downward. 'You should know better than to ask such questions, Claire. All you need to know about Jacques is that he is the boss. When he says jump, you jump! When he says lie down, you lie down!'

We'll see about that! Lotte thought but was wise enough to keep her own counsel.

XVIII

Michael Charles Holker was born on a blustery autumn day when the elm trees around the Dower House were alive with the raucous call of the rooks. It was the first sound that Rosie heard as she surfaced from the deep sleep she'd fallen into after the baby's birth. Then she heard a faint clucking sound interspersed with a kind of mew and she opened her eyes. Was her son demanding food already? But it was Great Aunt Bella who stood at her bedside, peering down into the old cot that had been brought down from the attics. She smiled at Rosie.

'Extreme old age trying to communicate with extreme youth and quite rightly being ignored.'

Rosie gave her a sleepy smile. She was very fond of Robert's aunt. Then her Aunt Kate came tiptoeing into the room and saw that Rosie was awake. She carried a tray of tea.

'Congratulations, darling! You're a clever girl! I thought you might like a cup of tea?'

'Thanks, I'd love one.' Rosie wriggled up in bed and peered down into the cot. A fuzz of dark hair covered the head that lay on the pillow. She put out a finger and stroked it gently. 'I am clever, aren't I?' And then her eyes suddenly filled with tears. Surrounded though she was by the love and care of a close-knit family, she longed with all her being for Charlie to be there. If only she could have written to him and told him the wonderful news, it would have been enough. Perhaps, she reflected, that was what she'd do anyway, when she was feeling a bit stronger. Not that the letter would ever be delivered but she could fool herself for a little while. Silly, of course, but weren't new mothers allowed to be a little irrational?

'When he dies,' said Maria's father, 'what do you propose to do with his body? It would not be right for us to bury him. We could get into big trouble. The Germans are on the run now although I have heard that they are holding out inland. Even so, they are gone from around here. You must seek out a British soldier. Or an American. And ask for help.'

Maria gazed down at the man on the bed and knew that her father was right. She had bound up the deep wounds on his head and on his arm and had bathed the many lacerations caused by the rocks on which he must have been dragged to and fro by the tides before she had found him. She had dribbled soup laced with brandy into his mouth and twice he had regained consciousness but only to babble some incomprehensible phrases. His face was ashen pale except for two scarlet spots high up on his cheekbones and his arm was now erupting into angry sores.

She found help in the shape of a platoon of Americans resting by the roadside. She picked out one with three stripes on his arm and approached him. Once she had convinced him that she wasn't trying to sell them wine or tomatoes or eggs, it wasn't difficult to make him understand, especially when she pointed at one of their number who wore an armband emblazoned with a red cross. Two of them, at least, she insisted, must come with her – and with a stretcher.

The examination was swift and their diagnosis clearly not good. For a moment or two, they argued among themselves and Maria grew afraid that they would not take her soldier but then they picked him up and gently placed him on the stretcher and carried him away up the rocky hillside to the track.

As she watched them go, Maria wept unashamedly. Her father put his arm around her shoulders.

'You did your best,' he said gruffly. 'More than I would have done.'

But it wasn't enough, Maria thought sadly. And now, she

would never see England or America and nor, she feared, would her soldier.

Twenty-four hours later, in a military hospital in Algiers, two American doctors stood beside the bed on which Charlie Johnson's inert body lay.

'Just been flown in from Italy,' one said, 'with some of our guys. What d'you reckon?'

'If you'd asked me that a little while ago,' said the other, 'I'd have said no way! But now, with the new penicillin drug available, I'd say it's worth a try.'

'Let's go to it, then!'

Mair – proud of her role as godmother – held the scrap of humanity that was Michael Charles Holker and prayed that the baby wouldn't cry. At the moment, he seemed far too preoccupied with the shiny buttons on her tunic. She glanced up and caught Rosie's eye, which immediately closed in an enormous wink, and Mair, suppressing an urge to giggle, hurriedly transferred her gaze to Mat, who was standing next to Rosie. Immediately, she lost all sense of merriment as she saw the expression in his eyes as he looked down at the baby.

He's besotted, she thought, and knew a moment of cold despair. She doubted if even Charlie, had he been there, would have shown a greater, more overwhelming emotion. It was this tiny scrap of humanity she was holding in her arms that would bind him to Rosie. And would it stop there? She doubted it.

At the very moment that his son was christened, Charlie opened his eyes and found himself gazing up into the face of an angel. Or perhaps, he reconsidered, a kind of celestial Girl Guide, for she seemed to be wearing some sort of uniform. Either way, he liked what he saw, but where the hell was he? Perhaps the angel would know.

'Hello!' he croaked in a voice that didn't sound at all like his. At least, he didn't think so. 'Where am I?'

'Hi!' she said. 'Welcome back!'

160

He closed his eyes while he considered her answer. It certainly didn't tell him where he was, but did seem to indicate that he had been away. He opened his eyes. 'What—' he began but was interrupted.

'My turn to ask a question, I think. What's your name? And no need to worry where you are. You're in an American hospital in Algiers and that, as I'm sure you know, is in North Africa. And you're getting better. The big thing is we don't know who you are. No identity tags, no pay book, no nothing. You're our mystery guest!'

She waited expectantly. Charlie frowned. Not only did he want to be able to tell her what his name was, he'd rather like to know it himself. Perhaps if he lay still for a while and didn't think about it, it would come to him, like things often did when you left them alone. Meanwhile, he rather liked the sound of his angel's voice – something familiar there, he thought. He'd work on it when he didn't feel quite so tired. 'Don't go away,' he said to the angel and drifted back to sleep.

'It happens,' said the psychiatrist, gazing down at Charlie. 'Battle trauma, or whatever you like to call it. I've seen it time and time again.'

'But it's been several days now,' the army doctor pointed out. 'Most of which he's spent fast asleep. Like he is now.'

'The best medicine there is,' said the psychiatrist cheerfully. 'Do you know anything at all about him?'

'All we can be sure of is that he's British,' said the doctor. 'Apparently, he was found just south of Anzio but several days after the original landings and all he was wearing was a singlet and combat troueers – definitely of British make. Shouldn't we have him transferred to a British hospital? At least they could work out which outfit he belongs to. That would narrow it down a bit.'

'Eventually, yes,' the psychiatrist agreed, 'but give him a bit longer here before moving him. Any day now, he could wake up with total recall.'

XIX

They had been climbing steadily and fast through the forest for a good hour. Several times, Lotte would have welcomed a short stop while they stood and breathed in the resinous scent of the pines but, ever mindful of Victor's views on her stamina, she had kept doggedly on, grateful that at least he was not wasting any breath upon speech. Now, however, after they had reached a jagged outcrop of granite shaped like the head of a lion, he signalled to her to stop. Putting his clasped hands to his mouth, he blew into them, producing an extraordinary lifelike cry of an owl. It was followed, after an interval of a few seconds, by three answering cries, coming from about a hundred yards ahead.

Beckoning her to follow, Vincent moved on. Two minutes later, they had entered a clearing in the forest, in the centre of which was a rough shack constructed, as far as Lotte could make out, of roughly hewn logs, roofed with thickly interwoven branches. Several large trees were dotted around the clearing, under which small bivouacs had been constructed, again roofed by branches. The camp, Lotte guessed, would be invisible from the air. Only the granite outcrop nearby might act as a marker to an informed eye and there were, she knew, many such outcrops in the Vercors, terminating in the massive escarpment of the Veymont ridge itself.

A titillating smell of herbs wafted across the clearing and Lotte saw that a fire had just been doused under a tripod from which swung a massive cast-iron cooking pot. A line of men, probably about twenty, she thought, had formed with billy-cans in their hands and were filing past the pot from which a swarthy-looking man was ladling out portions of stew; rabbit, she decided, and felt a pang of unexpected hunger. A man with a rifle slung over his shoulder swung himself down from the top of a boulder from which there would have been a clear view of the forest below, and blocked their way.

'Victor! *Salut!*'

'*Salut*, Jean!'

The two men clasped hands but Victor made no attempt to introduce Lotte.

'And this is?' Clearly, Jean took his duties seriously or else wished to steal a march on his fellow Maquis, Lotte decided.

'A visitor,' replied Victor curtly. 'Jacques knows of her coming. She may not be staying.'

'Pity!' said Jean, giving Lotte a lecherous wink.

'Jean! Back to your post!' A tall, blond giant of a man had come out of the shack and now stood before them. Jean raised his hand to his forehead in a sketchy salute and began to climb back on to his boulder.

'Jacques! Good to see you!' Victor went to embrace the blond giant even though, Lotte noticed, he had to stand on tiptoe to do so.

'Victor!' Over Victor's shoulder, Jacques' eyes were like blue steel as he gazed at Lotte. Victor turned towards her.

'This is Claire. I told you about her and her unfortunate acquaintance with an officer in the SS.' He made it sound as if the situation was entirely of Lotte's making.

And now her hand was taken in a grip so firm that it took all her control not to wince. 'And where, may I ask, did you make this unfortunate acquaintance, Claire? And how long ago?'

'In the winter of 1938 and here, in the Vercors. We were in a party of students who had come for a few days skiing.'

'You are French, Claire?'

'Half German, half English. I am trilingual.' No harm in letting him know of her qualifications.

'Were you lovers?'

'No,' she replied evenly, 'we were not lovers.' No doubt, she reminded herself, it was necessary for him to know if she was emotionally involved with Karl Bluthner. But her lips curled into a tiny smile at the idiocy of such an idea.

'Why do you smile, Claire?'

'Because if you knew this man, you would realize the absurdity of such a question. Not only is he cruel and uncaring, he is physically most unattractive.'

A mocking light came into the blue eyes. 'Attraction, as the poet implied, is in the eye of the beholder, Claire. And are there not some women who like their men to be a little cruel?'

Her gaze remained steady. 'I am not one of them, m'sieur.'

He raised a sardonic eyebrow. 'Some day, perhaps, you will enlighten me as to the sort of man who would appeal to you – a woman with such a diverse background. But for now, it will be sufficient if you describe this man for me in as much detail as you can manage. Not only his physical appearance but also his personality. It is always useful to be aware of the qualities, or lack of them, of the enemy.'

'I have already told you that he is cruel,' Lotte said. 'I doubt if he would show mercy to any living creature if it got in his way. As for his face, if you can give me pencil and paper, I will show you exactly what he looked like.'

At that, both eyebrows shot up. 'Ah, an artist as well as an interpreter! Your talents know no bounds.' He turned to Victor. 'Clearly, we must not let such a paragon slip through our fingers!'

Victor, who had followed this exchange with his face as impassive as a lump of dough, nodded morosely. 'If you say so.'

'Come with me, please.' Jacques turned on his heel and led the way across the clearing towards the shack, giving the ladler of stew a curt command as he passed. Inside the shack, he indicated a couple of upturned wooden boxes. 'If you are going to stay with us, you had better get used to our lack of conveniences.'

'This is fine, thank you.' Lotte seated herself on one of the boxes and Victor took the other.

Jacques took a notepad from a makeshift table and a pencil and gave them both to Lotte. At the same moment, a man came in and placed three bowls of stew on the table, cast a curious eye at Lotte, who was already bending to her task, and went out. Immediately, Jacques and Victor began to eat. Two minutes later, she had finished. Handing the drawing to Jacques, she too began to eat. Clearly, there was no standing upon ceremony here.

Jacques inspected the drawing closely then looked at Lotte. 'You expect me to believe that this man meant nothing to you and yet you are able to remember every little detail of his face, including even the wart above his right eyebrow and the tiny scar at the corner of his mouth?'

For answer, she picked up her pencil again and, without looking at Jacques, drew with quick incisive strokes, then handed him the pad and continued to eat.

It was all there: the long blond hair curling slightly on to the collar of his shirt, the gold chain around his neck, the high forehead above the strong, aquiline nose, the deep-set eyes, the determined chin with a deep cleft at its centre, even the stubble on that chin. He gazed at it for a long moment then gave her a wry smile. 'Had I known you were coming I would have shaved!' He studied the picture for a few more moments then pulled a box of matches from his pocket and deliberately set fire to the drawing, holding it by a corner until it was no more than a charred mass. Then he dropped it on the earthen floor and ground it in with his heel. 'That is not an indication of the value I set upon it, only that if it were to be seen by the wrong people, it would be as good as my death warrant. You have a rare talent, Claire.'

'So, may I stay?'

'You may stay!'

'We shall be coming back to the cottage when Mike's a few weeks older,' Mat said.

It was the day after the christening and he and Mair were strolling in the grounds of Holker Hall.

'I thought you'd be staying here for a while,' Mair said.

'Well, I've still got to have several more ops before the medics write me off, so it will be easier for me to be nearer to the hospital. Besides,' he added turning to smile at her, 'young Mike won't want to be too far away from his godmother! Anyway, now that the bombing's eased up on London, Rosie will probably decide to take him up to see Charlie's parents.'

'They really seem to have accepted the situation now, don't they? Rosie must be very relieved.'

'She is, although she guessed Charlie's mother would change her tune once the baby had arrived. His father's always been on Rosie's side. I'm not sure if they think I'm a good thing or not, but at least they can see it's better for Mike to have some sort of a father than none at all.'

'I don't think you're going to be "some sort of a father", Mat. You obviously love him to bits.'

'I know! To be honest, I'm amazed at how much. But I am his second cousin, remember. We're blood relations, after all. But apart from that, I'm beginning to look at children with a new eye. Even to the extent of wondering if I might have a future in teaching.'

'Really? That would be wonderful!' In her enthusiasm, Mair stopped walking and turned to face him. 'That's the best news I've heard in ages. I'd been wondering . . .' She stopped abruptly and her cheeks turned a delicate shade of pink.

'What sort of a career a chap with a face like mine could possibly follow,' he finished for her.

'No!' Mair protested. 'Not that! There are many, many things you could do and do well. But I doubt if there are many you would want to do. But teaching – well, that's something different. You'd be wizard at it – especially with your history.'

'You mean that a face like mine wouldn't necessarily be a handicap?'

'I wish you'd stop going on about your face,' said Mair with asperity. 'It's not as bad as you make out and you've just said they hope to improve it even more.'

'And children? How do you think they would react to it?'

'Children are good at knowing what a person is really like inside. Anyway, look at little Maggie. She still thinks you're the bees' knees.'

166

Her face was alight with her enthusiasm. He had rarely seen her so animated. And on his behalf. He felt strangely humbled. And pleased. Suddenly he heard himself ask, 'And what do you think of me, Mair? Do you think I'm wonderful, too?'

A baffling sequence of emotions chased each other across her face. Surprise? Resentment? He found he was holding his breath as he waited for her reply. And then his heart gave a sudden extraordinary lurch of disappointment as he saw that her eyes were brimming with mischief. She cocked her head to one side.

'Wonderful? You must be joking! You can't even scramble an egg!' Mat's inability to cook, even such a simple dish as scrambled egg, was legendary. The moment of emotional tension was over as he laughed with her.

'One day I'll show you!'

Arm in arm, they wandered back to the Dower House, their talk now on the safe subject of young Michael Holker. But Mat found himself strangely confused. He'd love to know what she really thought of him. And what, come to think about it, did he really think about her?

In Italy, Allied troops continued to move steadily northward and in Algiers, Charlie Johnson continued to baffle the medical staff. He also continued to baffle himself as he tried desperately to remember anything from the past.

XX

Ruefully, Lotte considered the state of her nails. Digging her own latrine hadn't improved them but Jacques had been insistent that, in that respect, at least, she should be treated differently from the men. She had already competed in a contest to establish the fastest time for the stripping, oiling and reassembling of both Sten and Bren guns and had shared second place with Jean. Jacques was first. She had plotted a course through the forest and followed it on compass bearings, ending up within yards of her target. She had taken part in a knockout bout of unarmed combat and had survived into the penultimate round. She had been included in the guard roster and had taken an early morning watch with a taciturn individual called Paul.

But what she had valued most was her own personal assignment from Jacques to sketch the layout of the several villages within a ten-mile radius of the camp. So far she had provided him with one of St Tomas, remembered from her two visits there. To do the others, it had been decided that her appearance must be changed in case she came under the eagle eye of Karl Bluthner.

'I think,' Jacques said soon after she'd arrived, 'we should change the colour of your hair and also cut it shorter.'

So Lotte had been presented with a bottle of hair dye and a pair of scissors and told to get on with it with the aid of a tiny piece of cracked mirror. Her hair was now dark brown, as were her eyebrows, and hacked into an uneven cap of straggling, unkempt locks.

She had spent an absorbing couple of hours with Jacques with a map of the area spread out before them while he painstakingly explained the advantages and disadvantages of particular places from the point of view of the Resistance.

'No doubt you are already familiar with the 'goulets', the name we give to the incredibly deep and precipitous gorges that have been carved out of the limestone by the River Vernaison. In the last century, a road was built – a road that was a marvel of civil engineering as it followed the river from Pont-en-Royans in the west of the Vercors through many tunnels and cuttings of the Petits Goulet before it began its perilous climb up the side of the gorge through yet more tunnels and using a series of hairpin bends to reduce the steepness of the gradient. This is the Grands Goulet and it ends at Les Barraques-en-Vercors, the village that was especially built to house the constructors of this incredible road.

'Besides the goulets, there are also many underground caves or "grottes" in the area. One of these, a particularly large one, we use as a hospital. Such an area is near perfect for the ambush of German troops who may come up from the Rhône Valley and therefore must use the road up through the Grands Goulet. There are several villages of which it would be useful to have detailed plans. Les Barraques, Chapelle-en-Vercors, Vassieux-en-Vercors and its strategic bridge over the Vernaison. As you make these plans, you will familiarize yourself with the area. But before that, we are expecting an arms drop at the same place where you were landed. I should like you to be there along with Paul and Maurice. There will also be a small packet containing crystals for a wireless set that is urgently needed by one of our operatives. I would like you to take responsibility for its safe collection.'

'You're late!' said Mat, looking up from tickling Mike's stomach as he lay, spread-eagled and cooing ecstatically, on a rug in front of the fire.

'Head wind,' Mair explained, peeling off her greatcoat and carefully concealing her pleasure that he'd noticed.

'Here, let me!' Mat unfolded himself from the hearth rug and took her coat from her. 'Cup of tea?'

'Smashing! Thanks.' Mair knelt on the rug and took over the tickling. 'Where's Rosie?' she called after Mat's retreating back.

'Having a lie down,' he said over his shoulder.

'OK, is she?'

Mat turned back. 'Yes, I think so.'

'Only think?'

'Well, she's getting these periods of depression. But I gather that can sometimes happen after you've given birth. But I do wish her day didn't revolve quite so much around the postman. When the only post is a letter for me from the Air Ministry or a parcel from Charlie's mum enclosing yet another pair of hand-knitted leggings or whatever, she just fades away.'

'But surely she still loves the baby?'

'I'm sure she does but I'm not sure that that's enough. When he cries these days, it's usually me that goes to see what's up. Sometimes, I think it's me he's bonding with and not Rosie. Not that I mind! I love it. But it worries me rather. All the euphoria she felt when Mike was born seems to have faded away.'

Mair suddenly wrinkled up her nose and sniffed. 'Talking of bonding, how are you on nappies? Because I think . . .' She sniffed again.

Mat came back and knelt on the rug. 'Well, I'm not that bad. If you could just give me a hand?'

They knelt either side of the baby as if they were high priests at a votive offering.

'At least I know how to take it off.' In spite of the still limited use of his hands, Mat removed the soiled nappy deftly enough while Mair took a clean one from the pile on a nearby chair. She folded it into a triangle.

'That's right, isn't it?'

'Perfect. Now, if we plonk him down, *comme ça* . . .'

'Then pull it up between his legs . . .'

'. . . and cross over the two side bits, like so . . .'

'What did you do with the pins?'

Mat sat back on his heels and looked around him. What had

he done with them? And then he saw them on the coffee table in front of the fire and leaned over to pick them up.

'Don't bother!' said Mair suddenly.

'Why? What?' And then he saw what Mair had already discovered. Young Master Holker, chortling his head off, had just demonstrated, yet again, his expertise at filling nappies. 'Oh, no!'

'Oh, yes!' And then, suddenly, they were helpless with laughter.

'How many nappies have we got?' Mair asked, wiping her eyes.

'Three more until the last lot have aired,' Mat said and she thought, goodness! He's having to do everything. Rosie must be in a bad way. But there was one thing, at least, that he could not do. Rosie would have to be awakened soon for Mike's food.

But she came down of her own accord, bleary-eyed and apologetic, but with a strange, haunted look in her eyes.

'I'm worried about her,' Mat confided to Mair a couple of hours later as he went outside to see her off. 'But she flatly refuses to see a doctor. I don't like the idea of leaving her on her own when I have to go back to hospital next week.'

'Moneymoon Manor?' Mair suggested but thinking how much she would miss her visits to the cottage.

'Just what I was thinking. I'll ring them tomorrow. Meanwhile, thanks for all your help this evening. Champion nappy changers, that's us!'

'My pleasure! Anyway, the experience may come in useful one day, you never know.' Some imp of mischief prompted her to make the seemingly innocent remark, just to see his reaction.

For a split second, there was none. And then he said, 'Is there any chance of you and Andy. . . ?'

'None,' she said firmly. 'Mat, I'll be all right now, truly.' For he seemed all set to escort her back to the main road, the fields having been dismissed as unsafe in the dark, even though the moon was nearly full.

'Are you sure? Why don't I get the car out? There should be enough petrol.'

'Mat, I shall be all right, honestly. And the wind will be behind

171

me this time. I shall probably become airborne!' She took the bike from him and stood with one foot on a pedal, her face a white blur in the moonlight.

'Goodnight, then. God bless!' And he bent, as he often did, to give her an affectionate peck on the cheek. But this time, either his aim wasn't so good or his mouth had a will of its own for his lips found hers and stayed there for several seconds before she turned and pedalled quickly away.

Mat stood there, gazing after her until the faint red glow of her rear light disappeared around a bend. What had come over him? She was his good friend, for God's sake! What would she think of him? Taking advantage of her present lack of a boyfriend to 'try it on'? That was the last thing he wanted from her. But what did he want?

Deeply confused but unable to forget the cool sweetness of her lips, he turned back to the cottage. Probably it had just been a reaction after Rosie's strange behaviour. But as he retraced his steps, he smiled to himself. She'd looked so sweet, kneeling on the hearth rug, laughing her head off. Somebody would be a lucky guy one day.

Meanwhile, Mair was being blown back to camp, her spirits soaring as if she really were a bird on the wing. She'd always remember the gentleness of that kiss. She tried to be sensible, to exert some sort of control over her emotions. But it was no good. She was happy, happy, happy!

Pedalling up the hill towards the camp gates and the guard room, she smiled to herself as she remembered the password.

'Paradise,' she called out as she rode up to the sentry. But he'd heard the word too often that night for it to have any romantic connotations for him.

'You wouldn't think so if your feet were as cold as mine,' he grunted. 'But paradise it is. Goodnight, Corp!'

'Of course Rosie must come to us.' His grandmother's response was as Mat had expected. 'Apart from anything else, it will be wonderful to have a baby in the house again. The children will love it.'

'All all right, are they?' Mat asked. 'Maggie still doing well at school?'

'Brilliantly, I understand. She reads to your grandfather every night from *Tom Brown's Schooldays*. He tried her on *Alice* but she said that was boring.'

Mat chuckled. 'I wonder if she'd enjoy my old *Boy's Own* annuals? I'll dig them out next time I'm home.'

'Just up her street, I should think, and your grandfather would certainly enjoy them. You'll drive Rosie and the baby over, then?'

'Yes – next week, probably. Thanks, Gramma!'

'Maybe we'll all have Christmas together. That would be lovely.'

The drop had gone perfectly as far as Lotte was concerned, not that there hadn't been moments of sheer, stomach-churning terror. Paul and Maurice were old hands but she doubted if even they would have got through it with such apparent ease had it not been for the flasks she knew they carried in their pockets.

It was a clear, starry night but with no moon. Ideal conditions for them but also for any German reconnaissance party that might be in the neighbourhood. As it was, she did as she was told and, literally, kept her head down, glancing skyward from the comparative security of the bush she was crouched behind only when she heard the drone of an approaching aircraft. It was a Whitley again, she thought, and wondered if the same sergeant was on board. But there would be no way of knowing for it was only a drop of arms and supplies and the aircraft would only circle over the dropping zone before heading back to England.

England! Briefly, she thought of her grandparents existing stoically in their wartime accommodation and of Holker Hall and Aunt Bella, Kate and Robert and then of Moneymoon Manor and its little 'colony'. Did she want to be there? Would she exchange the dangers and deprivations of her present life for the comparative safety of England? And she knew that she would not. This was where she wanted to be, even with these annoying tremors in the pit of her stomach, even with Jacques constantly telling her what to do and keeping an eagle eye on her every movement. Perhaps, she conceded with a wry grin as she pointed her torch skyward and flashed it three times as Paul and Maurice were doing at their corners of the triangle, it was because of Jacques. There seemed to be something about situations such as these, when every nerve was quivering with anticipation and fear, that made one see things as they really were. And no amount of telling herself that agents should not, must not, become personally involved while in the field was making the slightest difference. She was – heaven help her – already deeply involved. But at least she would keep the knowledge to herself.

Her mouth dry, her heart beating like a sledge-hammer, she watched while the aircraft circled, came low and disgorged its load. As far as she could see, all the boxes with their attendant parachutes seemed to be landing on target. The aircraft dipped its wings in farewell and turned for home and then all three of them were racing towards the parachutes.

'Here, this one is for you, the boss said.' Paul handed her a package smaller than the others. 'He said you would look after it.'

Don't forget to bury the 'chutes, Jacques had also said. And they did, using the spades they had brought with them for the purpose of digging a hole between the bushes, covering it with dead leaves and grass as camouflage.

'Now we go! And quickly!' said Maurice. There was no way of knowing if the drop had been spotted by the Germans. Even as he spoke, an army lorry full of armed men could be driving up the road towards them and they would be like moths caught in the lights. They dragged the boxes to where they had parked the van belonging to Philippe and heaved them on board.

Lotte felt blood oozing from her fingertips but wasn't conscious of pain until they were in the van with Maurice at the wheel. At first he drove in low gear but gathered speed as they followed the tracks that wound down the mountainside into the darkness of the forest.

XXI

For the war-weary British people, Christmas that year was a time for wary celebration and, above all, hope. For on Christmas Eve, the appointment of General Dwight D. Eisenhower as Supreme Commander of the Allied invasion of western Europe was announced, with General Montgomery, hero of the battle of El Alamein, as his field commander. It was not so much the appointment of these two individuals that gave them cause for hope as the admission thereby that there was to be an invasion of Europe. And not before too long.

'Mind you,' said Professor Moneymoon to his wife, 'I don't know how they'll get on with each other. Monty's a great chap but I don't think I'd like to work with him. Like working with a fire-cracker.'

'Just as well you don't have to, then, isn't it?' said his wife with some asperity. 'And if you're going to sit and read your newspaper all morning, would you mind doing it in the study? I've got a lot to get through.'

Professor Moneymoon laid down his *Manchester Guardian* with a sigh. He knew when he was beaten. 'What would you like me to do, my dear?'

'Sprouts, please,' said his wife immediately. 'And then bread-crumbs. And after that . . .'

But she was interrupted by the scrunch of tyres on gravel and Maggie's excited shout from the first-floor landing window where she'd been keeping watch since breakfast-time. 'They're here!' Followed at a slower pace by her step-grandparents, she ran outside.

'Hello, sprog! Happy Christmas!' Stifling an impulse to try and pick her up and whirl her around above his head, as he'd used to do, Mat contented himself with bending down and wrapping his arms around her in a clumsy embrace. At the same time, he smiled up at his grandparents over Maggie's shoulder. 'Gramma! Gramps! And Port and Star! Great to see you all!' For Stella and Polly had been hard on Maggie's heels; quickly abandoning all pretence at the adult decorum they strove for these days, they lined up behind Maggie to kiss their uncle.

At the same moment, Tom, his arms full of holly and mistletoe, came round the side of the house, an enormous grin on his face. 'Tom!' cried Mat. 'Well, this is a welcome and no mistake! Now, come and meet his lordship!' And he turned back to the car.

Rosie stepped out first, then turned to take her son from Mair's arms. Was that how it had been on the journey? Mrs Moneymoon wondered. Had the boy been cradled in Mair's arms and not his mother's! And was there something almost furtive in the speed with which Rosie immediately transferred him to his great-grandmother's arms? But she soon forgot such thoughts in the pleasure of holding her great-grandson.

The next half-hour was spent in the warmth of the kitchen with everyone standing around 'billing and cooing', as Mat put it, over the charms of Master Michael.

'Can I hold him?' Maggie asked, her eyes enormous with longing. 'I'll be ever so careful.' It was then they discovered that Rosie was no longer with them.

'She's gone up to unpack and then maybe take a rest,' Mair explained. 'She said she felt a bit tired after the journey.'

'But . . ' Mrs Moneymoon began, for it couldn't have taken longer than an hour, but then caught Mat's eye. He gave a tiny, warning shake of his head.

'It's very nice of you to invite me for Christmas,' Mair said quickly, clearly changing the subject. And Mrs Moneymoon went along with it – for now.

'My dear, we look on you as one of the family. How long can you stay?'

'I'll be going home on Boxing Day,' Mair said, 'if that's all right. I'll still have several days with my parents. Dada's always so busy at Christmas time and Mam, too; they won't really miss me. Anyway, Mam wants to hear all your news.'

'That will be lovely,' said Mrs Moneymoon. 'Now . . .' She glanced back over her shoulder at the pile of sprouts on the draining board. 'I must get on.'

'We must *all* get on,' said her husband dutifully, but unable to resist a furtive glance at the rocking chair by the stove with his discarded newspaper still on it. 'Unless Mat . . .' He glanced hopefully at his grandson. He might like to share a pre-lunch drink of the rather inferior sherry he'd managed to acquire. A chat with him would be even better than reading the paper.

'I'll help, too,' said Mair swiftly. 'Just let me go and change this scrap and put him down and I'll be with you.' And she swept the baby up into her arms and bore him away with the sort of practised ease that spoke of familiarity.

'I'll help you,' said Mat, just as matter-of-factly, and left the room with her, followed by three adoring girls. Tom had long gone and was busying himself in the hall, balancing sprigs of holly along picture frames and twining ivy up the stair rail.

What was going on? Mrs Moneymoon wondered.

Lotte found the café in Pont-en-Royan where she had been told to be at three o'clock on Christmas Eve, went inside and looked about her. According to Jacques, her contact should be waiting for her and would immediately get to his feet and wave to her to join him. Once she had done so, they would talk animatedly for several minutes while they drank their coffee and would then exchange wrapped Christmas presents in the affectionate and light-hearted manner appropriate for cousins. Only they would know that Lotte's 'present' contained the wireless crystals picked up at the last drop.

Her eyes searched the café. She had been told that her contact would be facing the door and would be wearing a sprig of mistletoe in the lapel of his jacket. The 'present' intended for her would be prominently displayed on the table in front of him. She, clutching her 'present', would go to him immediately and say, 'Cousin Henri! How good to see you! And how is my Aunt Isabel?' He would then reply, 'As well as can be expected. She sends her love.'

The café was crowded, with most of the tables occupied. Even so, it was easy to pick out the person sporting a bunch of mistletoe in their lapel and who had a large, square parcel wrapped in white paper and bearing a festive bow of crimson ribbon. Her own parcel was practically identical. The only difference from what she had expected was that the person was a woman – and a woman whose heart-shaped face with its determined little chin and big grey eyes she would have known anywhere. It was Sarah.

Their eyes met. At least, Lotte thought, recognition in these circumstances was permissible. She felt a surge of joy and the unexpected bonus of being able to sit here, for all the world to see, and chat to her old friend. She began to move forward but then realized that the expression in Sarah's eyes had become a cold stare as if she was gazing at a complete stranger and then there came an almost imperceptible shake of her head. And then her eyes slanted downward to the table top and Lotte saw that there was another cup there. The chair in front of it had been pushed back and a German army greatcoat had been slung carelessly over the back of it. And then she became aware that Sarah's eyes were now focused on a corner of the café where an arrow indicated the position of the toilets. Coming through a door was Sturmbannführer Karl Bluthner, heading for Sarah's table. At the same moment that Lotte turned away, a man and a woman got up from a table just beside her and prepared to leave. Immediately, she took one of the vacant chairs, positioning herself so that she sat behind Karl but with a clear view of Sarah's face.

She ordered coffee from the waiter who appeared at her elbow and placed her 'present' on the table where Sarah could see it. Why was Karl Bluthner sitting at her table, anyway?

Surely there could be no sinister reason for him doing so, for he was now leaning forward and she was giving him a small, tentative sort of smile. At the same time, she lowered her eyelids and glanced at her watch. She was, Lotte decided, looking as attractive as ever in spite of her drab skirt and jacket, and she remembered how one girl in the pre-war skiing party had had difficulty in repelling Karl's advances. Exchanging presents was going to be difficult. Her eyes strayed to the door beyond which the toilet was located.

Five minutes later, she finished her coffee, rose to her feet and picked up her parcel. Slowly, she walked past Sarah's table, keeping her face turned well away from Karl.

The toilet consisted of just one cubicle but, to her great relief, was unoccupied. Slipping inside, she stood with the door very slightly ajar and waited. Two interminable minutes later, Sarah came through the door from the café and Lotte pushed open the toilet door so that she could slip in beside her. Then Lotte sat on the seat of the toilet as, with great difficulty, Sarah managed to close and bolt the door. There was hardly enough room for her to turn around to face Lotte.

'Breathe in!' said Lotte and immediately they both dissolved into a fit of silent giggling which made the manoeuvre even more difficult. Giggles over, they hugged each other briefly then launched into rapid explanations.

Sarah, Lotte discovered, was working in a bakery in Pont-en-Royan and Karl Bluthner had become a regular customer and far too interested in her for her safety. Fortunately, Robert, the owner of the bakery, was also a member of the Resistance and had appointed himself as her protector, aided by his wife, Louise.

'Karl thinks I'm his mistress,' Sarah whispered, 'which is great. Robert should have been here instead of me but he's gone down with a stinking cold and Louise put her foot down. And, of course, as luck would have it, Karl saw me and followed me into the café. Now, tell me about you.'

So Lotte gave her the bare bones of her story, giving only the essential details and leaving out anything that it would be safer for Sarah not to know. But she did explain about her previous acquaintance with Karl. 'So it's imperative he doesn't see me,' she finished. 'What's happening now? Is he waiting for you to come back?'

Sarah nodded. 'Just as well, probably. At least we know where he is. How are you getting back to wherever you've come from?'

'I'm being picked up.' Philippe, the dogsbody, was waiting a few streets away in his van. 'And, by the way, I think we'd better unwrap my present to you so that you can take out the crystals and we'll leave the wrapping in here.'

'Fine! And I'll just say my cousin hasn't turned up to collect her present so she'll just have to do without it until after Christmas! What a shame!'

'Come for a walk,' Mat suggested. 'After a meal like that, you can do one of two things. Go to sleep or walk it off. And as you're going home tomorrow, I'm blowed if I'm going to waste time sleeping!'

Mair already felt pleasantly warm – there was a plentiful supply of wood for the fire that had been lit in the little sitting room – but now she glowed inwardly at Mat's implied compliment. There was nothing she'd like more than a walk with him. And Mike could safely be left in the care of his doting great-grandparents. Rosie had retired to bed for her regular after-lunch nap and the children were in the kitchen, taking it in turns to play table tennis with the set Tom had been given for Christmas.

They walked down the lane that ran at the side of the house, then took a field path towards a coppice of tall beech trees.

'I love scuffling through dead leaves,' said Mair when they reached it.

'Especially beech leaves,' Mat agreed. Side by side, they scuffled happily, sending up great plumes of russet-coloured leaves and releasing the warm, pungent smell of the rotting vegetation beneath. Emerging eventually from the wood, they found themselves on the bank of a wide stream, so wide it had been spanned by a stone bridge.

'This was where Gramps and I used to play Pooh Sticks when

I was very small,' said Mat.

'The perfect place,' Mair agreed. 'Come on!' They scrambled down the bank and collected their sticks then climbed back up and positioned themselves in the centre of the bridge, leaning over the stone parapet.

'Now!' Mat shouted and they each released a stick into the swirling current then rushed to the other side of the bridge.

'That's mine!' Mair shrieked as a stick emerged.

'No, it's mine! I distinctly remember. It had a cleft in it.'

'So did mine!'

'Right! We'll have another go!'

This time, the sticks were clearly identifiable and this time, Mair's was clearly the winner. 'There! That proves it!'

Her eyes sparkling, her cheeks flushed, she turned and looked up at him. Before coming out, they had helped themselves from the collection of assorted outer garments that always hung in the lobby of the Manor and she had pulled on an ancient oiled-wool jersey of his grandfather's. It reached almost to her knees and her hands were invisible inside its sleeves. Her cropped head nestled in the folds of its roll-neck collar like some exotic flower bud emerging from a corolla of dead twigs, he thought fancifully.

'You're so beautiful!' he said and, quite without premeditation, bent his head and kissed her full on the lips.

It was not a long kiss and his lips stayed upon hers for no more than a few seconds his – 'new' lips were still tender and would not, in any case, allow anything longer – but when he withdrew his mouth, he could have sworn he could hear singing. Or was it just the sound of the water rushing beneath them that he now seemed to be hearing with a heightened perception, as if his senses were suddenly awakening from a long sleep?

'I love you!' he said. And the wonder in his voice matched the wonder in his eyes.

XXII

'It's happened,' said Victor, making one of his rare appearances in the camp and this time on skis. 'Just as I said. The Germans have come up the Rhône Valley and up the Grands Goulet road to Les Barraques.'

'Where were the Maquis?' asked Jacques.

'Where they should have been,' said Victor proudly. 'They ambushed them twice and killed over twenty.'

There came a cheer from the men gathered around him. 'Not all roses, though, said Victor. 'They burned down houses and hotels in Les Barraques in retaliation.'

'And where are they now?' Jacques asked.

'That's why I've come,' said Victor. 'It seems likely that some of them are coming in this direction towards Rousset. I wondered – a little harassment, perhaps? Something to see them on their way or rather – to slow them up? Wire across the road, perhaps?'

'Or our old friend the tyre buster,' said Jacques. 'Thanks, Victor, for letting us know. We'll just have time before it's dark.'

Minutes later, Lotte among them, a group was at the Rousset road. Besides the equipment they needed for their 'harassment', they also carried skis for a quick getaway.

'Right,' said Jacques. 'Paul and Maurice, you do the wire. And make sure it's the right height for a motorcycle. Preferably garrotting the rider but certainly unseating him. You others, help me lay the tyre traps.' These consisted of bunches of sharp metal prongs laid strategically across the road. 'Cover them with just a light sprinkling of snow,' Jacques ordered.

They had only just finished and withdrawn to the side of the road among the trees when they heard the sound of approaching vehicles.

'Skis on!' Jacques ordered.

In seconds, their feet were clamped to the long, narrow cross-country skis, ski sticks poised.

'When you go, go in twos,' said Jacques, 'and take different routes back to camp. Claire, you will stay with me.'

They waited just long enough to see the motorcyclist that led the convoy fall to the ground as if he'd been shot, he and his machine sprawling across the road in an untidy heap. 'Go now!' commanded Jacques as the first vehicle screamed to a halt and two soldiers, obeying a shouted command, ran forward.

Four of the Maquis slid silently away between the trees and into the gloom of the forest. Jacques put a restraining hand on Lotte's arm. 'Wait!'

They waited for several minutes while the motorcyclist was picked up – whether alive or dead, they couldn't tell – and both he and his machine carried on to the vehicle behind before it moved off again. Seconds later, there came sounds like pistol shots as the tyres were pierced and once more the vehicle skidded to a halt and two soldiers, urged on by a furious voice inside the cab, ran forward.

'That should keep them occupied for a while,' Jacques whispered. 'Let's go!' And then they, too, slid away. But this time, a shot rang out from the vehicle, followed by another, and a voice roared out a command in German. 'After them!'

He was on the edge of remembering. It was like walking along a dark passage and suddenly seeing light ahead around a corner, but when he'd turned that corner, it was still ahead around the next corner. It had started that morning when he'd dropped off to sleep again after the early-morning round of temperature taking.

Vague shapes – of people, sometimes of places and buildings – swam up into his consciousness, teasing him into awareness. One of them, he was sure, was his mother but there was another, less blurred, more demanding, and he was aware of a vague sense of unease where she was concerned – he was sure it was another woman – so that he tended to try and dismiss her. At the same time, he knew that she was important to him. And then he'd woken again, properly this time, and the images faded – but it was a beginning.

'When shall I see you again?' Mat asked. He and Mair were on Oxford station waiting for the South Wales train.

'I don't know. I'll cycle over to the cottage as soon as I'm back from leave but you'll be back in hospital by then.'

'Yes. I will, more's the pity. But I daren't ask for a postponement. They're so busy there.'

'Of course not. But I'll go over anyway. Rosie will expect it.'

'It's possible she'll be taking young Mike up to London to see his grandparents in the New Year. I'll try and fix it so I'll be back before she comes back.'

'Mat, is that wise?'

'Wise, be blowed! Darling girl, if I don't see you on your own before long or at least have it to look forward to, I shall blow a gasket!'

Mair smiled at him and, hoping that there were no WAAF officers on the platform, for they were both in uniform, put up a hand and gently stroked his cheek, a cheek that in the raw December air was bright pink and even more puckered than usual. Mat caught the hand in his and kissed it gently.

'I still can't get used to it,' she said. 'That you really love me.'

'Nor I you. When I think of all the time I've wasted! If only this had happened before . . .'

'Mat, there's no point in going over all that again. There's nothing we can do about it.'

'No, you're right. It's strange, isn't it? I think with most people, it's usually love at first sight and the good friends part comes later – if you're lucky, but with us, the good friends bit came first. And I think that's probably the best way. There's more chance of a lasting relationship. Don't despair, my darling.

We'll find a way somehow. Not at the moment; Rosie's in too bad a way. But we don't know what the future will bring. When she's more her old self, she could easily meet someone else.'

Mair didn't say anything. As far as she was concerned, Providence had already been magnanimous enough in allowing Mat to care for her as much as he clearly did. It was chancing your arm, she considered, to hope for a neat solution to the problem that their love had caused. But she wouldn't leave him on a downbeat note. She smiled up at him. 'We'll just have to wait and see.'

'And meanwhile, no more talk of getting yourself posted. Right?'

'Right!' she agreed but with her fingers surreptitiously crossed. When you were the daughter of a Methodist minister and his equally strait-laced wife, it was difficult to imagine any action but the moral one.

'And here's your blasted train! Look after yourself, my darling!'

Throwing all discretion to the wind, Mair hugged him as tightly as her great coat allowed. 'I love you!' she almost shouted, determined to make herself heard above the hissing of the engine.

'I love you, too!'

From the beginning, they knew there was someone after them. After the shouts had come the command. 'Follow them! Don't let them get away!'

For what seemed an eternity but was only minutes, they sped onwards, drawing in great gulps of the freezing air, Lotte slightly ahead of Jacques. Only that morning, she and Jean had patrolled up here. She doubted if Jacques knew the trails as well as she did. She thought quickly. Very soon, they would reach a place where the path came out of the trees and traversed a wide open space before disappearing into the trees again. The distance was not great but it would be sufficient to allow someone with a gun to take aim and fire – at a target that would be clearly visible against the snow. But just before the clearing, the paths divided.

185

'In about a minute,' she hissed at Jacques over her shoulder, 'take the path to the left. There is a hut a few hundred yards along it. Wait there! I'll be back.'

'But . . .' he began.

'I know what I'm doing. Trust me!'

Seconds later, she was indicating the path with one of her sticks and obediently he took it. She grinned wryly. It made a change for him to be the one to obey orders!

Almost immediately afterwards, she was at the edge of the clearing. Stooping low, she sped across it. She had almost reached the far side when a shot rang out and she felt a searing pain in her left arm. But the impetus of her skis carried her on into the shelter of the trees. Once there and gritting her teeth against the pain, she bent and released her skis, picked them up and stepped off the path.

Seconds later, the German soldier shot past at great speed. But she still waited. And then came the sound she had hoped for and yet dreaded; the cry of a man who realizes too late that he is on the edge of an abyss and that there is nothing but space – and eternity – below him. As he fell, his cries grew fainter and eventually stopped altogether and Lotte felt her stomach curdle. But it had been him or her. Thank heaven she knew, as the German would not have known of the landslide that had caused the path to virtually disappear.

Fighting nausea, she leaned on her sticks for a moment until she saw drops of blood on the snow in front of her and realized that it was her own. She must get back to Jacques while she still had the strength.

But even as she stepped out on to the track and bent to put on her skis, a tall figure loomed above her.

'Claire! Are you all right? When I heard the shot . . .'

The next moment, his arms were cradling her and she felt his cheek cold against her own. 'I couldn't have born it, my darling, if . . .' And then he kissed her and everything – her arm, the German soldier, the war, even – vanished in the ecstasy of the moment.

*

'It's been great having you,' said the elderly major blandly, 'but it's time for you to go. We're expecting a pretty heavy intake of wounded from Italy. We guys don't hang about, you know. We'll be in Rome any day now but it's taking its toll. So we're going to need all our beds, I'm afraid.'

It was on the tip of Charlie's tongue to say that the British army didn't hang about either but he bit it back. They'd been pretty good to him, one way and another.

'When do I leave?' he asked.

'Transport arranged for 0800 hours tomorrow,' said the major.

'Where to?'

'Tunis,' said the major. 'They'll have a look at you there and then, with any luck, you'll be catching the next boat home. I wish I was in your shoes!'

I wish you were, too! Charlie thought apprehensively.

XXIII

They had walked to the top of Wittenham Clumps and were now leaning against the broad trunk of one of the elm trees.

'I love you so much,' Mat said. He traced the contours of Mair's face with a gentle finger. 'I still can't believe I had you under my nose for so long and never realized how lovely you are.'

Mair smiled at him. 'Let's just say you had . . . other people in your sights.'

He smiled ruefully. 'You mean Lotte?' He pulled Mair closer to him and rested his chin on the crown of her head. 'She was very beautiful, I grant you. I think we just got caught up in the emotions and urgency of that time. I knew she was probably going off on some dangerous mission and she knew that one day I might get shot down. What she couldn't cope with was my being shot down and surviving – like this. I think that Lotte, perhaps because she is so physically perfect herself, demands perfection in others, certainly in any man she decides to live with.'

'You've no idea where she is now?'

'I'm pretty sure she'll be in France somewhere. Mum tells me that her parents receive postcards occasionally. They've always been posted in England and they all say just one thing – that she's alive and well. Presumably if she wasn't, the postcards would stop. Anyway, enough of that. I shall always wish her well but I'm not going to waste any more of this precious day in talking about other people. I can't tell you how wonderful it was to see your cycle wobbling down the lane just now.'

'I honestly thought Rosie would have been back with Mike by now.'

'She was supposed to be but apparently the Johnsons persuaded her to stay on for a few more days. Wouldn't you have come if you'd known that?'

'I would have done my best not to. But . . .' And now Mair put back her head and pulled his down so that their lips were nearly touching. 'I doubt if I could have stayed away.'

'Good!' And he lost no more time in words but brought his lips firmly down upon hers. What seemed like an eternity later, she broke away from him. 'Mat, we've got to talk. Decide what's best to do. For all of us. There's Rosie and Mike to consider, not just us.'

'Darling, I know, I know.' He nuzzled his mouth into her hair. 'And we will talk – later.'

'Mat, I don't think I should stay for supper.'

'Why not? You told me you weren't on duty again until midday tomorrow.'

'You know perfectly well why not!'

Charlie knew now why he'd been moved on from the American hospital in Algiers with what at the time he'd considered unseemly haste. Towards the end of January, news had come through of the surprise landing by British and American troops at Anzio, just thirty miles south of Rome, and their swift thrust northwards.

One of the objectives was the capture of the airfield that had once been the international airport for Rome. After that, it would be Rome itself.

'We've got them on the run now, mate,' observed a British private standing at the rail next to Charlie as the hospital ship they were on steamed away from Tunis. He didn't know that Charlie was a sergeant but that was hardly surprising since Charlie didn't either.

On the third day out, he was nodding off over a much-thumbed Agatha Christie he had found lying around when he became aware that the sun had suddenly disappeared and yet, a moment before, when his eyelids had first started to droop, the sky had been cloudless. His eyes flickered open at the same moment that a voice said:

'My God! It can't be!'

Charlie's eyes came wide open. A tall figure stood in front of him, blotting out the sun; a figure clad in khaki shorts and shirt like everyone else on the ship, but with a sergeant's stripes on his sleeve. He was leaning heavily on a stick but still managing to lean forward and subject Charlie to intense scrutiny as if he were under a microscope. The expression in the man's eyes was one of disbelief coupled with joyful astonishment. 'It is, isn't it?' he almost shouted. 'It's my old mate, Charlie Johnson! Back from the dead!'

Lotte's eyes flickered open, closed again then opened wider. Where was she? It looked like some sort of huge cave; the walls – what she could see of them in the dim light – seemed to be roughly hewn from the living rock. She turned her head and glanced about her. There were other beds there besides her own, each with what looked like an orange box beside it. There was one, she now noticed, beside her own bed and on it was a carafe of water and a tin mug.

Water! For the first time, she became aware that her lips were dry and cracked and her throat felt as if iron filings had been forced down it. She started to pull herself up on to her elbows but the next second had crashed back on to the bed as excruciating pain shot through her shoulder like a battery of red-hot needles. Her exclamation brought a figure from somewhere out of the shadows – a woman dressed in what seemed to be a man's white shirt and dark trousers.

'Careful! You'll burst your stitches if you're not careful. Was it water you wanted?'

Lotte nodded, incapable of speech.

'Hold on, then, while I help you up.'

The woman poured water into the tin mug, then slid one arm behind Lotte's shoulders, raising her a few inches while she held the mug to her lips. The water was like nectar – the finest wine

190

could not have been more welcome. Lotte sank back on to her pillows.

'Where am I?'

'The hospital near Rousset.'

She remembered now. Someone – it must have been Jacques – had told her about the makeshift hospital created by the Resistance in the huge cave near the village of Rousset.

'They brought you in yesterday,' the nurse continued. 'Jacques, was it? He said that he'd be back after we'd removed the bullet. The bullet in your upper arm,' she added as Lotte continued to gaze at her, clearly puzzled. 'Don't worry about it now,' she added quickly. 'I'll get you some soup and then you must sleep. Sleep is the best medicine now,' and she moved away down the 'ward'.

Lotte lay back on the hard mattress. She had a vague recollection of Jacques tearing his shirt into strips to bind up the wound, of the concealment of her skis and sticks and then the laborious, agonizingly slow return to the camp when she had had to balance herself as best she could on the back of Jacques' skis and put her good arm around his waist and simply lean on him. He was a fit man but even so, they had had to stop several times while he drew breath. She must have passed out towards the end because she had no recollection of arriving back at camp.

Presumably, she would have been bundled into the back of Philippe's van and brought here. What was it the nurse had said? 'He'll be back after we've removed the bullet.' Lotte gave a small sigh of contentment and snuggled into her pillow. She was asleep before her soup arrived.

Bit by bit, it was coming back. At one point, he'd had to tell Nobby Clarke to shut up for a moment or two while he tried to take it all in. Nobby, of course, hadn't realized at first what had happened to him; thought, in fact, that he was pulling his leg when he'd asked him things like his name and rank and what he'd been doing in Italy anyway.

'I can understand you wanting to forget about Salerno,' Nobby said. 'It was a shambles. I tried to find you when it was all over but no luck. So I decided you must have been blown to bits. A lot of the lads were. So what did happen to you? Or can't you remember?'

Charlie shook his head. 'All I'm sure about is waking up in hospital. An American hospital. What happened to you?'

'Copped it at Anzio. So did Fred. Remember Fred? He did Charlie Chaplin impressions. He's on board, too. I'll go and get him.'

But Charlie wasn't ready yet for more visitors. 'In a minute, Nobby. I'm still getting to grips with things.'

And then it all came flooding back – in a great tidal wave that he couldn't stop. Rosie! And there was a baby on the way! 'Nobby,' he said urgently, 'what's the date?'

Nobby thought. 'To be honest, I'm not quite sure. Not to be exact. One day's just like the other when you're at sea. But round about the middle of February, 14th or 15th.'

But Charlie wasn't interested in precision. 'Then I'm a father, Nobby! At least, I hope I am!'

Nobby suddenly clapped his hand to his forehead. 'Going senile, I am! I forgot all about your letter! It was a mistake it ever came up the line after you went missing. But it did and I picked it up. Thought the least I could do was get in touch with whoever had written it if I ever got back to England and try to explain what had happened. Not that I knew, really. It's in my kit. I'll go and get it before I look for Fred.' And he went.

Five minutes later, he was back with a somewhat tired-looking envelope, which he handed to Charlie. 'I'll leave you to read it, mate. Back in a little while with Fred. If I can find him.'

Charlie took the letter and stared at it then began to turn it over and over in his hands. He'd know that writing anywhere – black and sprawling, a no-nonsense hand.

His fingers were trembling so much he could hardly open the envelope.

'Dearest Charlie,' Rosie had written, 'I know that the chances of you ever reading this are as unlikely as Thanksgiving in May. I know that it will eventually come back to me, stamped 'Missing, believed killed', but I still have to write it. I'm no shrink but maybe it's something to do with trying to rid myself of the guilt I feel – the feeling that I've betrayed you, even though I know, deep down inside, that what I did was the right thing for our son. But I'll tell you the good news first – Michael Charles was born on October 18th and Charlie, he's the most beautiful baby you could imagine. He was born at the Dower House of Holker Hall with my Aunt Kate in attendance and Mat waiting downstairs. And that brings me to the second piece of news – the news I feel guilty about.

'It was Mat's idea. He hated the thought of the baby – his second cousin – being born a bastard which, to put it crudely, he would have been. Believe me, my darling, if we hadn't had the news you were missing, if Mat hadn't checked out the chances of you still being alive with his uncle, I would never have considered it. I'd have ridden out the storm until you came home and made an honest woman of me, but as things were, it seemed the most sensible thing to do. Mat and I were married just before Mike was born so I am now Mat's wife and the baby is Michael Charles Holker.

'There, I've said it. And in a crazy way, I feel the better for having put it down on paper even though I know you'll never read it. But oh, my darling, I miss you so! No matter what happens in the future, Mike will be told all about his real father one day, Goodbye, my darling. Your ever loving, Rosie.'

Charlie read the letter twice – then once more to make sure he'd got it right. Then he folded it carefully and put it in his shirt pocket. He hoped Nobby Clarke wouldn't be back for a very long time because time was what he needed now to try and make some sense of the emotions that were threatening to swamp him.

Once he had remembered about Rosie and the baby, there had been overwhelming joy, shot through with anxiety. How was Rosie? Had the baby arrived safely? Was his mother still being difficult? When Nobby had given him the letter, he had thought that all his questions would be answered. And they nearly all had been, although there still remained a question mark over his parents' reaction to the birth. But when he'd reached the second

193

part of Rosie's outpouring, he'd felt as if his legs had been knocked away beneath him. Mat Holker! The guy he'd been so envious of even before he'd met him. The guy that represented all that Charlie had ever wanted but never had. But surely Lotte had been his girlfriend? What had happened there? And then he remembered that Rosie had written to him and told him how Mat had been shot down and had survived but with a terribly disfigured face. Perhaps that was something the beautiful Lotte hadn't been able to cope with. So maybe Rosie, his sweet, generous Rosie had been used to fill the gap. He felt a surge of anger, almost choking him, and he took out the letter from his pocket and screwed it up in his fist. What if Rosie hadn't needed much persuasion? She'd always been close to Mat. It wouldn't take long before proximity brought them even closer.

Mid-February, Nobby had told him it was now, so they'd been married for four months. By now, they would be a cosy, supportive little family. Wouldn't it be easier if, as far as they were concerned, Charlie Johnson simply remained 'missing, believed killed'?

XXIV

'You won't be able to use a Sten for a while,' said the doctor. 'Not with any degree of accuracy. That shoulder's going to be stiff for some time.'

Lotte glanced at Jacques. Both men were sitting on the empty bed beside hers and she was sitting, fully dressed, on her own. Jacques had come to 'take her home'.

'What do you think?' she asked him. 'Should I go back to England? I don't want to be a liability.'

'Do you want to?' he asked.

The doctor got to his feet. 'I'll leave you now.' He bent and kissed her formally on both cheeks, then walked away.

Jacques leaned across and took one of Lotte's hands in his. 'Do you want to go back to England?' he repeated his question.

She shook her head vehemently. 'You know I don't. Now, less than ever.'

He relinquished her hand and came to sit beside her then slid an arm carefully around her shoulders. 'I cannot hold you as I would wish but one day . . .' He left the sentence unfinished as he bent his head and kissed her gently on the mouth.

She felt weak with longing.

'If this were peacetime,' he said, 'I would take you away to Norway.'

'Norway?'

He nodded. 'That is where my mother came from. Where I was sent each year for the summer holidays. To a village beside a lake among the mountains in Telemark. My father met my mother there when he was in his early twenties – he was climbing there with a friend – married her and brought her back to Paris.'

'So that is why you are so fair. I had wondered. And your parents now?'

'Both dead. When the Germans entered Paris we left in our old Renault. But we didn't get far before we were strafed by German dive-bombers and my parents were killed and the car was wrecked. I was the lucky one, I suppose. But I had to leave their bodies there, by the roadside.' His grip on Lotte's shoulder tightened and she winced. 'Forgive me, *chérie*, I am a thoughtless brute but I can hardly bear to think about it, let alone talk about it. Although it was what my parents had told me to do, if this were to happen, it is something I shall never forget. I still have nightmares about it and probably always will.'

'There was nothing else you could have done,' she said gently. 'Now, tell me,' she urged, wanting to lead his mind away from the past. 'How are we getting back to camp?'

'In Philippe's van, of course, and sadly, that means Philippe will be with us!'

'And so,' Mair informed Mat, 'I'm off to Liverpool in the morning.'

'Liverpool? In the morning? That's not possible!' And then, as he saw from her expression that it was indeed possible, 'You went to see the Queen WAAF, didn't you,' he accused, 'and asked to be sent as far away as possible as quickly as possible?'

Mair sighed. 'Mat, please try to understand. You know we can't go on as we are. Not after the other night.'

'The other night was the most wonderful night of my life,' said Mat obstinately. 'And I thought it was for you, too.' He knew that he was behaving like a small child who had been denied the fairy at the top of the Christmas tree but he couldn't help himself. This was no Christmas fairy but the person he loved most in all the world. The person who was now sitting next to him in the public bar of the George Inn in Wallingford – where she had insisted they meet rather than at the cottage because 'it's safer that way'.

He knew what she meant, of course. Perhaps things might have been different if she hadn't stayed over at the cottage the other night, if they hadn't both ended up in his bed. 'For the second time!' she'd reminded him before abandoning herself so completely to the urgency of her need.

The next morning, there hadn't been time to do more than make sure Mair had something to eat before cycling back to camp. 'I'll ring you,' she'd promised. And she had, which was why they were sitting here, surrounded by other people and talking about a future which had suddenly become as bleak as anything he could imagine.

'Actually,' she said, 'there's something else I've got to tell you. I won't be in Liverpool for long.'

His face brightened. 'You'll be coming back?'

She shook her head. 'No, I'll be sailing for the Middle East. Now the war's virtually over in Africa, they need WAAF personnel out there.' Unable to meet his eyes, she stared fixedly into her glass, waiting for an explosion of angry words. But they didn't come and she looked up. What she saw was worse than any anger. He was like a man suddenly stunned, his face ashen, his lips drained of colour.

'You can't mean it,' he said. She put out a hand to him but he pulled away.

'Mat,' she pleaded, 'you know there's no future for us. Rosie depends on you. Mike depends on you.'

'Rosie doesn't even notice if I'm in the same room as her,' he said.

'But she will. Give her time, Mat.'

'Time,' he said bitterly. 'You talk about time when you deprive me of it so completely! And without even talking to me first'

'It was the most difficult decision of my life,' she protested. 'D'you think I want to go to the Middle East? To know that I won't see you again for years, if ever?'

He put a hand up to his forehead. 'At this moment, I don't know what I think. I am quite incapable of logical thought. All I know is that the bottom has fallen, quite literally, out of my life.'

He stared straight ahead of him for a moment and then turned to face Mair. 'You are the most wonderful thing that has ever happened to me. And you are going away – for ever. That's all I know. And I simply can't take it.' And without another word he rose to his feet and walked out of the bar. And he didn't look back.

Charlie sat in the café opposite his parents' public house, wondering what to do next. It was as well, he thought, that it wasn't the old Shoulder of Mutton where everyone around had known him. As it was, he'd sat here for a good hour, half obscured behind a morning newspaper, without attracting anyone's attention at all, other than occasionally walking up to the counter for a refill of his coffee cup.

Ever since Nobby Clarke had given him Rosie's letter, he'd been in a terrible quandary. If only she hadn't married Holker! How simple it would all have been if he could just have cabled her from Cape Town, told her that, against all the odds, he was alive and longing to see her.

He'd bought the newspaper more as camouflage than a wish to read its contents, although he'd been temporarily diverted by a headline that told him that, according to Mr Churchill, his hour of 'Greatest Effort' was approaching. He was right, Charlie had decided – in more ways than one!

Half an hour after he'd arrived in the café he'd been rewarded by the sight of his father, coming out in his braces and shirt sleeves and with a cloth and a bucket of water to clean the windows of the pub – and had felt an almost unbearable urge to go and tap him on the shoulder and then to envelope him in one enormous bear hug. But, he had cautioned himself, there was no way he could be 'alive' to some members of his family and 'still missing' to others. He must make his decision in a mood of cold reasoning and logic. And again, he was afraid that the old boy, given his advancing years, might suffer a heart attack or worse if he were suddenly to materialize in front of him.

And then his father had started to whiten the doorstep before moving on to the window-sills. Charlie had frowned then – in astonishment. They must be starting to spring-clean earlier than usual this year. Usually, his mother let the vagaries of March weather pass before starting it.

He was further puzzled when, half an hour later, his father had re-emerged, this time done up in what had looked suspiciously like his best suit or, at least, his second best, and set off briskly in the direction of the main road. Clearly, he had an assignation and what was more remarkable, he was seen off by Charlie's mother, still in her pinafore and with her hair still firmly netted. At the sight of her, Charlie's heart had swelled with love, especially when he saw her put up a hand and tweak his father's tie. Just so had she seen him off on any errand all the years of Charlie's life. There was no way, he now realized, that he was going to allow them to go on thinking he was dead. But he still stayed where he was. What right had they to look so happy when their only son was presumed killed? There was quite a spring in his father's step as he set off, almost jauntily, down the street, turning to wave as he reached the corner. And the wave and smile he got in return seemed to be full of anticipation. Of what exactly? Surely not Auntie Mabel and Uncle Alf's annual visit? They had always brought as much annoyance as pleasure.

Charlie bought himself another cup of coffee and this time a Chelsea bun. He had the feeling it might be a long morning.

XXV

Charlie glanced at his watch. Twelve-thirty. If something didn't happen soon – like his father coming back with whoever he'd gone to meet – he'd be driven to having a proper meal. He'd had sight of his mother once more since she'd seen his father off but that was only to open up the pub. She'd come out on to the step, glanced up and down the street and gone back inside, leaving the door propped open. Now, as Charlie watched, a sailor in bell-bottoms, probably home on leave, went inside. Close behind came a middle-aged man in ARP uniform. Possibly his father, Charlie decided and frowned, wishing that his own would turn up.

And then, suddenly, there he was, turning the corner of the street and – the extraordinary sight brought Charlie to his feet – he was pushing a pram. And walking beside the pram was a young woman, and now, all previous resolutions forgotten, Charlie was almost running out of the café. For the woman was Rosie.

It was as well the street wasn't a busy one for he crossed it – really running by now – looking neither to right nor left, drawn as by some invisible cord towards the woman in the shabby green coat whose face was pale beneath her mop of unruly black hair. He reached the pram and put out a hand to halt its progress. Startled, his father looked up.

'What's up with you, mate? What. . . ?' And then the words died on his lips. 'My God! It can't be!' Rosie, too, had stopped, her face even paler than before, rigid with shock. 'Charlie!' The word was no more than a whisper.

It was Charlie who caught her as she fell, who gabbled incoherently to his father that everything was all right, that he was sorry he hadn't written to say he was coming but shouldn't he get Rosie inside pronto? But then, on the step, he remembered his mother and turned, Rosie a dead weight in his arms..

'You go first, Dad. Tell Mum I'm coming.'

But his father seemed incapable of movement and there was the pram to consider, to be manhandled up the step first. His mother, alerted by their voices, had already come out of the bar. It was the ARP man, hovering solicitously behind her, who rushed forward as she put out a hand, groping for the door frame for support.

'On leave, unexpected, is he?' he asked.

Lotte's arm was almost back to normal. Waiting for it to become so had been a tedious affair. 'Light duties', Jacques had insisted upon for several weeks. These had mostly consisted of helping with the cooking, a move greatly appreciated by Anton, who had become the camp chef.

To relieve the monotony, she had started to sketch the wild flowers that had begun to appear in grassy clearings in the forest as April gave way to May.

'That's beautiful!' said Jacques on one occasion as he dropped down beside her on the grass where she was sketching a particularly lovely orchid.

'Does anyone know you're here?' Lotte asked.

'They have a rough idea. They will give the owl signal if I'm needed.'

Lotte turned on to her back with her face uplifted to the sun. 'Shall we pretend, then, just for a few minutes, that there is no war on? That we are just a man and a woman spending a day together in the mountains?'

He took up her story. 'And soon, we shall eat our lunch of bread and sausage. Perhaps a tomato or two. And some wine, of course. And then we shall sleep for a while, before we wake up and make love.'

201

She looked up at him. 'We don't have bread and sausage and we daren't sleep. But we could make love.'

Jacques looked down at her without saying anything but his eyes were full of longing. Lotte sat up and looked around them. They were on the summit of a small, rocky hill. The only way up to it was by the path that they had both followed, clearly visible from where they lay.

'It isn't likely,' she pointed out, 'that anyone will disturb us. But if they should, we shall see and hear them coming.'

Still he hesitated.

'It wasn't that I was hesitating over,' he said.

'What, then?'

'I think perhaps you are still a virgin?' he asked bluntly.

Lotte nodded. 'Yes, I am.'

'Such a step must be of great importance to you, then?'

'Of course!'

'So you must be very, very sure before you take it.'

'I am very, very sure, Jacques. If . . . if . . .' Her voice trembled slightly. 'If anything were to happen to you – to either of us – then I should regret very deeply that we had not taken it.'

There was complete silence on the hillside. The scent of wild thyme, crushed beneath their bodies drenched the air. As slowly as their feelings allowed, they explored each other's bodies, before coming together in a final act of fulfilment. When it was over, Jacques lay back and put out a hand to smooth back a lock of hair from Lotte's forehead. 'I am so glad that I was the first for you,' he said.

And the last, I hope, she thought, but did not say it for fear of tempting providence.

They still could not believe it. Charlie's mother, in particular, could not have enough of him and it took all her husband's coaxing and persuasion to make her, eventually, leave Charlie and Rosie alone together.

'Come along, woman,' he said, half laughing, half serious, 'you've fed the boy until he can't hold a mouthful more, so leave him to sleep it off or . . .' With his back to his wife, he gave

Charlie an enormous conspiratorial wink before leading his wife from the room.

Charlie was stretched out on a sofa. He looked across at Rosie, where she sat opposite him in an armchair. 'Come and sit here!' And he swung his legs to the floor and made room for her beside him. He had kissed her as he had kissed his parents and baby Mike, hugging them all to him in one mighty embrace, but he had not kissed her properly – and perhaps, he thought, he no longer had the right to do so. But he put his arm around her shoulders. 'Rosie, I'm so sorry for causing you so much grief.'

She looked up at him. 'If you mean Mike, that was hardly grief. Not at first, anyway.'

'And afterwards? Surely things were much easier after you married Mat?'

She drew slightly away from him on the settee so that she could look up at him properly. 'How did you know I'd married Mat?'

He explained how he had received her letter telling him so, also announcing the birth of the baby. 'A long story but it didn't catch up with me until a few weeks ago, on board the ship bringing me home. It was only then that I knew who I was.'

'So you didn't know about Mike until then?'

'No. Nor that you'd married Mat.' He tried not to sound accusatory but clearly it didn't work, for she frowned up at him.

'Charlie, please try to understand. It was he who suggested it.'

His face flushed angrily. 'I'm sure he did! He's always fancied you.'

'Charlie, that's not true. I married Mat because, under the circumstances, we both thought it was the best thing for Mike.'

'And what now?' he asked. 'Mat isn't likely to agree to give up his conjugal rights just because I've come back from the dead.'

She looked up at him in amazement. 'Conjugal rights? You surely don't imagine I've slept with Mat?'

'But . . .'

'Oh, Charlie!' She gazed up at him. 'I could no more sleep with Mat than – than Ike Eisenhower!'

Charlie made a sound somewhere between a laugh and a sob.

'General Eisenhower to you! And chance would be a fine thing! They say he's rather busy just now!'

Next morning, Rosie rang Mat at the cottage. 'Mat, you'll never guess what's happened!'

'Mike cut his first tooth?' He knew from the bubbling happiness in her voice that it was good news and all he could think of was that, in some bizarre, feminine way that a mere male would never understand, her maternal instincts were functioning at last.

'Don't be absurd! He's far too young!'

'What, then?'

'Charlie's home! He's alive, Mat! All this time, he's been in hospital in North Africa, with his memory completely gone. But he's all right now. He'll have to be careful about what he does – probably be invalided out of the army – but he's OK. Mat, isn't that the most incredible news?'

'Incredible!' he echoed. And indeed it was but his mind was racing down a completely different avenue from Rosie's. Rosie, who had no idea how he and Mair felt about each other.

'I don't suppose Mair's there, is she?' Rosie was now asking.

He gave a dry laugh. 'Mair's somewhere in England, waiting to be sent overseas.'

'What! When did this happen?'

'Sometime last week. It was a very rushed affair.'

'But you have to volunteer for an overseas posting. Whatever made her do that?'

He mustn't spoil Rosie's happiness by telling her the real situation. Not yet, anyway. 'Search me!' he told her. 'I'd be the last to know.'

'Well, I sure am sorry I didn't see her before she went,' Rosie said, but then returned to the main reason why she had rung. 'Mat, we'll have to talk soon, won't we? I've explained to Charlie how things were – why we got married – and he understands. But . . .'

'Don't worry,' he told her. 'I'll get on to the solicitors straight away. You'll be a free woman before you know it.'

'Thanks, Mat. And for everything.'

She rang off and Mat, too, put down his receiver. But then, almost immediately, picked it up again. Time to pull a few strings.

XXVI

In May, what remained of the town and monastery of Cassino was finally occupied by the Allies. In France, Hitler appointed Field Marshal Rommel as the anti-invasion commander-in-chief. One of his first actions was to cancel all passenger trains and to ban all communication between Vichy France and neutral countries, thus depriving the Resistance of several lines of communication. In the Vercors, as in other parts of France where the Resistance was active, rumours were rife and a sense of urgency kept everyone on their toes.

'The word is,' said Victor, arriving at the camp one morning in early June, 'that the Vercors Maquis as a military force is to be officially recognized by the appointment of a commander, one Colonel Huet. His line of command will have British, French and American officers. As we have known for a long time, the Vercors is recognized as being of great strategic importance once the invasion begins. Up here, in our eyrie, we will have the view of an eagle, high above the rest of the world.'

'I've never known you so lyrical,' said Jacques with a grin and indeed, Victor's usually lugubrious countenance was almost radiant with anticipation.

'Now,' he told them excitedly, 'there will be more drops of ammunition. Perhaps even the anti-tank guns we need more than anything.'

He ate a quick meal with them then moved on to spread the news to other groups. 'The "sedentaires" have been called up. Our numbers are increasing by the hour.'

The 'sedentaires' was the name given to those men who had enrolled with the Maquis but had not yet joined it, waiting for a major event such as invasion before leaving their homes and their jobs. Jacques' own group had already been joined by local people eager to help now that the situation was moving to a climax.

Such a man was Paul Duval, a priest from one of the nearby villages. 'I do not wish to carry firearms,' he had told Jacques, 'but there may be things I could do to help. At one time, before I became a priest, I had begun to study medicine. And in any case, more than half my flock is already with you. Soon, I shall be preaching to an empty church.'

Jacques' eye fell on Lotte where she was sitting with several of the men as they unpacked one of the containers that had been dropped on the previous night. There were Bren guns, Stens and explosives but still no anti-tank guns as they had requested.

'It could be,' he said thoughtfully, 'that I will first ask you to perform a rather unexpected task. One that I am sure was not in your mind when you joined us. If all goes as I hope, I will speak to you of it very soon.'

When the container had been unpacked, he called Lotte to one side. 'I want to ask you something.' He did not wish to be out of sight of the men so he had to content himself with leaning, arms akimbo, against the trunk of a tree with Lotte doing the same against another tree.

'You know that I love you.'

'As I love you.'

'And under normal circumstances, I would be asking you to marry me.'

'And I would say yes!'

'And then, no doubt, begin to do all the things that women do on these occasions. A white dress, perhaps, a reception for many guests. Champagne.'

'I'd say yes to the champagne but I could do without all the other things.'

'I can't even promise the champagne but Claire, will you marry me?'

*

Sitting on a train that rumbled up through the heart of England on its way to Liverpool, Mat wondered if he was being completely mad. His contact had been helpful up to a point in telling him the location of the transit camp that Mair was probably at. 'I'm told there's usually a three-week waiting period while they all get kitted out for wherever they're going and have their inoculations, etc. But more than that, I can't tell you. My chap wouldn't stick his neck out any further.'

And with that meagre information, Mat had had to be content. Quite what he was going to do when he got there, he had no idea. Brave the station commander in person and request that Corporal Mair Corben be taken off the draft on compassionate grounds? What chance did he have of persuading the powers-that-be to listen to a word he said? On the face of it, he was a married man with a child, who had no business to go chasing half across England to see a WAAF who, as far as they knew, could easily have applied for an overseas posting just to escape his unwanted attention.

What would they make of a garbled story that the real father of his child had now turned up and that in a matter of months he, Mat, would be a free man?

The ceremony could not have been quieter, at times verging on the clandestine. Lotte and Jacques had arrived at the church separately, slipping in unobtrusively at the vestry door. Inside, they had found Paul in his vestments and Victor and Sarah, who were to be their witnesses.

Sarah, who had now joined their group of the Maquis, was utterly delighted to be there. 'I couldn't be happier,' she told Lotte as she enveloped her in an enormous hug. 'Not exactly part of our training but they did tell us to always use our initiative!'

The ceremony was as brief as possible. Even when it was over and they were signing the register in the tiny vestry and Lotte had discovered that she had married one Charles Vouvray, she could hardly believe that it was over. And she had no visible proof to take away. The marriage certificate would remain where it was – 'until you have need of it,' Paul said. Even the ring they had used in the exchange of their vows was returned to Victor from whom it had been borrowed.

As they left the vestry, a man cycled past, softly whistling the 'Marseillaise'. When he saw Victor, he dismounted and bent down as if to inspect the cycle's brake blocks. Victor went over to him and joined him in his scrutiny.

'The Allies have landed,' the man whispered. 'In Normandy. It just came through on the radio.'

He'd been lucky so far, Mat reflected. He'd worn uniform, of course, which more or less guaranteed him an entry in to the camp once he'd proved his identity, but from then on it had been a matter of the personal approach and, he was ashamed to admit, a certain subterfuge.

He'd felt extremely guilty when he'd spun a young flight officer the yarn he'd invented on the train – that he'd just happened to be in the area visiting a poorly grandmother and having been unable, through a spell in hospital, to see Corporal Corben when she was on leave, had seized this opportunity of perhaps seeing her before she embarked. Would it be possible for him to do this and perhaps, if it was convenient, take her off camp for a couple of hours? He had then paused hopefully.

But her reaction hadn't been what he'd expected. True, she'd agreed that he could certainly see Corporal Corben and take her off camp for a couple of hours but, she'd added, only if Corporal Corben wished this to happen.

'But of course,' he'd stammered. 'That goes without saying.'

'I only mention it,' she'd continued, 'because you must understand, Flight Lieutenant, that you are not the first young man to present himself here and make such a request and I'm afraid these visits have not always been appreciated. One girl, in fact, was so upset she refused to see the young man at all because she knew he would try and persuade her to remain in this country.'

At that point, misery had engulfed him because she had, perhaps unwittingly, put into words his deep-rooted fear that that might, indeed, be the case with Mair. But he had said nothing more, just nodded to acknowledge what she had said and she had then gone out of the room and left him to his thoughts – and worries.

'The Germans are getting lively up in the north,' Victor reported. 'Particularly in the village of St Nizier. There was strong resistance and it took them three days, but it seems they occupied it in the end, in spite of massive air drops during that time.'

'How about St Nizier?' Lotte asked. 'Reprisals?'

Victor nodded. 'I'm afraid so. The bastards burned several houses. But even so, morale is high and getting higher. They've even hoisted the Tricolour on the mairie in Villard-de-Lans. Things going all right here?'

'Exellent!' Jacques replied. 'More and more men are joining us and we've managed a fair bit of harrassment. But it goes without saying that it hasn't all gone our way. The Germans have occupied the airfield at Chabeuil, near Valence, and that's meant an increase of air reconnaissance and some bombing. There've been several drops but no anti-tank guns, of course, but at least we've got machine guns and some bazookas.'

After Victor had drunk his coffee and gone, with Jacques walking with him to the perimeter of the camp, Lotte sat on under the trees, deep in thought. She'd been married for just one week and already, and to her great astonishment, her attitude towards the future was changing. It had begun immediately after the ceremony when she and Jacques had been huddled in the back of Philippe's van and on the way back to camp.

'I find it difficult to explain exactly why I think it so important that we are married,' Jacques had told her. 'There's precious little I can give you in the way of worldly goods but at least I can give you my name. And giving you my name makes you part of my family and that, in turn, gives me hope that we will add to that family, that we will somehow manage to come through this war unscathed or, at least, alive.'

'But different!' Lotte had smiled and kissed him long and hard. Now, as she watched Jacques shake Victor by the hand then turn and start to walk back towards her, she thought, now we have yet another reason for defeating the Germans. *Our future!*

XXVII

Mat looked at Rosie and marvelled at the change in her. A miracle indeed! Charlie coming back from the dead, as it were, had been like a single stone cast into a pond – the ripples it had caused had spread and spread, affecting more and more people. And as for the difference it had made in his and Mair's lives well, that was something he couldn't quite get his head round just yet. He was continually finding a foolish grin of pure happiness spreading across his face which he could do nothing to stop – and nor did he want to. Even though it was hardly appropriate just now when he was helping Rosie clear away the breakfast things. She saw it and smiled.

'Come on!' she said. 'Neither of us is really responsible for our actions at the moment. And it's time for Mike's constitutional. Let's go down to the river.'

So, taking it in turns to push Mike's pram over the rough ground, they walked down to the river and sat under a tree. The same tree, Mat realized, under which he and Mair had sat when he'd told her he intended to ask Rosie to marry him. What an insensitive lout he'd been!

'When will Charlie be coming down?' he asked Rosie.

'Tomorrow,' she said happily. 'I wondered if you'd look after Mike while I went into Oxford to meet his train.'

'Of course!' he said. 'Take as long as you like. And then I'll push off. Go and stay with Gram and Gramps for a bit and then

Mum and Dad and Aunt Bella. I'm due for a medical board, too.'

'Mat, you don't have to. It seems awful to turn you out of your own cottage.'

'What? And play gooseberry to you and Charlie? Not on your life!'

'It's really good of you. But a week or two of quiet country life is just what he needs at the moment. He's got a board coming up, too.'

Mat settled himself more comfortably against the trunk of the tree. 'Did I tell you Mair sent her love?'

Rosie laughed. 'At least twenty times!'

He ignored her mockery. 'I shall never forget the relief when she came into the room, crossed straight to me and put her arms around me. And apologized to me! *She* apologized to *me*! After all those things I'd said to her!'

'Then what happened?' Rosie asked obligingly, although she'd heard the story at least three times before.

'Well, after we'd hugged each other until we were both breathless, I said did she really have to go? And she said yes, she did. Which I knew, of course. And then she pointed out that nothing had really changed, had it? Although she was so pleased that at least we'd be parting as friends. And then *I* said but things had changed and would she please go and get her cap and coat because I'd been given permission to take her out for the evening, and would it be all right if we went now and she said yes, she thought it would.' He stopped talking then while he thought about what happened after that. Even with Rosie, his confidante since childhood and now so wonderfully restored to him, he couldn't share the magic of that evening.

There were no taxis, of course, to take them into the city, and not a bus in sight so they had hitched a lift on an American jeep already packed to the gunnels with American servicemen hell bent on enjoying a night out. It had taken a great deal of persuasion to convince them that neither he nor Mair – no offence meant – had any wish to join them. But at last they had managed to extricate themselves and had found a tiny municipal park

213

where they had sat on a bench under an enormous lime tree and Mat had told her about Charlie's return. Her delight – and her dismay – had been immediate.

'Oh Mat!' she had kept repeating. 'If only I hadn't been so headstrong. If only I'd waited a few more days!'

'We won't go down that road,' he'd told her. 'The most important thing is that we now have a future – together. And I've been thinking. When the medics let me go – and that shouldn't be long now – maybe I could manage a posting out to the Middle East.'

It had been quite dark by this time and an elderly park-keeper had approached, clanging a bell. 'Don't want to be locked in here all night, do you?' he said.

'Can't think of anything I'd like more!' Mat had muttered under his breath as they got to their feet. After that, they'd found a coffee stall selling not only coffee but also bread rolls stuffed with sausage and fried onions, and discovered they were hungry.

'Hot dogs!' a familiar voice had said behind them. 'Not as good as the ones back home but not bad at all. You Brits are learning fast!' It was the driver of the American jeep that had brought them in and more than happy to offer them a ride back.

'What will you do now?' Mair had asked when they were finally put down outside her camp gates. 'Maybe you could get a bed in the officers' mess.'

'I won't bother. I'm too happy to sleep anyway and I won't push my luck by suggesting I take you out to breakfast!'

Their goodbyes had been brief even though the guard was tactfully looking the other way. 'Love you!' they'd whispered then held each other close. After that he'd turned and walked away and, some hours later, had found himself outside the railway station. Tired but content, he'd caught the next train south. When he'd finally reached Oxford, he'd bought a morning paper. 'Caen falls to the Allies' screamed the headline and he wondered, then, how Lotte was faring in all this.

*

Life had never been so exhausting, Lotte decided, and yet at the same time so exhilarating. Towards the end of June, the first part of the reinforcements they had been promised arrived in the shape of British and American officers supported by an American commando unit.

'Where are the French?' Jacques had muttered. But then, they too had come under the command of an air force officer called Pacquebot whose job it was to prepare a landing strip where Allied planes could bring in arms and equipment.

'Anti-tank guns at last?' asked Victor. Hopes were roused when thirty-six Liberators dropped 800 containers at Vassieux. This was the first of several drops but sadly no anti-tank guns were among them although one massive operation involved forty-eight planes dropping over 1,000 containers. Sleep among the Maquis became a luxury and food was eaten when they could find it. But the Germans weren't giving up without a fight. Overall, their artillery was still stronger than the Maquis' and at this stage of the war, many of their troops had become experienced in mountain warfare.

On the morning of 21 July, nineteen German gliders landed on the plateau above Vassieux, taking the Maquis completely by surprise. The village was occupied and many Maquis killed – but they were not beaten. Under the command of General Huet, they surrounded the village and attempted to retake it. But in vain – the German mortars prevailed and the Maquis were ordered to withdraw and disperse into the forest.

During the fighting, Jacques had become separated from the others and now, he, Lotte and Sarah found themselves on their own and climbing wearily up through the trees.

'We'll rest here for a few minutes,' said Jacques, flinging himself down under a tree, 'and then make our way to Les Hirondelles. That's where the others will go.' Les Hirondelles was an abandoned summer house where they had rested overnight before the attack.

'What will happen next?' Sarah asked as she joined him.

'Oh, we'll regroup. Huet will see to that. And then it will be a matter of waiting for the Allies to land in the south of the country. Huet seems confident they will before long.' He gazed up at Lotte. 'Sit down for a few minutes. You deserve a rest.'

He was right. They all deserved a respite. The fighting had been exhausting along the scrubby hillside, a matter of hide and seek and who could aim the fastest. She alone had killed – or so she thought – at least three of the enemy. They had been lucky, she and Jacques and Sarah but Jean, she knew for a fact, had been killed.

She smiled down at Jacques. 'I need the bushes first but I won't be a minute.'

She had relieved herself behind an accommodating tree trunk and was pulling up her trousers when she saw him – a German soldier, creeping like a shadow up the hillside, flitting from tree to tree towards Jacques and Sarah. Lotte swore under her breath. Why hadn't she brought her Bren with her instead of laying it down on the grass with the others? All she could now do was to try and reach them before the German. But she doubted if she could. It would be better to cry out and draw his fire, giving them a chance to pick up their guns.

Suddenly there came into her mind the memory of an English rose garden and a grief-stricken woman imploring her to 'keep an eye' on her daughter. And Jacques? She would willingly sacrifice her life for him. She opened her mouth.

'So you see,' Mat told his grandparents, 'it's just a matter of sitting it out until the war's over and Mair comes home. Or even better, maybe I could wangle a posting out there, once the medics have finished with me.'

They were sitting, cups of coffee in hand, in the little garden outside Mrs Moneymoon's sitting room. Maggie – surely a good two inches taller than the last time he had seen her, Mat thought – lay sprawled at his feet and trying to thread daisies through the eyeholes of his shoes.

'And then will you be getting married?' she asked.

'Definitely!'

Maggie gave up on the daisies and propped herself up on her elbows. 'But how will you unmarry Aunt Rosie? And what about the baby? Who will he belong to?'

'It's a bit complicated, Mags, but Auntie Rosie's real husband – the one we all thought had died—'

'I didn't know we thought he'd died. I thought . . .'

'Maggie,' Mrs Moneymoon broke in, 'it's one of those things we'll explain when you're a bit older.'

'Like the Facts Of Life?' Maggie asked, pronouncing the words as if they were the title of a book.

'That's it, dear.' Mrs Moneymoon sounded unusually flustered. Mat came to her rescue.

'Maggie, there's a rather interesting parcel on the top of my overnight bag in my bedroom. It just might have your name on it.'

Maggie was up and away in a flash. 'It's only some sweets I managed to get hold of in Oxford this morning,' Mat explained. 'So when is Maggie going to be told the facts of life? I doubt I'd be much good at it'

His grandmother looked worried. 'She's nine this year and Mary thinks she should be at least twelve before she explains things to her. Stella and Polly were. But Maggie's such a forward child in so many ways and yet very naïve in others.'

'We really need someone like my Mum,' said Mat. He thought for a moment. 'How about if I take her home with me for a few days? It's school holidays, after all.'

'Well now, let me look at you,' said Aunt Bella, adjusting her glasses. 'Bless me, but you've grown!'

'Gramps says I'll soon be able to reach things off the kitchen mantelshelf,' said Maggie proudly.

'Good for you!'

'I've never seen such a transformation,' Aunt Bella confided to Kate later that evening. 'When I think what a little monkey she was just a few years ago!'

'She's a great credit to Ma and Pa,' Kate agreed. 'But apparently there's one bit of her education that's being left to me.'

'What's that?'

'Telling her the facts of life. I gather that's what Maggie calls it. Dan's wife thinks she's still too young but Ma doesn't. Just doesn't know how to tell her.'

'Sooner you than me!' said Aunt Bella unhelpfully. 'Now, what do you think about Mat and this young Welsh girl?'

'Very pleased. Apart from the christening, I hadn't met her since she was a child but I know her mother very well indeed. Salt of the earth! My only worry is that any child of hers might be brought up too strictly.'

'Is that possible these days?'

'Cynic! But apparently that's why she's set off for the Middle East. Because she didn't think it right to form a relationship with Mat while he was married to Rosie. But now that Charlie's come back, it alters everything.'

'What complicated webs this war has woven with people's lives. It's a tragedy there's been no news of that nice girl, Lotte.'

'I know. Prissy says her parents are worried sick.'

'Let's hope they'll hear soon now that we've landed in Normandy.'

'And there's news just in that the Allies have landed in the south of France and are fighting their way up the Rhône Valley. If only we knew where she was.'

'Coming for a walk, Maggie?' Kate asked. 'I've got to go up to the farm for some eggs.'

'I'll go for you, if you like, Aunt Kate. I like going up to the farm.'

'Thanks, but I rather wanted to have a chat with you.'

Maggie's face clouded with anxiety. Kate noticed. 'Don't worry! You're not in trouble. It's about what I think you call the facts of life.'

'Oh, good! I really want to know about them. I think it might make life a lot easier.'

'*Would* it? Hang on a moment while I get a basket for the eggs.'

Five minutes later they were strolling – at least, Kate was strolling, Maggie was doing a sort of rhythmic hop, skip and jump – through the coppice of beech trees on the way to the farm.

Kate racked her brains, trying to remember what her mother had told her. Precious little, she seemed to remember. If her memory served her well, she and Prissy had simply been taken to a neighbouring farm and told to watch while a stallion, with the aid of a farmhand, had mounted a mare. The process had seemed quite revolting and nothing at all to do with how she and Prissy had arrived in their mother's stomach. Knowledge about this had eventually been acquired in dribs and drabs, as was so often the case for women of her generation, and mostly through whispered conversations among her school friends. No wonder her mother had baulked at instructing this precocious child! She drew breath.

'Maggie, do you know how rabbits are born?'

' 'Course! Out of their mothers' tummies.'

'Have you ever wondered how they got in to their mothers' tummies in the first place?'

'No.'

Kate stopped dead in her tracks. 'You *haven't*?'

' 'Course not! I've known *that* for ages.' And now it was Maggie's turn to look astonished. 'Is *that* what you meant by the facts of life? About men's willies and what they do with them?'

Kate put out a steadying hand towards the bole of a tree. 'How – how did you know about men's . . . er . . . willies, Maggie?'

Maggie gazed kindly upon her adopted aunt. 'Mostly,' she explained, 'through old Ossie Ogshaw. Ma Ogshaw was always telling him to put it away but he never did. Said he liked the feel of the air on it.' She peered more closely at Kate. 'You feeling all right, Aunt Kate? I didn't mean to shock you. I know I'm not supposed to talk about things like that any more but you did ask!'

'I understand, Maggie. And you're right not to talk about it now but Maggie, tell me one more thing before we talk about something else. What did *you* think I meant about the facts of life?'

'Oh, things like how not to fart in company. I find that *very* difficult. Especially after baked beans.'

Kate looked at her. It was ironic that Lotte, who had had such an important, albeit brief, effect upon this child's life and her brother's was now probably dead. One day, she promised herself, she would make it her business to tell Maggie all about her and the part she had played in her life.

XXVIII

It was the summer of 1948. The war had been over for two years. In the mountains of Telemark in southern Norway, two young women sprawled on the grassy bank of a lake. At least, one of them sprawled; the other sat more demurely, her back leaning against the bole of a massive pine tree, one of many that grew around the shores of the lake. A crutch lay on the grass beside her.

'What does this remind you of?' asked the one who sat demurely, gazing across the still, steely expanse of water towards the tiny, rocky island at its centre.

'Scotland,' said the other immediately, 'and that damn awful night when we had to row around the island.'

'Exactly! I'm so grateful this leg doesn't stop me from rowing. On a good day, I spend hours out there, fishing.'

'Fishing? Lotte *you* fishing?'

'I know! But I love it. And don't mock, Sarah! Market gardening doesn't sound all that exciting!'

'Oh, it isn't. But I can't tell you how satisfying it is to sift good, friable soil through my fingers and to plant things and watch them grow. So different from . . .'

'Killing Germans? I know how you feel – it still haunts me.'

Both girls, back on a sunlit French hillside, fell silent. Lotte lived again the moment when she had stood up and shouted at the German soldier who had been creeping up on Jacques and Sarah. All that she had been aware of at the time was that her shout – as she had intended – had caused him to swing his gun

221

in her direction and to fire. Then there had come a searing pain in her groin and she had lost consciousness. Much later, Sarah had told her what had happened next.

'When you shouted, Jacques and I immediately reached for our guns. It was then that I saw there was another German on the other side of the clearing and aiming at Jacques. Jacques didn't see him; by then, he was already firing at the German who had shot you. I aimed at the second German and got him but by then it was too late – he'd already killed Jacques. There were only seconds in it.'

When this conversation had taken place, both girls were in an American field hopital near Lyon. As Jacques had predicted, Allied troops had landed in the south of France and swept up the valley of the Rhône; the Vercors had been liberated. Lotte had already been told of Jacques' death; had, in part at least, come to terms with it and was now hungry for details.

'His body?' she'd asked. 'Has anyone. . . ?'

'It's all right,' Sarah had replied swiftly. 'It's been recovered. And been given a temporary burial in a marked grave. It will be up to you to decide where . . .' She'd left the sentence unfinished. 'Are you sure you're up to this? You're still pretty weak, you know. Lucky to be alive, the doctor said.'

Lotte had smiled at her. 'Lucky in the sense that you were with me. I still can't believe you carried me all the way up to Les Hirondelles.'

'Well, you were a bit heavy!' Sarah had conceded with a grin. 'But where we were both lucky was finding Victor there. It was he who dug out the bullet. I didn't know until then that he'd been in the French army medical corps before Dunkirk so he had some idea of what he was doing. But it was still a very risky business, although there was nothing else we could have done. We knew the hospital at Rousseau had been destroyed by the Germans so we just had to sit tight and wait for the Allies. When that happened, Victor went off for help and they came out and got you.'

Now, Sarah sprawled on her back, lifted her head and gazed across the lake to the island. 'It must have helped a bit when you found out you'd inherited . . . all this.'

'It did,' Lotte acknowledged, 'but most of all, it was finding Jacques' family. Talking about him to people who'd known him far longer than I had and in many cases, all his life. His grand-parents had both died but there were uncles and aunts and cousins – like Harald, whom you met last night.'

'The man who's so like Jacques, it's uncanny?' Sarah asked.

'That's right. He was in the Norwegian resistance during the war, including the raid on the heavy water plant at Ruyken. He's being enormously helpful.'

'Not to mention being rather fond of you?' Sarah suggested, lifting a quizzical eyebrow.

'Nonsense!' said Lotte briskly. 'Nothing more than a cousinly affection!'

Sarah decided not to pursue the matter for the moment. 'Whatever you say! But I'm still not clear how you found out about all this in the first place.'

'Through our marriage certificate. Until we were married, I didn't even know Jacques' real name.'

'Were there any relatives still in Paris?' Sarah asked.

'Only an uncle who'd decided to stay in Paris when the Germans occupied it. He was living in extreme poverty and very ill but he was able to fill me in about Jacques' Norwegian family.'

'Weren't they astonished when you turned up out of the blue?'

'Completely. And at first, they didn't believe me. But when I produced our marriage certificate, they were fine. They couldn't have been more welcoming.'

'Even Harald?' Sarah asked. 'Didn't you say he stood to inherit the entire estate once Jacques had died?'

'The estate was equally divided between the two of them so he has half anyway. And it's working out well. He owns the farm and lives in the farmhouse on the estate and I live in the family house and, as you know, intend to run it as a hotel. You're by way of being a guinea pig! And the others, of course, when they arrive at the weekend.'

'Tell me again who's coming.'

'Rosie and Charlie and baby Mike, now a two-year-old toddler and into everything, Rosie says. Mat and Mair and young Maggie and Tom, two children I first met in the London blitz. They live in Oxfordshire with Mat and Rosie's grandparents.'

'Quite a houseful!'

'And it's all being repeated the following week when the "oldies" appear. Parents and grandparents and an elderly great aunt. And that includes *my* parents – they're back in Germany now and Rosie's parents, all the way from the States and Mair's parents from Wales. They've all promised to be absolutely honest and complain bitterly if everything isn't just right. Ah, here comes Harald!'

Through the trees behind them came a tall, blond giant so like Jacques it still took Sarah's breath away to look at him. She glanced at Lotte beneath lowered lids, trying to assess her reactions, and was struck afresh by the beauty of her face; although the features were sharper now, the cheekbones more defined, the mouth firmer and the eyes? It was in the eyes that the change was most apparent; they were gentler now, more thoughtful and, at this moment, brimming with affection. Was she wrong to imagine that that affection might grow into something deeper, something that must take time to come to fruition? She thought not and Jacques, she felt certain, would wish it to be so.